The Best Day Of My Life

LYNDA THROSBY

Dedication

To all my family and friends,
thank you for the support and encouragement
you have given me.

The Best Day Of My Life

Nobody is perfect
Everyone is cracked
It's the cracks that let our light shine through

Prologue

10 Years Earlier

S HE'S GONE.

My life is gone with her.

This was supposed to be the best fucking day of my life.

It's turned into the worst nightmare of my life.

This can't be real.

I have to wake up.

I'll find her sprawled out beside me like she is every morning. Me cursing as I'm hanging off the bed because she's taking up all the room. She says it's because of the size she is now, that she needs to spread out but it's not, she's always done it.

I love her.

Time to wake up.

Except I can't.

I'm standing here in the emergency room. I can hear babies crying, but she's just lying there. They haven't covered her up — I wouldn't let them.

I remember screaming at them when they called time on her.

I scream when they try to cover her.

"What the fuck are you doing? Why are you covering her?"

The doctor tries to put a hand on my arm, but I shrug him off.

"Fix her!" I cry

"Just fix her..." I fall to my knees on the floor, my head in my hands. Trying to wake up from this nightmare.

My wife is gone.

I can't fathom what happened. It was a birth. They do this day in and day out, multiple times a day, so why did my wife die?

"What happened? Why is she gone? She was giving birth. You do this all the time. WHAT THE FUCK HAPPENED?" I scream at them.

The doctor crouches down to be eye level with me.

"I'm sorry, Mr. Tourney. Your wife had eclampsia and went into cardiac arrest. We did all we could for her, but, unfortunately, we couldn't save her. It's not common to have deaths in childbirth these days, but especially with twins, eclampsia can be a complication." I stare at him, not quite understanding

"She had a heart attack? She's only 27. How the fuck could she have a heart attack?"

He winces slightly at my outburst. "Mr. Tourney. I'm so sorry. I know this is hard for you, but you have two healthy babies over there." He nods his head in the direction of the crying babies

"They could probably do with meeting their daddy. Being born is stressful enough, but they've lost their mother. I believe they'll know that they've lost a connection. Would you like to meet your son and daughter?"

Would I?

Do I want to?

Did they kill her?

What the fuck do I do now?

I can't look after two babies on my own. They need their mother.

"Bring her back, doctor. Just bring her the fuck back. They need their Mommy. I need her. She's my life."

I break, collapsing backward on the floor. I'm curled up tight, tucking my legs into my chest as tight as I can get them. I start rocking and wailing. How pathetic must I look? A grown man curled up on a delivery room floor …

Not something they see every day.

Chapter 1

10 years later
Present

"EVELINA, EVANDER, COME TO DADDY, please. No more hiding. It's school, and we need to finish getting ready," I shout to the terrible twosome.

They do this most mornings. Have breakfast then disappear to play instead of getting ready for school.

My mother in law, Sonia has made the lunches for them. She comes over every day and waits for them to get back from school and looks after them for me. She makes dinner just in time for me getting home from work. I insist on having dinner with them every night. They have baths and are ready for bed, and Sonia does their lunches for the following day. It's quite a well-oiled machine now. To be honest, I couldn't have done any of the last ten years without the help of Sonia and Arnold, Evelyn's parents.

The school bus will be here for them in thirty minutes. If they don't get ready now and get to the end of the driveway, they will miss the bus, which means I will end up taking them to school yet again, which in turn will make me late for work.

"Evelina, Evander! I won't tell you two again. I'm getting really annoyed now. Get your little butts down here now for school." I can hear the murmurs from them upstairs somewhere, Evelina muttering, "It's dad, not daddy. We're ten, not two." Cheeky madam. She calls me Daddy when she's creeping for something like dolls or ice cream.

Why do I have such an enormous house? It's easy to lose them in this place. Maybe I need a smaller one. I just want them to have a good life and everything I can give them without spoiling them. Raising twins on your own is hard work. Evelyn had a good upbringing with everything she needed, and she turned out to be amazing. I'm just hoping the Evs — as I call them — turn out as good as she did.

Evelina is sassy already. God love her, she drives me crazy with her smart mouth. She is the spitting image of Evelyn in looks, but I'm not sure where her little spitfire personality comes from. I sometimes put it down to not having a Mom. Evander is like me both in looks and personality. He will be and, in fact, is a nerd. Takes after his dad — 100%.

I haven't dated since the twins were born. I couldn't. I love Evelyn and always will. She was my college sweetheart. I've had sex since I lost her, but that's all it ever was. I never had feelings for anyone. Even having sex with other women felt like I was cheating. Plus, I don't have the time for a relationship. I have work and the kids. That's my life, and it's all I have time for.

"Ok, you two. Down the stairs, now. It's a good job I don't have a boss to moan at me when I'm late for work."

"That's because you are the boss, Dad," Evelina shouts at me from over the galley at the top of the stairs.

She's right. I am the boss, but it doesn't mean I like being late. We started the company together, Evelyn and I, back in college. I fell for the hot nerd, and she said she fell for the hottest guy in the school.

Chapter 2

18 years earlier

WE STARTED DATING IN COLLEGE — both of us majors in computing.

Evelyn was gorgeous. She was my crush.

I wasn't a jock. I was a typical nerd, so she wouldn't be interested in me.

I admired her from afar because she was way out of my league. I'll never forget the day she walked into the lecture hall. I felt sure she was in the wrong room. This class was full geeks and nerds; she didn't belong here, but wow, was I wrong …

There are lots of empty seats, but she chooses a place just one away from me on my row. I start to sweat and try not to look at her. It's hard concentrating, that's for sure. I'm lucky I excel in computer programming and gaming. Let's face it, what else does a nerd have to do every night? It's not like we're out partying with the popular kids.

About two months into the semester, our tutor pairs us up for a gaming project. I'm stunned and start to panic. I can't believe my luck, but when I look over to Evelyn to acknowledge her, she looks as shocked as me. Just trying to speak to her has my heart racing and sweat beading my brow. I do it somehow but make a fool of myself stuttering out the words. We arrange to meet in the library at lunch to discuss how to go about this and see what ideas we have.

I'M NERVOUS, TO say the least. I get to the Library early so that when she walks in, I can watch her, only I don't get the chance. It's like she had a radar or something because as soon as she comes into sight, she looks straight at me.

I nod my head up in a kind of hello gesture and watch her walk towards my table and put her laptop and bag down. She mesmerizes me.

"Hi, Theon." She looks as embarrassed as I feel, and I wonder if she doesn't want her friends seeing us together, looking around I don't see any of her friends so we should be good for now.

She's a popular girl, and I've seen all the jocks hanging around her. I did notice however she didn't like all the attention that much.

"Hi, Evelyn." I'm a little uncomfortable. I blush. I can feel my cheeks burning. I grab my bottle of water from my bag and quickly gulp some down, trying to hide my awkwardness. The problem is, I gulp too fast and start choking, drawing attention to myself. Oh god, kill me now. I'm going to die of embarrassment. Evelyn rushes behind me and starts patting and rubbing my back. I stop choking, I think from the shock of her touching me

"Thanks, Evelyn," I manage to choke out. My throat is burning.

"Call me Eve if you want, Theon. Everyone else does."

"I like Evelyn." I shrug, and she smiles at me.

We start to discuss the project, and how we are going to work on it. Evelyn says we can work at her house — only if I wanted to. She explains her parents are hardly home, mainly just the housekeeper, and she has her own office set up in her bedroom. She seems a little shy when she suggests it.

I'm seriously out of my league here. Housekeeper and her own office! Her parents must be mega rich.

I'm glad she offers her house though. I would be too ashamed to take her to my place. I live in a trailer. It's just my grandma and me. She brought me up. My mom got pregnant at sixteen, and my dad didn't want to know her or the baby. She didn't want me either. She was seventeen and wanted to party. I never knew her — she died when I was two from a drug overdose. My grandma is my hero. I love her to bits. She works hard to keep me.

I got a scholarship to college. Otherwise, I would have been working somewhere to help her out. I feel bad as it is, so I make some extra money by tutoring in the evenings and weekends. I make good money this way.

We plan to go to Evelyn's after college to brainstorm and put our ideas down. I already know what I want to do. I've been working on creating games for a while now.

I wait for Evelyn on the steps as soon as college finishes. She arrives just seconds after me.

"Hi, Theon. We can walk to mine from here, it's not that far, if that's okay with you, unless you drive?"

"Hi, Evelyn, no, I don't drive, so walking is good with me." We start walking, and I'm surprised at how easily the conversation flows. I can't believe I'm actually here with her, talking about games and nerdy stuff. She is unexpectedly easy to talk to, and my embarrassment seems to be subsiding. It turns out Evelyn has been creating her own games as well. I tell her what I'm currently working on, and she seems impressed. We have so much in common. I'm in awe of her — beautiful and a nerd.

We reach her house, and I have to pick my jaw up off the floor.

"You live here?" I ask, just gawking at this huge house in front of me. It's set back from the road with a sweeping semi-circle drive up to it and lots of garden to the front.

"Fucking hell," I whisper to myself but judging by the look on Evelyn's face she hears, and she looks down in embarrassment.

"Oh god, sorry, Evelyn. I didn't mean to say that out loud. It's just … well … I've never been to a house like this. It looks like a mansion."

"I've never brought anyone here before, Theon. I never wanted people to judge me based on my parents' wealth."

I feel terrible and look away wondering if I should leave. We could have done this in the library at school.

"Maybe I should just … erm … go, Evelyn. I'm really sorry if I offended you." I look everywhere but at her. I feel like a real ass now,

"No, I don't want you to leave. I know you didn't mean anything by it. Come on." She links my arm like we are best friends, and we head up the drive. I try to keep my mouth shut because the closer we get, the bigger it gets — it's huge. I feel her glance at me a couple of times, but now, it isn't the mansion in front of me making me gawk, but rather the girl at my side who thought nothing of linking me as though it's something we do all the time, even though this is the first time we've spent any time together. She's touching me, and that alone is doing things to me. Things I like but don't have much control over. I'm going to embarrass myself. I just know it.

I look in awe at our linked arms and smile. She suddenly drops her arm from mine.

"Sorry, I didn't mean to be so forward. I just automatically did it. It's what I do with my friends."

"No, please don't be embarrassed. I, erm, I like it," I said shyly not looking at her. I hadn't realized we'd stopped walking.

"Come on, let's go round the back and through the kitchen. I don't think my parents will be home yet. Not that it's a problem if they are. On the rare occasion they are home at this time they like us to have dinner together, but it's not often they get home early."

"Can I ask what your parents do?"

"They are both plastic surgeons. They have their own practice in the city and well, this being L.A., you can imagine how busy they are."

"Oh," is all I manage as she links my arm again and we head around the massive house. We pass another building to the right. I glance over at it, and Evelyn must notice.

"That's the garage." She shrugs.

"Wow, that's bigger than most houses."

"They have a lot of cars. Daddy is a bit of a petrol head."

We carry on walking, and out the back is the biggest swimming pool I've ever seen, complete with built-in cave and slide. I gasp and quickly try to cover it with a little cough, but I'm not sure I pull it off. Over behind the pool is another building.

"That's the pool house." Again she shrugs but looks a little embarrassed. We walk past the pool, and there's a lanai at the back of the house with an outdoor kitchen and stunning outdoor furniture. This is a completely new world to me. I feel out of place. I feel uncomfortable. I want to leave, but then that's me judging her. She doesn't act like she's spoilt, and I would never have thought it if I hadn't come here. She doesn't drive a flashy car that I've seen. In, fact, I've never seen her drive.

"Do you have a car, Evelyn?"

She looks at me trying to gauge where this is going.

"No. Well, yes. I can drive, and my parents bought me a car, but it just sits in the garage. I didn't want it, and they didn't ask me first. I like walking places," she says on another shrug. She's not stuck up or spoilt, which makes me fall for even more.

We enter the kitchen where there is a lady pottering about and cooking.

"Hey, Maggie, this is my friend, Theon. We have a computer project to do together, which counts towards our final marks. I'll just grab some drinks and cookies."

"Hello, Eve. Hello, Theon. Nice to meet you. Don't have too many cookies, Eve, your parents just phoned. They are on their way home, so you're having dinner with them tonight."

"Ok, thank you. Did they say when they would be home?" She turns to me as she opens the huge fridge. "Theon, would you like to stay for dinner?"

Shit, no, I can't. I need to get back to Grandma.

"Sorry Evelyn, I can't stay too long. My grandma will have my dinner ready."

"They said they would be home for six," Maggie says.

"Oh okay, Theon, no worries. What time do you need to be home for dinner?"

"I said I'd be back for six thirty."

We head through her house up the stairs to her room. I try hard not to let it show just how much in awe I am. Her room is huge. It's at the top of the house in the attic. We move through it, I notice there are lots of sea turtle ornaments on some shelves, and posters on her wall of them, her bed is big but looks small in this room, which also has its own sitting area, we head to the back where she opens the door to a very large office with desks and computers. Not just one computer, oh no, she has two computers that I can see and four screens set up. We move to the biggest desk, and she wheels a chair over so we can sit side by side.

"Evelyn, this place is amazing. You look like you have everything you need right here. I envy you," I say looking down as I start getting my laptop and notebook out of my bag.

"I know how lucky I am, believe me, I do. I just don't like to flaunt it, which is why I never bring anyone home." I look up at her in admiration yet again. She amazes me. She is the most beautiful girl I know, with her short auburn hair, her sparkly green eyes, and pixie-like features. She has a stunning figure, not too skinny like those cheerleader girls who I think barely eat. She is just amazing, but if I carry on thinking like this I may need to use the bathroom.

"Will your parents mind you bringing me up here? Just not many parents would allow their teenage daughter to bring a boy up to their room to study." Way to change the subject, Theon.

"I've never brought anyone home before, but I don't think it will be a problem. They are easy-going, and they trust me. I'll check with them later when they're home."

We brainstorm for the rest of the time. We have some amazing ideas working together, we bounce off each other perfectly, and I can't believe how relaxed we are in each other's company. But, it's almost six, and it will take me a good half hour to walk home from here.

"I best make a move, Evelyn, before your parents get home. I need to get home in time for my dinner." I really don't want to go. I don't want to leave her.

"Yeah sure, Theon. That was a great couple of hours. My head is full of so many ideas. I think we made a great start. You're amazing with all this, and your ideas are truly remarkable."

"Ditto, you really know your stuff too. You amazed me. When you walked into the lecture theatre, I thought you had the wrong class."

"Why do you say that?"

"Well, you're not exactly a nerdy type, are you, Evelyn?" I can feel myself getting very red again, as I pack my stuff up and rush to the door without looking at her before she can question my comment

"Right, I'll see you tomorrow in class." I rush for the stairs. I hope I can remember my way out of here, it's like a maze it's so big, and I didn't exactly pay attention walking up here. With following behind Evelyn, my mind was elsewhere.

"Hey, I'll show you out. You look like you're in a rush?"

"Yeah, thanks, just need to get home."

"Do you want me to take you?"

"No, it's okay. I can run home, thanks anyway. I need my run, I didn't get it in today, I was distracted," I say with a small, shy grin.

She distracted me.

I would have run home from school like I usually do. I may not be a big muscled Jock, but my physique is pretty good for a nerd. I lift weights in the college gym then run home, but it looks like I won't be doing that for a while. I'll have to run in the morning, go to the gym, shower, then let my school day begin.

We pad quietly down the stairs, not speaking. When we get to the bottom into the vast hallway, Evelyn overtakes me and heads to the front door.

"Here, this way is quicker. I can't hear any talking, so I take it my parents aren't home yet."

We stand on the steps, and I'm just about to turn to say goodbye when a car rolls into the drive. Shit, I didn't want to meet her parents, not yet anyway.

The car is a Maserati, not that I know much about cars but the Maserati emblem of the trident on the front grill gives it away, I have no idea of the model. I hardly know anything about Fords or Chryslers never mind these expensive types of cars. It is a beauty.

"Too late, Theon, you didn't escape my parents, sorry." She has a great smile, and it's aimed right at me as I turn to her.

"Hello, darling, what a nice surprise, having you here to greet us when we get home. I usually have to tear you away from your computer. Hello there, I'm Sonia, Eve's mother and you are?" She reaches her hand out to shake mine — shit I'm sweating. I wipe my palm on my top before shaking her hand,

"H-h-hello Mrs. Westcott, I'm Evelyn's friend Theon. Theon Tourney." I'm so nervous my voice is shaking. Just then her dad comes around to us. He eyes me suspiciously. I'm still holding Mrs. Westcott's hand. I drop it.

"Hello, darling." He leans in for a hug and kisses Evelyn on the cheek.

"I miss you, darling. I'm just glad we were able to get away to have dinner with you tonight. I want to hear all about your week." He puts his arm over her shoulder facing me.

"And who might this be?" he asks Evelyn looking directly into my eyes.

"This is Theon, my friend from school. We've been paired to do a project together. We were having a brainstorming session." Mr. Westcott puts his hand out to shake mine. I take his hand, stuttering again, "Nice to meet you s-s-sir." Shit, I feel stupid.

"Good to meet you too, Theon."

"Sweetie, would you like to join us for dinner?" Mrs. Westcott asks me

"He has to get back home, mother. He's having dinner with his grandma. I'll be inside in a couple of minutes. I'm just saying goodbye to Theon." I think that's Evelyn politely telling them to leave us. Thank god. She's good at reading me. She can see how nervous I am.

"Nice to have met you, Theon," Mrs. Westcott says as she heads inside.

"You too, ma'am. Sir." Mr. Wescott just nods, appraising me for a second, kisses Evelyn's temple then puts his hand on the bottom of Mrs. Westcott's back, directing her gently inside. I let out a breath I didn't realize I was holding.

"Tense huh?" Evelyn says to me. I run my hand through my black mass of curly hair that needs a cut.

"You could say that." I laugh.

"I must get going, Evelyn. Thanks for this. I had a great time. We seemed to get a lot done today, I'll see you tomorrow."

"I agree. I love sharing my ideas with someone who understands and is as enthusiastic as me. Bye, Theon. See you tomorrow."

I turn and walk down the steps and out of the drive heading home. I have a definite spring in my step. As soon as I turn the corner at the end of the road I set off running. I can't stop smiling when thinking about Evelyn as I run along the streets home. You would never know she comes from money, she doesn't act like she does and that puts me at ease. I'm pretty sure she won't judge me based on where I live, but it's not info I will freely share yet.

That was by far the best couple of hours of my life, and I'd say the best day of my life so far. There is no doubt I've fallen for this beautiful, unassuming girl. I can't wait for tomorrow.

Chapter 3

THE EVS ARE IN MY CAR, SETTING OFF to school. They just missed the bus again. It's getting to be a regular thing.

"This has to stop, you two. It's happening more and more, and I'm late for work most days."

"But, Dad, it's better when you drop us off. We get to spend a bit of time with you before the day begins. Don't you want that, Daddy? I mean, to spend more time with us?" The little madam has those puppy dog eyes that she knows gets me every time. I know her game.

"Don't give me that look, Evelina. I know what you're playing at. You just don't want to get up any earlier. Well, I'm sorry, but the pair of you need to get up half an hour earlier." She tuts and rolls her eyes, and Evander looks up from his games console and into the rearview mirror also giving me an eye roll.

"Less of that, thank you. That's what happens, up, dressed, then breakfast, in that order. No matter how you want to play it, we leave the house at 7.45 a.m. every morning. Got that, you two? In fact, I'm banning any games being played after breakfast from now on." I look at them in the rearview mirror. Evelina is pouting and sulking, with her arms crossed high up. Only her. Evander cool as a cucumber

"Works for me, Dad. It's Lina who messes around. I'm always ready, just laying on my bed until she's done." I see Evelina give him a filthy look and pull her tongue out at him and laugh to myself.

As we approach the wait line at school, I notice Evelina looking a bit forlorn.

"Are you still sulking, Evelina? You've been quiet back there. That's not like you."

"I'm okay, Dad. Nothing to worry about." Well, that's an odd thing to say.

"What would I be worried about?" She doesn't look at me. She's raking her teeth over her bottom lip which is her tell that something is bothering her.

"Come on, poppet, spit it out. What's wrong?" She's worried. Maybe she thinks I will be upset with her.

"Evelina, you know you can tell me anything, right? No matter what it is. I will always listen to you, poppet."

"I didn't want you worrying about me, Daddy."

"Well, now you are making me worry. What's wrong?"

"I've not been feeling well sometimes." Is this a ploy? Is someone picking on her at school?

"In what way?" I edge along in the car as the vehicles in front finish dropping their kids off

"I keep getting pains in my tummy and head. It's not all the time, Daddy, just sometimes. I was sick as well, about four times now ..." She looks at her hands, which are now in her lap. This isn't like her at all. I haven't noticed her not being herself.

"When was this?"

"It's just been a few times over the last couple of weeks. But I was sick again after my breakfast today. My tummy really hurt."

"Does it still hurt now?"

"No, Daddy. That's what's strange. It happens fast then it's gone. It doesn't always make me sick. Daddy, when I went to the toilet when my tummy hurt, there was some red in the toilet when I got up to flush it." Oh shit, is it blood? She's too young for her monthlies, isn't she?

"Is it always after breakfast?"

"No, it's different times." She shrugs. Evander is looking at her like he doesn't believe her. His eyes have gone to slits and are boring into her.

"What's up, Evander. Did you know about this, son?" He doesn't look at me but keeps looking at Evelina.

"Lina, you said you weren't going to tell Dad." Wait, what's going on here? Why don't they want to tell me? I edge the car forward — we are nearly at the front of the line.

"Whoa, whoa, guys. What's all this about not telling me? Why would you not want to tell me? I want to know everything that concerns you both."

"We just didn't want you to worry. You always worry about us."

"Poppet, it's my job to worry about you. I tell you all the time; you two are my life. If something is worrying you, then you need to always tell me. You got that? I love you two to the moon and back. Now I'm going to make an appointment to take you to see Dr. Harrow, okay?" She nods at me

"Sorry, Daddy."

"Don't ever be sorry, poppet. Just both promise you will never keep anything from me, okay. Promise?"

"We promise," they both say together. Suddenly there is a horn blasting, and I realize I haven't moved and the car behind is getting annoyed. It's my turn to let the kids out.

"Hey, give me a big hug and kiss, you two." I turn in my seat, and they both stand and throw their arms around me as best they can.

"Are you sure you feel okay now, poppet?"

"Yes, it didn't last long."

"Okay then, I'll make the appointment with the doctor for after school.

I will be here to pick you both up so don't mess around. Come straight out when school is finished, okay?" They both nod at me then scramble out of the car.

"Evelina, if you feel poorly at all during school you make sure you tell Ms. Thomas. Do you hear me?"

"Yes, I will."

"Love you both to the moon and back."

Together they both retort.

"Love you back from the moon to us."

God, I love them.

I GET TO WORK late. Aggie, my secretary, smiles at me as I get off the elevator on my floor.

"Good morning, Aggie. How are you today?"

"Good morning, Theon. I'm good, thanks. Here are your messages. You have a meeting at eleven with that new software developer, and I will bring you your coffee in a couple of minutes."

"Thanks, Aggie. Will you phone Dr. Harrow please and get an appointment for four this afternoon if she can fit us in? It's for Evelina. She's been a bit under the weather."

"Yes, of course, I will do that right now before I get your coffee. I hope the poor little thing is not too poorly, bless her."

"She seems fine, but she just told me she gets tummy pains and headaches and is sick sometimes. Then she said there was red in the toilet bowl this morning. Please tell me she's too young to start her monthlies, isn't she? She's not 11 yet."

"Theon, every girl is different. Some girls can start very young. It certainly sounds like it to me, but I'm no doctor. Good job you're getting her checked. I'll make the appointment now for you." I head to my office, thanking Aggie.

I really need to look at either seeing if I can take over another floor of the building or find a bigger space. We just keep growing and growing as a company, which is excellent. People still want to game, no matter what the financial market. It helps that we sponsor one of the biggest gaming competitions here in L.A. Which reminds me, we need to get that sorted as it's only a couple of months away now.

I look at the office directly across from me. I refuse to let anyone use it. With my floor-to-ceiling window next to my door, the office opposite is the mirror image. It was Evelyn's office. We loved that we could have our own space but still see each other through the glass. It still breaks my heart ten years on. I know I wouldn't be here if it wasn't for her and our first project together back in college.

Chapter 4

OUR FIRST PROJECT WAS GOING WELL. We only had a week left to hand it in for marking, I knew without a doubt we were going to get top marks.

We've spent every day together, including what time we could grab at the weekends to make this the best game ever.

I love every single second with her. I'm now starting to panic about what will happen when we've finished. Will we still be friends? Will she talk to me at all? I don't know how or if I will cope without her. After my computers, she's my addiction. We've been to her house every day after school, and I've had dinner with her parents, Sonia and Arnold, a few times. They are nice to me, but it took Arnold a while to come round to me being with Evelyn so much.

It isn't always studying though. A few times at the weekends, if I'm not tutoring, I go over, and we spend a couple of hours on the project then we hang around the pool.

I remember the first time I saw Evelyn in a red bikini. I had just come out of the pool house where I got changed, and she was already in the pool. She gazed up at me with water dripping down her face and neck toward the swell of her boobs, which were still slightly submerged, but not all the way. I followed the drips that traveled down between her breasts, and I licked my lips without realizing I was doing it. It was only when I noticed Evelyn watching my mouth while I stared at her that made me realize what I was doing. Then her eyes lowered, and I just knew she had seen the erection tenting my shorts. Shit. I turned beetroot. I could feel my cheeks burning. I moved my hands lower trying to cover myself up and squishing my thighs together as if that would help me out before I turned my back to her. I looked at her over my shoulder. I must have been the same color as my bright red shorts.

Evelyn, being classy, didn't mock me. She just smiled then pushed off the side of the pool and floated away on her back.

"That is not helping," I muttered to myself as I turned to watch. Her boobs were completely out of the pool now, and I could see her flat tummy and the small bit of material covering her bottom half. She was stunningly beautiful.

She was also taking in my physique — her eyes lingering on my abs. She licked her lips. I turned and walked painfully and slowly back into the pool house. I needed to calm myself down.

I was in the bathroom for a few minutes when I heard the door to the pool house open and shut. "Theon," she called softly near the bathroom door. "Are you okay in there?"

Oh God, what do I say? No, I'm hard as steel in here trying to calm down.

"Yeah, I'm good, Evelyn, thanks. I just needed the bathroom. I won't be long." Great, now she thinks I'm shitting in here. I don't know what's worse.

"Ok, I'll grab us some waters from the house." That was her way of giving me some space so I could get in the pool while she's not there.

I heard the door open and close again. I took a couple of deep calming breaths trying to think of something gross to free my mind of Evelyn. It didn't work. I made a run for it and jumped into the pool, just what I needed; the cold sharp shock of the water. A couple of minutes later she joined me.

We stayed in there for ages, swimming, splashing, and talking, getting to know each other and just generally having a great time. When we decided it was time to get out, Evelyn got out first and went into the pool house to get a towel to dry off before heading into the main house to her room to change, leaving me alone to get dried and changed in the pool house. She was the sweetest, kindest, most thoughtful person I knew.

I thought I might be in love with Evelyn. No, scrap that, I knew I was in love with her.

We did that a few times, swimming after hours of working. The project was nearly finished, just some tidying up on algorithms and tweaking some of the graphics. Other than that, we have an amazing game to hand in.

We've finished our game, It's the Saturday before we hand in the project. "Hey, Theon, as my parents are away for the weekend, shall we go out tonight and celebrate finishing our amazing game? Maybe we could go for a meal and then to the cinema. What do you think?"

What do I think? Hmm, hell yeah. But I have to tell myself it's not a date — we're just friends.

"Sounds great. Shall we go for pizza then see what films are on?" She nods enthusiastically, smiling that big beautiful smile. Her green eyes shine and sparkle when she smiles like that.

"Let's go for a dip in the pool. It's so hot today."

"Yeah, sure. You go and get ready, and I'll save everything."

We head down to the pool. We have a routine now. Evelyn change's in her room while I head to the pool house to get changed. Then she goes into the main house to get us some bottled waters while I jump into the pool. It saves any embarrassment. God I love her.

"Theon, you never talk about your parents or home life. I don't even know where you live?" I knew this would come up at some point. We've become inseparable over the last two months. Do I tell her? Yes, I'm not going to lie. I sit on the steps in the pool, and she comes and sits next to me.

"It's okay. You don't have to tell me. I know most things about you except that." I run my hand to slick back my hair that has fallen in my face. I let out a deep sigh.

"I don't want you to think any differently of me than you do, Evelyn. I think it would destroy me if you did."

"Theon, I could never think of you differently than I do. You're my best friend, no matter what." I'm all warm and fuzzy inside from her saying that. She's my best friend as well.

"I live with my grandma. She raised me from birth. My mother got pregnant at sixteen and had me at seventeen. My father didn't want anything to do with her once he found out she was pregnant, and I don't even know who he is. She didn't want me either once I was born. She wanted to party, telling my grandma she was too young for a kid. She died of a drug overdose. I never knew her. My grandma is my hero." I look at Evelyn, and I see a lone tear falling down her cheek. I wipe it away with my thumb.

"Please don't cry, Evelyn. I don't want sorrow or pity. I don't know any different. As for where I live, that's the hard part. We live in a trailer on a trailer park, north on Mission Hills." I look straight into her eyes to gauge her reaction. All I see is warmth and admiration — no pity, sorrow, or shock. I love her more if that's possible. She takes my hand and holds it between her two on her lap. She squeezes it, so I look at her.

"I can tell how much you adore your grandma. There is nothing to be ashamed of. Everyone is different, Theon. Where we live does not dictate who we are as a person. That's in here." She points at my head. "And in here." She rests her hand over my heart. "They are the most important things in a person." She leaves her hand on my chest and stares into my eyes. I stare straight back into hers, and I shiver from her touch. I feel sparks, and I have goosebumps all over. I wonder if she feels it too. I want to lean in and kiss her, but I'm terrified she doesn't see me that way, and I don't want to ruin our friendship. That would kill me.

I don't have to wonder for long. With one hand still on my chest and her other hand still holding mine in her lap, she leans in closer to my face, searching my eyes, checking if she's doing the right thing. I lean in slightly too, letting her know this is what I want.

I look from her eyes to her lips to her eyes again. She looks at my lips then leans in more. Her mouth opens slightly, and I can feel her breath on my face. We are mere inches away from our lips touching. I lean in just that fraction more resting my lips on hers.

"Tell me this is okay, Evelyn. I won't do anything unless you tell me it's okay," I say with our lips still touching.

"It's okay," she says with a slight nod to her head. That's all I need. I press harder on her lips. Her mouth's still open, giving me access with my tongue. I've never done this before, but I've watched enough movies. I slip my tongue into her mouth, and I move my lips on hers.

She does what I do, and our tongues start to duel. She tastes so sweet. I edge closer to her on the step. With our mouths still attached, she climbs onto my lap and straddles me. I moan into her mouth. She's moaning into mine. She wraps her hands around my neck trying to pull me closer. She shifts slightly on my lap then breaks the kiss. With our forehead's touching, she smiles.

"Oh," she says. She can feel how hard I am. It's like steel. I suck in a deep breath when she wiggles slightly, and I close my eyes, gritting my teeth. I can feel her core right on my hard shaft, and I shiver.

"Are you cold?" she asks

"No, no, not cold, it's just you when you wiggle like that right against my erection it kind of does things to me."

"Oh sorry." She giggles and edges back slightly. I need to move before I explode. I grab one of her hands from around my neck and edge her off my lap onto the step next to me, still holding her hand. I stand up, which is the wrong thing to do. My erection is now staring Evelyn right in the face.

Shit. I quickly pull her up to standing. She's blushing crimson red, but I think she just matches my face right at this moment. I kiss her lips again very softly and gently bring my hands to her waist.

I suddenly lift her up and throw her into the water. I need the distraction.

She comes up spluttering and glares at me. "Right, mister, this is war!" She splashes me then grabs my ankle and drags me off the step and climbs on my shoulders, trying to dunk me. She's no match for my size though, and I flip her around and dunk her instead.

We fool around for a while and keep stealing kisses all through playing. Now, this has to be the best day of my life. The day Evelyn Westcott became mine.

Chapter 5

Present

I PICK THE KIDS UP FROM SCHOOL, and we head to the doctor's office.

"How has your day been, Evs?"

"I got a gold star today for getting all my math right," Evander tells me.

"Wow, that's my boy. That's fantastic. Well done, son. I'm so proud of you." He looks really proud of himself too. Sitting down for an hour each night and helping with homework is paying off. Even when they don't have homework, we do extra math and English.

"What about you, poppet? Did you have a good day? You haven't been poorly, have you?"

"I was all right in school, but my tummy hurts again now. I can see she has both her arms wrapped around her middle. I hate seeing my kids in any kind of pain. It's like a knife being jabbed through my heart.

"How bad does it hurt? Is it bad like when Evander pulls your hair or like when he just pokes you in the side with his finger?"

"When he pulls my hair." I can see tears falling down her cheeks. I feel helpless. She's in the back, and she needs a daddy cuddle, but I'm driving. I need to get to the doctor's as soon as I can.

Ten minutes later, I'm parking the car. It's been the longest ten minutes ever. Evelina was crying in the back holding her tummy. Even Evander was comforting her, cuddling her. I can't believe I didn't crash the car with watching Evelina through the rearview mirror all the time. It broke my heart.

I get out of the car quickly, throwing the back door open and gently lifting Evelina into my arms. She wraps her legs around my waist and grips onto my neck tightly. She's crying but trying to be brave. I rub her back as I walk towards the doctor's office.

"Sshhh, poppet. Daddy's got you. I love you to the moon and back," I whisper into her ear, but she doesn't say it back. God, let her be okay. The receptionist sees we are distressed.

"You can go straight in, Dr. Harrow is ready for you." We enter the doctor's room with me still carrying Evelina.

I explain what Evelina told me this morning and Dr. Harrow can see she's in pain.

"Can you lay her on the bed for me please, Mr. Tourney so I can exam her tummy?" I lay her down gently. She clings to my neck, not wanting to let me go. The doctor starts gently pressing all around asking Evelina to say where the pain is. She takes her other vitals and listens to her heart with her stethoscope. I keep hold of Evelina's hand throughout the examination. She's so brave, my strong, sassy little girl.

Dr. Harrow asks us to go back to the waiting room for a few minutes, which worries me. Evelina is really clinging to me now. "How's the pain now, poppet?"

"It's going again now. It does that all the time."

Dr. Harrow comes out. "Mr. Tourney. May I speak with you please? The children can wait here. Stacey, can you just keep an eye on them, please?" She asks the receptionist. I start to get up.

"No, Daddy, don't leave me. Please don't." I get the sad puppy eyes. The ones I can't refuse. Dr. Harrow looks at me with quite a stern look that has me in a panic.

"Poppet, I just need to speak to the doctor. You stay here for two minutes, okay. Evander will look after you." She reluctantly lets me go, and I walk into the doctor's office.

"Please take a seat, Mr. Tourney. I'm going to send you to the hospital to get some tests done."

I look at her worried. "What kind of tests? What's wrong with her?"

"I don't know at this stage, and I don't want you to worry. I know that's going to be hard to do. I need some blood work and a urine sample, and I also want her to have an ultrasound." I start rubbing my hand over my face then through my hair. "What do you think is wrong, Doctor? I thought it might be her monthlies, but she's only ten?"

"I don't think she has started her menstruation, no. Her abdomen felt hard, and I need to get it checked out as soon as possible. I have just phoned the children's hospital on Sunset Boulevard, and they are expecting you in the next hour. Are you okay to take her over there now?" I must look like a deer caught in headlights. I don't speak. I'm just staring at the doctor.

"Mr. Tourney, can you take her over there now? It will probably take you a half hour to get there."

"Yes, yes of course. I'll do it now." I jump up out of my seat and head for the door.

"Take these notes with you and hand them to the reception desk when you get there. Please try not to worry, at least not until we know what's wrong with little Evelina." She gives me a half smile, but it doesn't reach her eyes. She knows there is something wrong. Shit, I need to keep it together in front of the kids. I nod at the doctor and then take a couple of deep breaths to calm myself before I walk out of the door. I put on a fake smile as I approach the kids. I don't want them to see me worried or alarmed.

I crouch down in front of Evelina putting my hands on her knees. "Right, poppet. The doctor wants you to have some tests done."

Her eyes go wide. "What tests? Like a math test?"

I smile at her shaking my head gently. "No, I need to take you to the hospital." Her eyes nearly pop out of her head. Neither of them has ever had to go to the hospital before.

"That's for really sick people, Daddy."

"No, poppet, not always. It's also where you have to go to get tests so that the doctor can find out why you don't feel well. We need to make you better and not feel so poorly." She nods her head at me. I stand up and take her in my arms. She clings to me chimp-style again.

"Come on, buddy, let's go and see if we can find out why your sister doesn't feel well," I say to Evander stroking my hand over his head.

Forty minutes later we are entering the children's hospital on Sunset. I head straight to reception and hand over the letter Doctor Harrow gave me. We are directed to a waiting area to take a seat.

"You okay, poppet?" I ask kissing the top of her head that's resting on my shoulder. She nods. "How are you feeling now?"

"Scared," she mumbles into my shoulder.

"It's okay, nothing to be scared about. We just need to know why you're feeling poorly. Is your tummy better now?" She nods a yes to me.

We are called through to a room where another doctor asks us questions. Doctor Cassidy is very good with Evelina and manages to get the answers to her questions. As she examines her, she continues to reassure her. "You are one of the bravest little girls I have ever met," she tells Evelina.

"I'm not so little. I'm a big girl now, aren't I, Dad." And we are back to dad now. I do love it when she calls me daddy. I hate to think of them growing up so fast.

"You are my big girl." I smile at her and kiss the top of her head.

"Well, as you are a big girl, do you think you can be brave enough for me to take some of your blood from your arm? I have to use a needle to do this, and it might sting a little bit. But big girls can handle a little scratch, can't they, Dad?" Dr. Cassidy asks me.

"Of course, Evelina can do that. If she can take the hair pulling and the smacks from Evander, then I'm sure a little scratch will be nothing compared to that. What do you say, poppet?" Evelina looks a bit shocked, but she nods her head.

"Well, Dad, if I am a brave big girl and let the doctor scratch me, can I have a treat, pleasssseeee?" And just like that, my little madam is back.

"Of course you can," I say ruffling her hair.

"Great. Evelina, can you sit on the edge of the bed for me and roll your sleeve up. I think if you keep looking at your dad and not at what I'm doing, it won't hurt so much." Evelina does as she's told. She keeps her eyes on me, I start pulling funny faces to distract her, and it works. The doctor has the needle in her vein and is filling up vile after vile of blood. Evelina barely flinches and hasn't looked once, just concentrating on keeping her eyes on me.

"Wow, you were amazing. So brave. Did you even feel the scratch?"

"Not really, Dad, it was your silly faces making me laugh."

"No, I think it's just that Dr. Cassidy is very gentle."

"Why, thank you. Now, Evelina, just a couple more things. Do you think you can go to the bathroom for me?" Evelina looks at the doctor and shrugs.

"I would really like it if you could try for me, Evelina. I need you to have a pee for me in this bowl. Do you think you can try for me?"

"Eww, no. I can't pee here and in that. That's just gross, Doctor." Dr. Cassidy laughs out loud at that, and so do I. Evelina isn't sure what we're laughing at.

"Poppet, you don't have to pee here in front of us. You go to the bathroom to pee. I don't want to see you peeing any more than you want to pee in front of us and I'm sure the doctor doesn't want to see you either."

"Oh, then yes. I can do that in the bathroom. I think I need a pee anyway, Dad."

"Great, Evelina. Then you can use my special bathroom just through this door here. My toilet is a little special because we can fit this bowl just inside the toilet to catch your pee."

"What do you want to catch my pee for?" Evelina asks scrunching up her nose in disgust.

"Well, I don't want it to flush down the toilet because I have to collect your pee from the bowl and put it into these special jars. Then they get sent away to the science doctors, along with your blood, and they look at them very closely to see if they can find out why you have not been feeling very well. Does that sound like a plan?"

"Huh huh. I just want to be better," she says nodding her head.

"Can I go pee now please? I'm busting after talking about peeing" she says holding herself. The doctor takes her to the bathroom and tells her not to flush but to wash her hands and that she will collect the bowl when she comes back out.

"Doctor, do we have any idea what we are looking at here?" I ask once the door is shut running my hand over my head.

"Until we have the results from the tests, Mr. Tourney I can't possibly speculate. It would be unfair to you. Please know that whatever it is we will get to the bottom of it."

"I'm just losing my mind with worry, Doctor. How long till the results are back?"

"Tomorrow. Make sure I have your contact details and Mrs. Tourney's. We just need an ultrasound next then you can go home." I look over to Evander who has been sitting quietly in the corner on his Nintendo switch. "There is no Mrs. Tourney. It's just me and the twins. I head to Evander. "You okay, son?" I ask rubbing his head before sitting next to him.

"Yeah, Dad, just worried about Lina, like you."

"I know, son, I know. I'm sure she will be fine." Just then she comes waltzing out of the bathroom with not a care in the world. God, I love her with all my heart.

"All done, it's in the bowl for you, Doctor. You can go and get it now," she says, smiling, all proud of herself.

"Dad, what treat do I get for being the bravest big girl ever in the whole wide world?" She's standing in front of me, hands on hips, head slightly cocked. I could just get her and cuddle her to death, so I do. She's wiggling and squealing in my arms, but she is no match for her big strong dad. Evander and Dr. Cassidy are laughing at us.

"Right, young lady, just one last thing I need you to do for me," Dr. Cassidy says to Evelina.

"I need you to come with me to another room. I want to take pictures of inside your tummy to see if I can find out what is going on."

"Will it hurt me?"

"No, not at all."

"Ok, then." And with that, she shrugs and heads for the door. I'm in awe of my baby girl.

We all head down the corridor and enter another room. This has a bed in it and the ultrasound machine next to it with a monitor. It's the same as when Evelyn had scans when she was pregnant.

"Ok, Evelina, can you pop onto the bed for me? I'm going to lift your top a little bit and edge your skirt down a little so I can see your entire tummy. Is that okay?" She shrugs

"I guess so."

"Right then, next thing I need to do is put some gel on your tummy. This is what it is." She puts a dab of gel onto Evelina's little finger

"It's a little cold when I put it on your tummy." I really like this doctor. She is good with Evelina, explaining everything she's going to do and putting her at ease instead of just bulldozing in there just because she's a kid. Evelina is rubbing the gel between her fingers

"Ok." She shrugs again.

"It's a bit like Jello. Look, Dad, it's like Jello." She holds her fingers out for me to see the gel. Dr. Cassidy puts a blob of gel onto Evelina's tummy, and I hear her intake of breath at the coldness. I smile to myself. She spreads it around then gets the probe and places it on the gel.

"What's that for?" Evander asks at the side of me.

"It sends little sound waves through the tummy, and they create pictures by bouncing off the organs in there. It's very clever. It's how you can see a baby in a lady's tummy. It's how your mum and I first saw you two."

"Oh, that's way cool," he says, and I laugh at him. I put my hand on his knee and squeeze lightly.

"Can I speak, Doctor?" Evelina asks.

"Yes, of course you can, sweetie."

"Dad, I know what I want for my treat." Here we go. It's probably a pony or something like that

"Okay, what is it, poppet?"

"Promise you won't be upset with me?"

"No, never, but it has to be reasonable, Evelina."

"I want a mommy like my friends have." Oh, shit. I freeze. That just floored me. Neither of them has ever said anything about not having a mommy. I have always told them about their mommy being in heaven. How she never got to meet her babies, and now she was an angel watching over them. I have always kept Evelyn around, they both have a picture of her in their bedrooms, and there are photos all over the house of her.

"Evelina, I said a reasonable treat, baby girl. I cannot give you a new mommy as a treat. Do you have a second choice and we can discuss the new mommy idea at a later date?" The doctor is finishing up the ultrasound and Evelina is glaring at me.

"Second choice, poppet," I say firmly. I'm not getting into this conversation in the hospital. She's tapping her finger on her lips thinking hard about a second choice.

"Ok, I really, really, need Clawdeen Wolf, Draculaura, Frankie Stein, Cleo De Nile, and Lagoona Blue, pretty, pretty, please, Daddy." She looks up at me. Oh boy, how can any dad deny their daughter when they look at them like no one else in the world matters? She has been so good. I see Evander snigger, and when I glance at him, he shrugs.

"Guess we're stopping at the toy store on the way home."

"May I ask what on earth you just asked me for? Your old daddy has no clue?"

"Duh, Dad, they are Monster High dolls. How can you not know that? They are the bestest dolls ever." I see Dr. Cassidy laughing to herself. She knows I have just been had. I can't help but smile.

"Okay, sweetie, that's it for today. You have been the best biggest girl ever. Thank you for that. You can go home now with your daddy and brother." I see her lean in and can just make out her whisper. "You have the best taste. I love Monster High. Make sure you get them all off your daddy, and I would get the Monsteriffic bus and the Monster High School for them as well." She winks at Evelina and smiles at me. A pony might have been cheaper.

We say our goodbyes and Dr. Cassidy says she will call me tomorrow. It's going to be the longest night of my life waiting for news on what's wrong with Evelina. We stop off at the toy store where I get bamboozled into buying the complete collection of Monster High dolls, accessories, school and bus because the doctor said so. I might need a word with Dr. Cassidy. I buy Evander a couple of new games as well, even though I can get them free at work — I can't leave him out.

We head home where Sonia is waiting. I had called her earlier to let her know Evelina was not too good. She's obviously worried about her and wants to see how we have got on. We have dinner with her, and then I send the kids up for showers and promise Evelina she can play with her dolls after homework and shower. I tell Sonia everything that has gone on today.

"I'm really worried, Sonia. I have no idea what could be wrong. I hope they get the results early and don't leave me hanging around all day. I can't see me getting much work done tomorrow. I won't be able to concentrate. My brain is already running away with all possible scenarios as to what is wrong with her."

"Will you ring me as soon as you find anything out, Theon? I'm going to be as concerned as you. Arnold is away for a couple of days, golfing with the boys. If there is anything you need, just let me know."

"Yeah, of course. I will let you know as soon as I know anything." I get up and give her a hug. She looks like she needs it, and to be honest so do I.

"You know I would never have survived all these years without you, don't you? Guess what Evelina wanted for her treat for being brave?"

She looks up at me furrowing her brow. "I thought it was all the dolls?"

"No, that was her second choice." I let out a deep sigh and move to the fridge to pull out some juice.

"She asked me for a mommy like all her friends have."

Sonia looks at me a little bit horrified. "What did you tell her?"

"To have a second choice and we would discuss this topic at a later date. She floored me. Neither of them has ever said anything about not having a mommy around before."

"Well, I think that was the right thing to say, Theon. Don't feel bad. I pray you do find someone to love and love you as much as Evelyn did. I know you still love her, and that will never change, but you do have a life. You do need to live again, sweetie. It will happen one day when you're ready and when you're least expecting it."

Her comments get me thinking about Evelyn again and our first date the night we celebrated finishing our project.

Chapter 6

18 Years earlier

W E ARE GOING ON AN ACTUAL date tonight.
How unreal is that?

The most beautiful girl in the school is going on a date with me, the computer nerd, of all people. After our little make-out session this afternoon, we decided that tonight would be our first ever date as girlfriend and boyfriend. It wasn't even me who suggested it.

The feelings I have for Evelyn are so deep already. I know we have been friends for only a few months, but I believe when you know the one for you, then you just know. I pray she feels the same. I'm scared this will screw up our friendship though.

I run home to get ready. Grandma knows how I feel about Evelyn, and I tell what's happened. She gives me the usual lecture about being responsible and not rushing into anything. But she doesn't have to worry—I know she's referring to my mom. I have no intentions of becoming a dad for some time. I want to build up my career first to give any children I have a good start in life. I promise Grandma I will bring Evelyn home to meet her and that she will love her just like I do. I love how my relationship with Grandma is so open and honest. It's one thing she's always insisted on.

I walk back to Evelyn's. I have on my good shirt and trousers. I ring the bell, and when she opens the door to me, I'm floored. I think my mouth is hanging open. She's breathtaking. Her auburn hair is up in a messy bun with little bits loose, her green eyes freshly made up but only very subtle. She has on a dusky pink dress that comes to her knees with buttons down the front, open at the shoulders, and a bit of sleeve.

"Wow, Evelyn, you are beautiful. You take my breath away." I step into the house, then lean in to give her a quick kiss on the lips. She holds my head and catches my mouth, and it soon becomes more than a peck. Shit, I'm rock hard now. It never takes much with Evelyn.

"You don't look so bad yourself, Theon." She's grabbing my waist now and pulling me farther into her. I know she can feel how hard I am because she has a knowing smile on her face. I think she loves how she can do this to me.

"Come on, gorgeous, let's get out of here for our first date before we end up staying in and losing control."

"Don't worry about that, Maggie's in the kitchen. When my parents are away for the night, and although I'm old enough to be left, they always have Maggie stay over so I'm not alone in the house. Just being protective I suppose." She gives me another kiss but again we can't seem to tear our lips away from each other until we hear a cough. We both turn our heads together and see Maggie watching us.

"Hi, Maggie," I say holding up my hand to give her a little wave.

"Friends, huh?" she says raising her eyebrows at us.

"Well, until today, yes, we were best friends, Maggie. But we both have feelings for each other. You know I do, we've talked about this," Evelyn says to Maggie. I look at her and raise my eyebrows.

"I think I want to hear about that conversation and when exactly it took place," I say winking at Maggie and smiling down at Evelyn who is still nestled in my arms.

"See you later, Maggie. Don't wait up. We're going for something to eat and then off to the cinema."

"Bye, Maggie," I say turning to the door so she can't see my front.

We go to a nice Italian restaurant at the plaza where the cinema complex is, and we share a pizza and drink water. We then walk hand in hand to the cinema. I let Evelyn pick the film, to be honest, I'm not that interested in what we watch as I know most of my attention will be on her anyway. We end up watching a film about a girl working in a club, and they dance on the bar, and she sings and falls in love. It's okay.

We are sitting at the back, and luckily there aren't many people in. I spend a lot of the time nuzzling her neck and kissing her. I can't get enough of her.

I still can't believe she wants to be my girlfriend, and on our way home my worries come tumbling out.

"Evelyn, why do you want to be my girlfriend? I mean, shit, you are beautiful, baby, and you have all the jocks asking you out on dates, I've seen it. Why do you want to go steady with me? You're gorgeous, and I'm well aware that I'm punching above my weight with you on my arm."

She stops walking and my arm jerks back because we're holding hands. I turn to find she is glaring daggers at me. "How the hell can you say that, Theon?"

Oh shit, she's angry, really angry by that look. I shrug. "Look at me, and look at you," I say to her.

"I AM looking at you, Theon, where has this come from? Don't you want to be my boyfriend, is that what this is all about?"

"No, No! Oh God no. You have no idea how delirious I was today when we kissed. I've wanted to do that since the first day I saw you. When you walked into the lecture hall that day, I nearly died. I'd noticed you before then, and I had the biggest crush on you. Then when we were paired together, that was the best day of my life. Until we kissed today then that was the best day of my life — THIS is the best day of my life. I haven't had many good days in my life, in fact, just a couple, and they both involved you. So, baby, no, this is not me trying to get out of being your boyfriend. It's just me making sure this is what you want before I fall even more in love with you — if that's even possible. It would destroy me, Evelyn, if this weren't what you wanted. I don't think I would ever get over it. It would break my heart." I hold her cheeks with both my hands and lean down to kiss her gently on the lips. "Just in case you missed it, I love you. I have been in love with you for a long time. And I would rather be in your life as your best friend if you didn't want to be my girlfriend than not in your life at all. I don't want us to try this for it to end badly and us no longer be friends. Evelyn, that would kill me, baby. I love you." I release her face from my hands and take a step back. The next thing I know, she's jumping up my body and is clinging to me like a chimp. She's hugging me hard, but she's sobbing into my neck.

"Shhh, baby, please don't cry. Hey, look at me." She slowly lifts her head to look me in the face. There's a smile there — okay this must be good …

"Baby?"

"I love you, Theon, I love you so much. You ask why you. Why not you? You are the nicest, sweetest, most unassuming person I know. I told you this afternoon where you live or how much money you have doesn't dictate the person you are, its what's up here," she points to my head, "but most of all it's what's in here," she puts her hand over my heart, just like she did in the pool this afternoon. "In here dictates who and what you are. I feel it in you, Theon. I've felt it for a long time. I'm yours. I'm going to keep you." She laughs. "I'm not and have never been interested in anyone else. You are the one for me. I love you, Theon, You." She wipes under my eye and then kisses the tears away from my cheeks. I spin her around, and we start to laugh out loud. Anyone watching us would think we were mad. We lean in at the same time, and we kiss hard. I can feel her love for me in this kiss. We break apart, and she slides down my body. That look on her face tells me she felt how hard I am again. I shrug.

"It's become the norm since being friends with you, Evelyn. He's always standing to attention. I'm getting used to it.' I wink at her, and she laughs.

"Come on, gorgeous, let's get you home before Maggie calls out a search party." I grab her hand, and we walk along together.

"Oh, just so you know, I told grandma tonight that we were officially together. She was happy for us. Told me to be respectful of you and responsible." I blush. "I told her I would take you to meet her. That she would love you as much as I do."

"I would love to meet the wonderful woman who brought you up to be such a perfect man." She pulls my arm down, which in turn brings me down so she can kiss my cheek.

We hand in our project and a week later are told we passed, top of our class. Our tutor asks if he can send our game to his friend who works for a games developer. We are working on a follow-up game to that one, and we still spend every minute we can together, usually in her office working, but now we do spend an awful lot of time making out. We both decide we aren't ready for sex. We are both virgins and rather than it being awkward between us, we talk about it like the adults we are — about us waiting until we are both ready. We talk about our feelings all the time. I have no doubt we will get married one day.

A couple of weeks later our tutor asks us to stay behind after class. He has heard back from his friend, and the company he works for, Bulldog gaming, wants to meet us both to discuss buying our game. We are ecstatic. We can't wait to get home and tell Evelyn's parents. They are happy for us, but not thrilled. They wanted Evelyn to follow in their footsteps as surgeons and thought she would grow out of her obsession with computers and gaming. It was never going to happen. My grandma, on the other hand, is jumping around for joy. She grabs our hands and we all spin around laughing and screaming. Grandma has met Evelyn a few times now, and she loved her immediately. Just like I knew she would.

Chapter 7

Present

I DROP THE KIDS off again the next morning. Evelina had some tummy ache but said she was okay to go to school. I went to work but found I couldn't concentrate. I'm lucky I have a great loyal team working for me. Some of my employees have been with me since the company started growing too quickly for Evelyn and me to manage.

I get a call from an unknown number at 11.55 a.m., and I answer straight away, my gut tells me it is the doctor.

"Mr. Tourney. Hi, it's Dr. Cassidy."

"Hello, Doctor, I take it you have the results back?"

"I do. Can you come in to see me today so we can discuss the results? Just you, no need to bring Evelina in with you." Shit, this doesn't sound good.

"Can you tell me now, Doctor, is it bad news?"

"I need to see you, Mr. Tourney, to explain properly."

"I'm on my way. Can you see me now?"

"Yes, of course. I have a patient due in very soon; then I'm free."

"Can I bring my mother in law with me?"

"Yes, of course, that's a good idea."

"See you soon, Doctor." I hang up without waiting for her to say goodbye. I sit for a minute with my face in my hands, trying not to fall apart. I know this is bad. I can feel it, and I'm not usually wrong, why else wouldn't she tell me if it's not bad news. Fuck! I dial Sonia.

"Theon, tell me, what did the doctor say?" No hello. She's as anxious as I am.

"She wouldn't tell me on the phone. She wants to see me. I'm going there now. Do you want me to stop by and pick you up? I think I need some support, Sonia. I know it's bad. I can feel it." The tears are flowing down my face. I can't lose Evelina. It almost killed me losing Evelyn. How I survived is beyond me. It was only the two tiny things that were a part of Evelyn that kept me going. If it weren't for them, I know I would be with her now — without a doubt. I know life goes on but when your heart stops beating it can't possibly go on. It was those two kids that made it beat again. I need them as much as they need me.

"Theon, Theon are you still there, sweetie? Theon?" I can't speak. I've been lost in my thoughts, and the lump in my throat is stopping me from saying anything.

"Theon, I'm on my way to pick you up. I think it's best if I drive. I'll be there very soon. Hang in there, sweetie. Whatever this is, we can get through it. Let's not jump the gun until we have spoken to the doctor. I'm hanging up now, wait for me." The phone goes dead.

The next thing I know, Sonia is walking into my office. She looks tired and worried. I haven't moved. I'm still crying, but with my head resting on my desk. How long has it been? I look at my phone — it's been twenty-five minutes since I spoke to Sonia. Why hasn't Aggie been in? Shit, I bet people passed my window and saw the state of me. Those that were around ten years ago would have seen me like this then. I was a shell of a man.

I go into my private bathroom and splash cold water on my face. I need to pull myself together. I have to for the Evs. I walk out with Sonia and mumble to Aggie to cancel any appointments I have for the rest of the day.

We are at the hospital twenty minutes later, waiting for Doctor Cassidy. She comes out and motions for us to come into her office. She starts talking to us, but I switch off as the words tumor, cancer, kidney, surgery, chemo, rare and something to do with Wilma come from her lips. I haven't taken anything in that the doc has been saying. Those words are swimming around in my head. Sonia has tissues in her hand, sniffling, but she is talking to the doctor. I think she is asking the questions I should have been asking.

"Who's Wilma and what does she have to do with my daughter?" I blurt out. It comes from nowhere. I just want to know who Wilma is. Of all the questions to ask when a Doctor is telling you your ten-year-old daughter has a tumor.

"I don't know, Mr. Tourney? Who is Wilma?"

"You said something about Wilma, you tell me. Who the fuck is she?" She doesn't even look shocked at my language, and I've shocked myself. She furrows her brow trying to think before it suddenly dawns on her what she's said.

"No, Mr. Tourney, not Wilma. It's Wilms' tumor. That is what Evelina has got. It's a rare cancer of the kidney. It usually affects younger children of around three years old, but it can affect older children and, in fact, adults. Although it's rare, it is the most common kidney cancer in children."

"What, are we having a popularity cancer contest now? I don't care how rare, or common or what fucking age she should be. All I want to know is will she …" I'm choked. I can't say the word. The tears are flying down my face now. I grab a tissue from the box on the table.

"It depends on the stage, Mr. Tourney. We need to do a biopsy tomorrow to see where we are at with it. Do you want me to run through the information about the stages with you now? I know you're in shock. I will answer any questions you have." I nod my head for her to tell me.

"I can't give you more information until I know the stage the cancer is at. Stage one is the best outcome we can hope for. Stage one means it's contained in one kidney and we can remove it and administer chemo. Stage two and the tumor has spread into the tissue of the kidney and the vessels. We can still remove the kidney, but she will need a more intense course of chemo. Stage three means the tumor can't be completely removed with surgery because it's spread to the abdomen and will need longer intense chemo and radiation therapy. Stage four …"

"Doc, please stop. I can't take all this in. What's the first step from now?"

"We have scheduled for you to bring Evelina in tomorrow and we will sedate her to take a biopsy. We will send that to the lab and have the results back the same day. The stage of the tumor will determine the next step." I can hear Sonia sniffling at the side of me. I grab her hand and squeeze. She squeezes back.

"What do I tell Evelina?" How can I tell my baby girl she's really poorly?

"She's a very intelligent little girl, Mr. Tourney. When I said she was brave yesterday, I meant it. I've seen older children go into meltdown from needles. She barely flinched. I think you should sit them both down and tell them she is very poorly and she will need an operation to make her better. I'm 99% sure she will be having chemo. You need to explain to her she will be having medicine that will make her feel more poorly than she is, but it will make her better eventually. It's imperative you tell Evander at the same time. Twins have a connection, as I'm sure your aware of, and when one is really poorly, in my experience, the other one also suffers. If you tell them both what's happening together, I believe it will alleviate a lot of his suffering."

"Thank you, Doctor. Really, I mean it. I'm sorry for swearing. It's not personal."

"Please, Mr. Tourney, there is no need to apologize. It's shock. It makes us do unusual things. You and Mrs. Westcott need to go and talk about this before the children finish school. You need to get over the shock, putting it bluntly, you need to pull yourselves together and show your little girl how confident you are that she will get better. You cannot fall to pieces around her. She needs her daddy to be strong and in control, now more than ever in her life. You cannot show her you are worried in any way. If she feels it coming from either of you, it could affect her recovery. It's hard for any parent to have a sick child and not lose control because it's out of your control, but be strong for her, Mr. Tourney, Mrs. Westcott." I nod at her and wipe my face. She's right. I know she is, and I will be so strong for my baby girl, but first I need to go home and break down.

"I've scheduled the biopsy for 9.30 a.m. tomorrow, that way we will know the stage by early afternoon. I have also scheduled surgery for her the following day because I am 99% sure we will be removing her kidney. The oncologist has checked the ultrasound and has said it doesn't look like the tumor is all that big. If it turns out it is too big or has spread, she won't be having surgery for a while. We will have to start the chemo and radiation to shrink it first, but we will cross that bridge tomorrow afternoon."

"Doctor —" Sonia looks at me as she says this, looking for permission to ask what I couldn't. I nod very slightly.

"In your opinion and with what you know of this tumor, without knowing more, what are her chances of survival?" The doctor looks at Sonia then at me

"These are the facts, not a diagnosis. You could do the research yourselves, so I can tell you that the chances of survival at stage one are 99%, at stage two it's 98%, and stage three is 90%. They are very high. I'm not going into stage four or five now until we know tomorrow because it's very rare that Wilms' Tumors are found after stage three or above. It's fingers, toes, and everything crossed. I will see you in the morning. Here's my card and if you have any questions at all, no matter what time, give me a call."

Sonia drives us home slowly, the last hour has been a blur, and we break down together as soon as we get to my house, but manage to pull ourselves together in time for the school bus dropping the Evs home.

They both come barreling in through the door, pushing and shoving each other with not a care in the world. I have to shatter their world very soon. But first, it's playtime.

"Dad!" Evelina shouts. "What are you doing home this early?" She runs to me, leaping into my arms hugging me.

"Well, I thought I would come home for when you finished school so we could go hang out in the pool for a bit. It's a hot day, and I need cooling down. What do you think?"

"Yay, come on Vander, last one in the pool is a stinky poo." She runs off to get changed. I don't worry about them in or near the pool. They are both excellent swimmers and have even got their lifesaver badges. I hear her running around, shouting to Evander to hurry up. He hasn't gone up the stairs yet. He's been watching me.

"What's up, son? Don't you want to go in the pool?" He doesn't say anything, just turns and runs up the stairs. My kids are too intelligent for their own good sometimes. He knows there is something wrong. He's like me. He weighs up situations and works them over in his mind. Unlike Evelina — because she's a little spitfire whirlwind. Very intelligent but barrels right in without thinking things through. I suppose them having two nerdy parents makes them super smart.

Ten minutes later, I'm the last in the pool, so I'm the stinky poo, who just so happens to get dunked all the time and splashed and climbed on like I'm a tree. I don't care. This right here is what I live for after losing Evelyn. This right here is my life with these two super little humans that were born from the love of Evelyn and me. I have no choice but to cherish them. They are precious.

I've got to get Evelina through this next stage of her life. I look up at the sky, silently asking Evelyn to guide her through this. To protect her. To make sure she makes it through what life is throwing her way right now.

I get dunked again by both of them, letting my guard down while asking Evelyn for help.

Chapter 8

17 and a half years ago

ARNOLD INSISTS ON US HAVING A corporate lawyer when we meet with Bulldog gaming. Once he found out it was one of the biggest game giants in the world that was interested in us, he did some research on payments for games and royalties and has realized Evelyn and I could be onto a winner. It's a good job we have the lawyer because Bulldog comes straight at us with a contract.

I think they were hoping that we were two naive kids who would sign anything for what we would consider a lot of money. I was a little annoyed they didn't pre-warn us. We were left by Bulldog to read over the contract with our lawyer.

"Bulldog want to buy your game from you for $500,000 and no royalties. They also want the rights to buy any other games you create, even if not related to this first game. As your lawyer, I am advising you to reject this offer and make a counteroffer. If they have already drawn up the contract, with no warning to you that they were going to, then they know your game will be a top seller. You two have the power here. You can ask for a substantial upfront payment with a further advance if sales reach a certain point and also royalties. You two have done everything on this game. It's your idea, graphics, music — everything. They have already beta tested it, so they know it's a great investment and when they are onto a winner. We can counter offer. If they don't accept, we go to another company. If Bulldog wants you that bad, then I'm sure Sony or Nintendo will too." I'm gawking at him. Did he say five hundred thousand? That's two hundred and fifty thousand each. I could buy Grandma a brand new house in a great neighborhood with that money. Oh my god. I would have just signed away if our lawyer hadn't been here. That's a huge amount of money for two kids in college.

"Evelyn, can you believe this? What do you think, baby?"

"I think we do what John is suggesting. What about you, Theon?"

"I agree with whatever you want to do. I trust you, baby." I bring her hand up to my mouth and kiss it. I've got the biggest smile on my face.

"Here's what I think the counter offer should be. You want $750,000 up front. Then, if they reach a sales target of $3.5million in the next 12 months, you want a further payment of $1million with royalties after that of 15% of sales for life, on all pc and console platforms. They don't have any rights to any follow-up or other games. You shouldn't be tied to them for life. You will take this one game at a time with negotiations for each game. How does that sound?"

I'm speechless. This could make me a millionaire, and they don't know about the follow-up game yet. Holy fuckeroo. I start laughing hysterically. Evelyn squeezes my hand and brings it to her mouth and kisses it. She nods at me, and I nod at her. We're happy with his suggestion. Who wouldn't be?

"Don't get too excited, the contracts aren't signed yet," John says.

We walk out of the Bulldog offices with more money than I ever thought imaginable. They agreed to our counter offer, no hesitation and they didn't counter offer. I grab Evelyn and lift her up, twirling us around. She's laughing at my giddiness.

"Oh my God, baby. Can you believe what just happened in there? It doesn't feel real, but they said we would have the money this afternoon. I don't even have a bank account, baby. I need to open one. I need to get home and tell Grandma to start looking for a house." I carry on twirling her then lower her so her face is level with mine and I kiss her hard, right in the car park of the Bulldog offices.

"That's what you're going to do with your money, Theon? Buy a house for your grandma?" I scrunch my brow up. Of course it is. Doesn't she think I should?

"Without a doubt, baby. I will spend it all on a lovely new house in a nice neighborhood and with everything brand new inside. It's the least I can do for her. I will spend every cent on her if that's what it takes. Why? Don't you think I should?"

"Oh, Theon, I wouldn't expect anything less from you. The minute they mentioned big money I knew straight away what you would do. You have a heart of gold. It's why I love you so damn much. Other people would buy flash cars, or designer clothes and jewelry before anything else. But not you. Not my Theon. I love you with all my heart. Come on, let's ask John to drop us off at your grandma's so we can tell her. I can't wait to see her face light up."

Once we tell Bulldog we have a follow-up game, they ask if they can see it. I have it on my laptop, so I show their team, and they want to buy that one as well, even before the first one is released. John negotiates a $1 million advance. We then get a further $2 million in twelve months and then $2 million twelve months after that for the second game plus we get 17.5% royalties an all platforms on all worldwide distribution, and that's on both games sales after twelve months. So we get over the course of two years a minimum of $5 million plus royalties and to show some loyalty we will let them have first dibs on any other games we develop. Holy fucking hell. I'm a millionaire — well soon, there will be $2.5 million coming my way.

We finish college, both getting top honors in our degree. We both decide we don't need to study anymore, we know what we are doing and how to do it, and Evelyn's parents and my grandma agree. I buy Grandma a lovely, brand new, three bedroomed ranch-style house in a quiet, clean neighborhood. I have enough money to fully furnish it and buy her a small car so she doesn't have to walk everywhere or take the bus, all non-negotiable as she puts up a fight telling me to save my money. I tell her she doesn't have to work three jobs anymore, she can quit them all if she wants, but she insists she will stay at one. I do buy myself a Harley Davidson with the bit of money I have left until our next advance comes through in a couple of months. I'm going to be a self-made millionaire, and I'm not even nineteen yet. The game becomes a number one top seller. It's the fastest selling game of all time, taking in more sales in the first week than any other.

Evelyn and I decide to start looking for offices to set up our business when the next advance comes through. We find the perfect place.

Chapter 9

Once the twins are ready for bed, I make them their hot chocolate with marshmallows as usual. We do this every night after their showers, and we talk until they finish. It's usually bedtime by then with Evelina talking our socks off.

I'm dreading today's conversation over hot chocolate. I don't want either of them upset. I sit on the stool at the breakfast island just staring into space thinking about how to tell them — I'm miles away. I don't even hear my little whirlwind come running in with her Monsters High dolls in tow and her stuffed turtle and stitch teddy she sleeps with — she loves that little alien and turtle — and Evander following close behind her.

"I need to tell you both something. I need you to sit here and listen to what I'm saying. It's very important. Can't you do that, poppet?" I know Evander can with no problem; it's my tornado of a daughter that will struggle. She nods at me, putting her dolls to one side but cuddling Stitch. I pull her stool closer to me so I can put my arm around her and she snuggles into me. I take a deep breath.

"Dr. Cassidy phoned me today. You remember she said she would have your results back from your blood test and your ultrasound?" I feel her nodding her head. I'm looking at Evander. He knows there is something wrong. I can see his face turning to a pained expression. I nod at him.

"It turns out you are poorly inside, poppet. You know we have organs in our body that help us live?"

"Yes, like our heart pumps blood around our body and our lungs help us breathe," she says all proud and clever.

"Yes, that's right. It turns out one of your organs is poorly."

"Oh, which one, Daddy? Is it my heart?"

"No, poppet. It's your kidney. Can you remember what your kidneys do?" She shakes her head no.

"You have two kidneys, and they help to clean your blood and the water in your body. They help take out any bad bits. One of your kidneys is poorly, so Dr. Cassidy needs you back at the hospital in the morning."

"I can't go in the morning, silly dad. It's school. We'll have to go after school. I don't want to get into trouble." I have to smile at her. I nod at Evander again, silently asking if he's okay, and he nods back.

"I will phone school in the morning, don't you worry about that. I will tell them you won't be in, probably for a few days. You won't get into trouble. I pinky promise you." We link our smallest fingers.

"In the morning, Dr. Cassidy is going to give you a special air through a mask over your mouth to make you sleep, and then while you are asleep, she needs to do a little cut so she can see into your kidney a bit better. You won't feel a thing, but it might be a little bit sore afterward. Do you think you are brave enough for that, poppet?"

"I am, Dad, yes of course, but I'm also a little bit scared. You pinky promise I won't feel anything while I'm asleep?" We link fingers again.

"I pinky promise, poppet."

"What happens after that, Dad?" Evander asks me.

"Well, they take a little bit of the kidney and send it to the science doctors to look at. They have to see it and then decide how to go about making Evelina better. Dr. Cassidy says that Evelina will probably have to have her poorly kidney taken out of her body." She gasps.

"But what will clean my blood and water. Will I have dirty blood and water?" She looks upset.

"No, poppet. Remember, you have two kidneys so you will still have one that will clean it, but it will just have to work a little bit harder being on its own. Now, if they have to take the poorly kidney out, that might happen the following day, so no school again that day or for a little while longer. You will be sore after they take the kidney out. So I need you to be extra brave for me. Can you do that?" She nods but doesn't say anything. She's not sure she can be that brave — what ten-year-old is? It's breaking my heart, sitting here, explaining something like this to her.

"After the surgery to take the kidney out, the next thing that will happen is not very nice, baby girl. I need you to be like Supergirl and be the bravest you can be." Her eyes are wide like saucers.

"Why? Are they taking more organs from my body? I won't have any left to live if they do and will be an angel like mommy." My heart just breaks. I have a lump in my throat, and I can feel my eyes welling up. Evelina can't see with her cuddling into me, but Evander is watching my reactions very closely. I see his eyes well up. I slightly shake my head, and I clear my throat by taking a sip of hot chocolate.

"No, baby. They are not going to take any more organs from you." Please don't ask me to pinky swear because I can't.

"But what they need to do is give you medicine for a few weeks. This isn't a nice medicine that you drink. It's a medicine that has to be put into your body with a needle, like when the doctor was taking your blood yesterday."

"If it isn't a nice medicine, how will it make me better?"

"The medicine will make you feel yukky and possibly more poorly than you have been already. It has to work really hard in your body to make sure you are all fixed. You will get better though, that's what the medicine does. After a while, it makes you all better. I know it's a lot for you, poppet, but we have to get rid of the poorly organ to make you better. Do you think you can be very brave for Evander and me?" She doesn't say anything, and I can see Evander struggling, but he manages to speak.

"I think Lina is the bravest girl in the world, Dad. I think she can do all this with us helping her. I was so proud of her yesterday. She didn't cry when the needle was in her arm. You are the bravest ever, Lina." He gets off his stool and comes over to hug us. I hug them both to me chanting: be strong, be strong, over and over in my head.

I get them both into bed. Evander looks sullen as I tuck him in and kiss his forehead goodnight. "Is she going to be okay, Dad?"

"I hope so, son. I really do. I've asked your mom to make sure she's going to get better. I'm sure she will. We have to be there for her, Evander. We have to be strong for her. Can you do that for her?"

"Yes, Dad."

"Good boy. I love you, Evander. Goodnight."

"Love you back from the moon to us, Dad. Goodnight."

I phone Sonia and tell her how it went. I'm in awe of Evelina. She's a tough little cookie. She reminds me of her mother so much.

Chapter 10

16 years ago

Last month, I turned twenty. What a birthday that was. It was nothing to do with partying because that's never been my scene, but everything to do with Evelyn by my side. We could do anything we wanted — we're millionaires. What did we do? Spent the day in our new offices, just the two of us, as usual.

It has taken us longer than we wanted, but we've finally picked out a floor of a building in downtown L.A. to rent. It's huge. There are fourteen offices, three meeting rooms, a conference room, reception area, kitchen and a couple of bathrooms. It's on the twenty-sixth floor, and we have fantastic views. It's just Evelyn and me working here at the moment, but we have no doubts we will be employing people to work for us in the next twelve months. Things are moving so fast now.

I'm busy in my office, which is opposite Evelyn's. I look up just as she walks in carrying a big chocolate birthday cake with a couple of lit candles. She's wearing a long trench coat, which I hadn't noticed her wearing earlier.

She puts the cake on my desk and sings 'happy birthday' to me. I blow out my candles and make a wish. I wish for an entire life with this gorgeous woman. She slowly walks around to my side of the desk, untying the belt on her coat. When she gets to me, she shrugs the coat off her shoulders, and it falls to the floor. Oh my god. She's standing in front of me in a basque, barely-there knickers, stockings, suspenders and high, red sparkly Christian Louboutin's.

I turn in my chair to face her, my jaw on the floor, just taking in the beautiful, gorgeousness that is my girlfriend.

"Like what you see, baby?" I look up at her face. She looks very shy and embarrassed all of a sudden, which isn't like Evelyn.

Although we still haven't had sex, we fool around a lot. We've almost gone all the way a few times, but one of us usually has the good sense to stop it.

"Fuck, baby. I love what I see, but holy hell, I'm not sure I can keep my hands off you. I never do, but with you looking like that? Well, I'm like the man of steel," I say looking down into my lap. I think he's going to bust through my trousers. We both burst out laughing.

"Baby, I want you to have me as your birthday present. I'm ready, Theon, I've been ready for a while. I love you with everything I am. I want to be yours in every way, I want to be your first and last, and I want you to be my first and last." She straddles my legs and sits on my lap, holding onto the back of my chair, getting as close to me as she can.

"Baby, I'm going to explode in a minute with you grinding on me. You know I can never help myself. How many times have I embarrassed myself? Do you really want to do this, beautiful?"

"I've thought of nothing else for weeks now, Theon. I'm more than ready. Are you ready?" Am I ready? It's been killing me holding off.

"Definitely. No doubt in my mind. I want to make love to you." So we did just that — there in my office. We fumbled at first, and it was a bit painful for Evelyn, which nearly made me stop, as I couldn't bear causing her pain, but she wouldn't let me. She clung on to me. It was quick the first time, neither lasting long, but thirty minutes later we were ready to go again, this time on the couch in my office. Slow and steady, staring into each other's eyes, having that connection as we both climaxed together, never looking away. That was making love. We didn't stop there. For the rest of the day, that's all we did, on every surface in our offices. It was the best birthday of my life.

It's Evelyn's twentieth birthday today, and although I want to give her a birthday present like she gave me, I have other ideas. We're not into fancy stuff. It's never been our thing, so I'm recreating our first date with a few added extras.

I arrive at her house, all done up in my new Armani suit. I'm not one for designer stuff, but Evelyn said I needed a tailored suit for our business meetings. We both went to Armani and they custom-made suits for each of us. I usually just walk into her parents' house, but I want to do this properly tonight. I press the doorbell and wait for the door to be opened.

"Hello, son, you look too nervous, are you ready for this?" Arnold held out his hand to shake mine. Mine was sweaty. I was nervous.

"Never been more ready, sir," I say.

Just then Evelyn comes bounding down the stairs and stops when she sees me standing there. I stop breathing — my heart skips a beat, she is breathtakingly stunning. Her long auburn hair is tied up at the back with strands falling down each side of her face, just like it was on our first date. Her make up is neutral, she never wears much, she doesn't need to, she's a natural beauty. She has on a figure-hugging soft pink sleeveless dress that falls just above her knees and her red Christian Louboutin's. She loves those shoes. I love them too, especially when those heels are digging into my backside when her legs are wrapped around my waist. She is breathtaking, and she looks just like she did on our first date, even down to the color of her dress.

"What do you kids have planned for tonight?" he says grinning at me, knowing full well what my plans are.

"We are going to the little Italian restaurant at the plaza for pizza and then to watch a movie."

"Oh, Theon. That's what we did on our first ever date."

"It is, baby." I smile at her. I hand her a big bouquet of her favorite flowers, lilies and there are lots in this bouquet, all in different colors.

"These are for you. Happy Birthday, Evelyn, and you look absolutely stunning. I love you, baby." I lean in and kiss her cheek.

"They are beautiful, Theon. Thank you." She puts them on the table in the hall.

"Not as beautiful as you," I say to myself, but she hears me and turns, smiling. I look at Arnold who is also stood smiling at the pair of us.

At the restaurant we sit in the exact same spot we did on our first date, I have already pre-ordered the same food and drink that we had that night. After dinner, we head into the cinema and are shown to our seats.

"Theon, what are we watching? I didn't catch what the film was?"

"Wait and see, baby," I say smiling and leaning in to kiss her. The theatre goes dark, and the screen comes to life.

She leans in and whispers, "There is no one else in here, Theon, its empty. It must be an old film." She's linking my arm, and I smile, feigning surprise. I look around. She has no idea I hired the whole screen just for us. The usher knew exactly what seats to put us in. The film starts, I hear her gasp as her favorite film, and the first film we saw together, Coyote Ugly, starts playing. After our first date and because of her love of the film, we'd created a game based on dancing, and it became a huge hit.

When the film finishes, we don't move. "Thank you so much, Theon. I have had the best birthday ever. Even after your best birthday ever." She laughs at me.

"I'm your first and last, baby, forever. I have something to show you." I stand up, remove my suit jacket and roll up my left sleeve. I hear her gasp when she sees the brand-new tattoo on my inner forearm.

First & Last Forever

"Oh, wow, that's beautiful, Theon. When did you get that done?

"It was last week. I wanted it to heal so you could see it today. I've been hiding my arm all week, and with this heat, it's been a killer. I'm just glad you didn't notice and question me." I lean in and kiss the tip of her nose. "Hold on one minute. Don't move. I will be right back. Stay put, you hear me?"

She nods at me. I don't leave the room. I stand at the back … waiting. Just then, the screen comes to life just as I planned. I've created a cartoon graphic that replicates Evelyn and me. It shows everything we have done tonight. Me arriving at her house and giving her flowers, us walking arm in arm along the street, in the restaurant having pizza, and then in the cinema watching her favorite film. This is my cue. I have some chocolates in a huge heart shaped box for her hidden in the back row along with a big stuffed sea turtle, her favorite animal, which I grab as I walk slowly down to the front where she is. The screen is playing exactly what I'm doing. I have to time this perfectly. I stand in front of her. She has her hands up to her face covering her mouth, and I can see tears flowing down her cheeks. I pass her the box of chocolates and turtle which she grabs and cuddles.

"These are for you, Evelyn. They are beautiful, but nothing in this world is as beautiful as you are." The screen behind shows me giving her the chocolates and turtle. I see her eyes going from mine to the screen behind me. I put my hand in my pocket, and I get down on one knee in front of her. I hold out my hand. I know cartoon me is doing this exact same thing with a Tiffany blue box held in his hand just like mine. Evelyn gasps and her hand shoots to her chest just as I knew she would and cartoon Evelyn does exactly that. I open the box to reveal a stunningly simple, platinum, brilliant solitaire diamond ring. I turn to make sure the screen behind is in time with me. And it is. I know as I start to speak, the words will appear on the screen

"Evelyn, you are my life. I want you in it for eternity, even though eternity is not long enough with you. You complete my life, baby. You are beautiful inside and out. I knew the first day I saw you that you were 'the one' for me, but never in my wildest dreams did I think I would be your 'one'. I never in my wildest dreams thought we would ever talk and that was the best day of my life. I never in my wildest dreams thought we would become best friends, and that became the best day of my life. I most certainly never in my wildest dreams thought you would become my girlfriend until that became the best day of my life. Will you make my wildest dreams come true again? Will you make this the best day of my life and do me the greatest honor of becoming my wife? Will you be Mrs. Evelyn Tourney?" I hold my breath, waiting for her answer. She flings herself at me, knocking me to the floor, flat on my back. She leans over my face, feathering it with kisses.

"Yes, Theon. Yes, a million times, yes. I would be so honored to be your wife. To be by your side for eternity — although I agree eternity is not long enough. Yes, to everything, Theon. Yes to all the best days of our lives. I love you so much."

"Yes." Kiss.

"Yes." Kiss.

"Yes." Kiss. She is smothering me in kisses. The graphic above us has stopped on me putting the ring on her finger, still on my knee in front of her and the words above say, 'First & last forever, Mr. & Mrs. Tourney.' We didn't get that far. I still haven't put the ring on her finger. I feel for the box at my side and take out the ring. I grab her left hand, and I place the ring on her wedding finger. She's crying happy tears, as am I. In a theatre, with my fiancée sitting above me, showing me how much she loves me.

When we arrive back at her parents' house, it's quiet, and she thinks they've gone to bed, but as we walk into the kitchen her parents, my grandma and Maggie are all there with champagne flutes raised and shouting congratulations to us. There is a big banner across the room that says: 'Congratulations on Your Engagement.'

"Oh my god, Theon. They all knew? You did all this for me?" She's crying again. All I ever do is make my fiancée cry. I kiss her nose and pull her closer to my side with my arm around her waist.

"You are my life, Evelyn. I would walk over broken glass and hot coals to get to you."

I know some will say we are too young but we are more mature than most twenty-year-olds and we are running a very successful business. We are both very traditional, and we talked about moving in together, but thought we would wait a couple of years. We wanted to do it properly by getting married, then moving in, then starting a family and growing our business. We have a ten-year plan. Getting married was going to happen during the sixth year, but I can't wait until we're twenty-six. I want her by my side permanently, as my wife. We both know it will happen, so why wait?

This is the best day of my life.

Chapter 11

Present

I GET THE KIDS UP EARLY AS WE HAVE TO be at the hospital for 8 a.m. to get Evelina prepped for surgery. The Evs are sullen, neither of them speaking much. I need to perk them up as best I can. I get Evelina's Monster High dolls and take them into the living room and put them behind the couch. I can hear them upstairs getting ready, and they come down together. Usually, Evelina is running around like the whirlwind she is, but today she's holding Evander's hand, coming down the stairs slowly. I just need to make sure she's feeling okay and hasn't got the pains again. I step out of the living room.

"Hey, poppet. How are you feeling this morning? Do you have any pains?"

"Yes, Daddy, and I feel sick. I don't want any breakfast." She looks at me waiting for me to demand she eats, but in all honesty, I was wondering how to broach the subject of her not being allowed to eat or drink anything this morning.

"Oh, poppet, come here." I lift her into my arms where she grabs my neck and rests her head on my shoulder with her legs wrapped around my waist, her usual chimp style, just like her mom used to cling to me. I sit on the couch with her, cuddling.

"Are you worried about going to the hospital?"

"A bit, Daddy, yes. I'm a little scared, but I'm going to be brave like I promised."

"That's my girl. We need to get you all better to make this nasty pain and sickness go away forever. You do understand what's going to happen, don't you, poppet?"

"I think so, Daddy. We go today. I have a sleep, and the doctor cuts me to see inside. Then tomorrow, I go to sleep again, and the doctor takes out my organ." She puts her finger on her lips thinking about what organ it is.

"Your kidney."

"Yes. Because it's broken, poorly sick, and can't be fixed. Then I have to have medicine that makes me sick again for a while but then makes me all better," she says with complete understanding and a proud look on her face. I kiss her forehead.

"That is spot on. Well done, my big brave girl. Shall we see if Evander has finished his breakfast and get on our way?" She nods at me but doesn't want to leave me, so I get up with her clinging to me, and we go and see how Evander is doing. As we enter the kitchen, I catch him suddenly pick up his spoon pretending to eat. His bowl doesn't have much in it, but I suspect that's because he didn't put much in it.

"You okay, buddy?" He nods.

"You ready to get on the road? Do you want to go to school, son, or to the hospital with us today? It will be a lot of waiting around, but you're more than welcome to come with us." I want to give him the choice. Everyone deals with things differently. He might need school and friends to take his mind of what's going on with Evelina, then again, he might not be able to concentrate and just want to be in the hospital with us. I'm not worried about him missing school as he is way ahead of all the other kids. He perks up a bit when I give him the option. Maybe that's what was getting him down. He thought I was going to send him to school when he wanted to be with his sister.

"Can I come with you please, Dad? I want to be there when Lina wakes up."

"Of course you can, buddy. I'm just going to run upstairs and get some things together. Evelina, baby, don't have anything to eat or drink because you're having that magic air to make you sleep. Okay, poppet?"

"Yes, Daddy. I don't want anything anyway." I put her on the stool next to Evander, run up the stairs, grab a backpack and put some nightwear and Stitch in the bag for Evelina.

At the hospital, we are taken to a private room that will be Evelina's while she's here. Dr. Cassidy comes in with another doctor.

"Good morning, Tourney family, and how are you all today?"

"Okay, Doctor. Just a little scared, but I'm a big brave girl." I am so proud of her.

"You most definitely are brave, Evelina. Did your daddy explain everything that was going to happen today?" She nods yes.

"Okay, that's good. Well done, Daddy." She turns to me and smiles. I smile back.

"Can you tell me what is going to happen, Evelina?"

"You are going to put me to sleep with magic air. Then you will cut me. Then the science doctors will do tests on my organ." She looks over at me, and I mouth 'kidney' at her.

"My kidney. Then tomorrow you will make me sleep again and take out my poorly kidney because its broken and you can't fix it. Then I will have some medicine that will make me sick for a while, but then it will make me all better again. That's it." She shrugs. Doctor Cassidy looks at me with awe on her face at the fact that my baby girl has told her exactly what is going to happen, and without any panic or worry at all.

"Wow, you know everything. Do you have any questions for me? Is there anything you are unsure about or are worried about?"

"No." She just shrugs again. I smile at her. They prepare Evelina ready for theatre. I hold her hand the whole way to the doors then I head back to her room to wait. They said it wouldn't be long before she was back in her room as it is a quick and simple procedure.

"How are you, buddy?" I ask Evander as I walk back into Evelina's room. He looks up from his game and shrugs.

"I'm just worried about her, Dad. I don't think she really understands what is actually happening. You know what she's like. I think she thinks everything is a game a lot of the time. Sometimes she makes me mad — when she acts like a baby. You wouldn't think she was ten or the same age as me. But I love her, Dad, she is my other half, and I would be lost without her. Is she going to be all right? It's cancer, isn't it?" Wow, I have never heard him speak like this before or say so much. He is so old-headed for his age, exactly as I was. I didn't even know he knew what cancer was. Before I can say anything, the door opens and in walks Sonia, puffing and out of breath.

"Oh no, I wanted to see her before she went into theatre. How was she, sweetie?" she asks me.

"Very good actually, Sonia. She wasn't scared, but maybe that's the good thing about being young and naïve." I say. She moves to Evander and kisses the top of his head.

"How are you, my little treasure?"

"Ok, thank you, Grandma. Where's Pops?"

"He's parking the car. He will be up in a few minutes." Right on cue, in strolls Arnold. He is semi-retired now, but he still always dresses smartly. I get up and shake his hand. He slaps my back.

"How are you doing, son? How is Evelina? How are you, Vander?"

"Okay," we both say together. We all make small talk, and it's not long before the doors open, and they wheel Evelina back into the room on her bed. She's wide-awake. I thought she would be sleepy and groggy from the gas they gave her but apparently not. I give her a kiss on the head, then I let Sonia, Arnold, and Evander make a fuss of her, and I walk out with the doctor.

"How did it go, Doctor? Did you get what you needed?"

"Yes, Mr. Tourney. It went really well, and we got a good sample from the kidney. It's gone straight to the lab, and I expect to have the results very soon. I will text you as soon as I get them. If you could come to my office so we can discuss it in there rather than in front of the children. Is that okay with you?"

"Yes, of course, and I agree better not in front of the kids. I'm just worrying now waiting for the results to see what stage she is. Why is she wide-awake? I was expecting her to be sleepy and groggy?"

"We only had to sedate her slightly, just enough to make her sleep for fifteen minutes. If we do the surgery tomorrow that will be completely different. She will be out for a good few hours. How are you doing, Mr. Tourney? You look a lot better than you did yesterday. I'm sorry for having to give you that news. It's not nice for anyone, let alone a parent of a young child." I run my hand over my head.

"Yeah, it was a shock, Doctor. I pulled myself together for their sake. They're my life."

"You did an excellent job in explaining everything to them. I have to say, you have the most adorable children I have met, and I have met a lot."

"Thank you, Doctor, that means a lot to me. It's hard being mom and dad at times but we manage."

She heads back to her office. I need to phone the school and explain everything to them. I head back into Evelina's room and see they are all laughing, thanks to Arnold's antics, no doubt. I tell them I'm going to make a couple of calls and will be back very soon. I motion Sonia to come out with me.

"Dr. Cassidy is going to text me when she has the results from the biopsy. She would rather discuss them in her office. Do you want to come with me?"

"Yes, I do, Theon. Most definitely." She gives me a hug. I head off to phone the school and let them know what is happening with Evelina. They are very sympathetic and say not to worry about keeping either of them off but to keep them informed. They are going to e-mail me any homework that needs doing so we can at least keep on top of their schoolwork.

I phone Aggie next and let her know I won't be in the rest of the week. I didn't get a chance to tell her about Evelina yesterday. I just left. I tell her to e-mail me anything that needs my attention but to cancel all my appointments for the next couple of weeks. I then speak to my number two at the office, Patrick. He was the first person Evelyn and I employed, and he runs the place when I'm not around. I trust him.

I'm outside of the hospital, and I come across a bench with a woman sitting on it, crying. She looks at me but turns away quickly, as though she doesn't want me to see her crying. I sit down on the bench. I can't just ignore her.

"Hello," I say to her. She lightly turns but doesn't look at my face — she's looking at her hands in her lap.

"Hi," she says to me but nothing more.

"Sorry. I don't want to be nosy or intrude, but are you okay?" She doesn't say anything for a while, and I see her shoulders shake as she cries.

"I'm sorry. I'm just having a hard time dealing with things. My daughter is very sick. The doctors have just told me the prognosis. It doesn't look good for her. I should get back to her. I'm sorry to lay that on you."

"Not a problem. Really. I don't like to see people upset. I know what you're going through though. My daughter is in there right now. She's very sick. I'm just waiting on the biopsy results to tell us what the next step is."

"Oh, I'm sorry. It's so hard when your children are ill, and you can't do anything for them. It makes you feel like a failure. We are supposed to protect them. How can we do that against diseases?"

"Oh listen to me. I asked you if you were okay then laid my problem on you. I'm sorry. But yes, it's the hardest thing in the world. She's only ten, my little whirlwind spitfire, and she's my life, along with her brother."

"Same here. I have three children, two girls, and a boy. It's my youngest girl Caroline that's sick. She's eight. She's so brave. She puts me to shame. I keep breaking down. How old is your son?"

"Evander is ten as well. They are twins."

"Oh my gosh, how bizarre is that? My other two are eleven, twins as well. A handful as well, huh?"

"Actually no, they are the best kids ever. Evander is old beyond his years, very intelligent. He's a computer genius, takes after his mum and me. Evelina is just a force to be reckoned with and has me wrapped around her little finger. It kills me she is so sick."

"My two, Bailee and Bryan, are great kids. It's Caroline who has me tearing my hair out at times. I wish she was doing that now instead of laying in that bed, almost lifeless." She hangs her head, and the tears flow again. I don't know what to do. I can't comfort her. I don't know her. I just pat her shoulder. Right then my phone buzzes, and I see the message from Dr. Cassidy.

'The results are back.'

My heart sinks.

"I'm sorry. I have to go. The biopsy results are back. I'm Theon, by the way. I hope things turn out well for your daughter. I really am sorry."

"Thank you, Theon. I'm Alana. It was nice meeting you and thank you for stopping and checking on me. I hope things turn out well for your daughter as well."

I head back into the hospital and text Sonia to meet me at Dr. Cassidy's office. I practically run there, and we get there at the same time. We knock on the door and wait till she opens it.

"Come in please, Mr. Tourney, Mrs. Westcott. Please take a seat." My heart is pounding, not just from the run here, but I'm a little hopeful. She seems a bit brighter, but maybe I'm reading too much into it.

"Doctor." I nod sitting down.

"Right. I'll get straight to it. It's good news. It's stage one." I cry like a baby. I let out the breath I've been holding, and I fucking cry big fat tears, and I don't care. I lean forward with my elbows on my knees and my head in my hands. It's the relief.

"Sorry, I just need a minute," I manage to say. Sonia is rubbing my back to comfort me.

I'm struggling to breathe. Dr. Cassidy places some water in front of me and hands me a tissue. I take the tissue and blow my nose.

"Thanks."

"Take your time, Mr. Tourney. I know the relief is overwhelming. Are you okay to listen if I talk?" I nod yes but don't look up.

"Ok, well it's stage one, which is the best possible scenario there is for Evelina. We can go ahead with the surgery tomorrow to remove the kidney. Once she has recovered from surgery, we will start the course of chemo. She should be okay to go home five to seven days after surgery. The chemo will be a six-week course, once a week, here at the hospital. She can go to school on the days she feels up to it. Usually, a round of chemo can knock a patient out for a couple of days so I would suggest we arrange the treatment on a Thursday, that way hopefully she can still attend school Monday through Wednesday.

Now, there are side effects from chemo. I will run through these with you before she is released from hospital, but just so you know, hair loss, vomiting, fatigue, weight loss, loss of appetite are all side effects. Do you have any questions for me? I know it's a lot to take in?"

"Can she live with only one kidney?"

"Yes. Many people live with one kidney. She should be able to lead a healthy normal life, only watching her diet. If she got a problem with her remaining kidney, then that's where the problems start, but we don't need to discuss that at this stage. Anything else?"

"No. Thank you." We leave the office, and I hug Sonia. We stand there for a while.

"Come on, let's get back to our girl. I need a cuddle from my baby."

I stay with Evelina for most of the day. Sonia and Arnold leave, but Evander wants to stay with us. He finds us some board games, and we play games all afternoon. The hospital brings food in for us all at dinnertime. I then sit on the bed, with Evelina cuddling into my side and Evander at the side of the bed, resting his head on my legs and read them a few stories. I feel Evelina fall asleep, and I gently moved away trying not to disturb her. She wakes up

"Don't leave me, Daddy. I don't want to be on my own. It scares me."

I kiss the top of her head. "I'm not going anywhere, poppet. Daddy will be right here all night."

"Vander, will you stay as well? You can share my bed?" He looks at me, and I gave him the slightest nod that he can stay.

"I wouldn't be anywhere else, Lina. I will stay with you."

The nurses never ask us to leave. They wheel in a cot for me to sleep in. Evander gets into bed with Evelina, and we all sleep there with her. Our family. I say a silent thank you to Evelyn for looking after our little girl.

Chapter 12

16 years earlier

I CAN'T BELIEVE THE DAY is here. It's Evelyn's twenty-first birthday and our wedding day. The day I make her mine for eternity. She wanted to get married on her birthday, exactly a year after I proposed.

We don't want anything big, so it's just Sonia, Arnold, Grandma, Maggie and then a couple of Evelyn's side of the family. We're having the ceremony on a private beach at Sonia and Arnold's house in Huntington Beach. We will then go for a meal at an exclusive restaurant. We've decided to go on a long honeymoon visiting Hong Kong, China, and Singapore. Then we will have a week relaxing in the Maldives. We haven't decided if we want to go to Europe yet. Why not see the world while we can?

Patrick, our first employee, will be holding down the fort while we are away. We have three other members of staff who are all working on different projects and can be trusted under Patrick's eye.

I arrive at the house with my grandma. We head straight to the beach to wait for Evelyn. I know we're a bit early, but I was ready and couldn't wait.

As long as my grandma is with me, and Evelyn's parents, I don't care about anyone else being at our wedding. Just Evelyn, she's the most important person in my life along with grandma. We sit watching the waves, waiting for Evelyn to arrive.

"Theon, you make me the proudest person alive. Your success and now, getting married to the girl you worship. Seeing you this happy melts my old heart. I couldn't have asked for a better grandson. I know it's been hard not having parents, but I hope you know I love you — like my son, not my grandson. You have done me so proud after I failed your mother. I hope you forgive me for that."

"There is nothing to forgive you for, Grandma. What mom did was her choice, no one else's. She got herself into the mess and couldn't get out of it. I love you like a mom, and you're the most important person in my life, well, along with my soon-to-be-wife, that is. I love you, Grandma." I lean down to kiss her on the cheek.

Sonia suddenly appears in a bit of a flap. "She's here, Theon. You need to stand up there with the minister, sweetie." I have butterflies in my tummy, and my heart is racing. I'm starting to sweat, I can feel it under my collar, and it's not to do with the heat. This is it. I'm marrying Evelyn — the girl of my dreams. I'm excited, nervous, anxious, and impatient — so many emotions. I stand at the front with the minister with my back to where Evelyn will appear. I'm scared to look. I don't know if I will break down at the sight of her, but I have to watch, my life walking towards me. The music starts. She's here. I can feel her presence. I turn slowly. She's walking towards me, linking Arnold. Her head is held high as she looks straight into my eyes, and she has the biggest smile on her face that makes her eyes sparkle. The tears fall down my cheeks. She's stunning. This, right here, walking toward me, is perfection. The most beautiful woman I know, and she's on her way to be mine for the rest of our lives — to declare her love for me. I can't take my eyes off hers. Her dress is simple, white silk, no veil. I didn't want her hiding her face. She has a crown of white daisies around her head and weaved into her hair that's tied up at the sides but long at the back. Her dress is straight and flares out behind her. It just flows. She looks like she's floating towards me. As she gets in front of me, Arnold places her hand into mine and my tears flow.

"Hi," I whisper and lean in to kiss her cheek still holding her hand. "You take my breath away. Happy Birthday, baby."

"Hi, yourself, handsome," she says and wipes the tears from my cheeks.

We turn to the minister who proceeds with the ceremony. Before we exchange the rings, we both have something to say. I go first. I face her and take both her hands in mine.

"Evelyn, my beautiful girl. You take my breath away. You will never know how happy I truly am because there are no words. I still pinch myself to see if all this is real — to see if you are real. You are my life. I will cherish you for the rest of our lives. My only aim in life is to make you happy. To love you with all my heart and to always be there for you, no matter what. Baby, eternity is not enough time to love and be with you. I want infinity and beyond for that. You're my first and last forever. Now, this is the best day of my life."

She has tears rolling down her cheeks. I reach up and use my thumbs on both cheeks to wipe them away. She grabs my hands and kisses both my palms.

"Theon, my beautiful boy. You make me deliriously happy. You take my breath away every day with the love you shower me with, and the adoration you have for me. You treat me like I'm glass. Like I'm the most precious thing you have, and I love you with all that I have for it. I agree to infinity — eternity is not enough. Your first and last. Forever, baby."

We exchange rings.

"It is my greatest pleasure to now pronounce you husband and wife. You may kiss your bride."

I do not need telling twice. I take her face in my hands and gently place my lips on hers, then kiss her, showing her all the love I have for her. I pull back, and we both have tears rolling down our cheeks, I rest my forehead on her forehead.

"Hi, Mrs. Tourney." She laughs and throws herself into my arms.

The day is amazing. One I will never forget. All my best days involve Evelyn.

We fly out on honeymoon and are gone for five weeks in total. We have an amazing time especially in the Maldives where we got to swim with sea turtles, they have become my favorite animal also. We do go to Europe: England, Paris, and Rome. We make love as much as we can. We can't keep our hands off each other.

We head back home, back to reality and our newly renovated house in the Hollywood Hills. It's the one thing we agreed we would invest some money in. It has an infinity pool, and the views of L.A. are stunning. It is quite a big house but Evelyn fell in love with it, visualizing what it could look like, and the extra rooms ready for when we start a family. I think it's too big, but Evelyn wanted it. All our things were put in while we were on honeymoon, so it's exciting heading back to our new home and spending our first night there together as husband and wife.

We concentrate on our business. We have eleven games being developed at the moment with three under contract — gaming is just exploding. We look at filling our offices with more employees. It's growing fast.

We both decide we want a few years to dedicate to ourselves and growing the business before we start a family. Neither of us is in a rush. We are still only twenty-one. We have plenty of time and want to enjoy each other.

Chapter 13

I WAKE UP WITH A START. It's a nurse coming in to take Evelina's observations and to start prepping her for surgery. I'm aching. This cot they gave me to sleep on is way too small for my six-foot-three frame. I look up and see the Evs sitting crossed legged on the bed, looking down on me.

"Morning, Evs," I mumble trying to get up. I slept better than I thought I would. Maybe with all the stress and lack of sleep the night before, then the relief. I hear them both giggle. I peep up and see them whispering.

"What's so funny?" I say yawning and trying to stretch the kink out of my neck before lifting my arms above my head to stretch. They both giggle again, and right now it's the best sound in the world.

"Dad, did you take your clothes off last night?' Evander asks me pointing to my bare chest. I look down and see what he's pointing at, then look to the side of me where there is a young nurse frozen, looking down at me. I follow her gaze and yep, sure enough, I'm naked to the waist with a thin sheet barely clinging to me and just about covering my modesty. I do have boxers on, but they are the skin tight ones. Looking down my bare chest and legs, it doesn't look like I have anything on. The Evs carry on giggling while I take in what the nurse is ogling at. Maybe it's my abs that have her frozen in place. I go to move, and she gasps and turns away. I smile, then pull the sheet around my waist and get up. I grab my jeans and slip them on underneath the sheet.

"You can turn round now, nurse. Dad's got his jeans on. He won't flash you," Evelina tells the nurse. I scowl at her.

"I had my boxers on anyway!" I say indignantly. The young nurse turns straight into my bare chest. She steps back blushing, and her eyes drag over my bare torso to my waist where my jeans are not fastened. She licks her lips and drags her bottom lip between her teeth. I don't think she realizes what she's doing.

"Ahem," I say, and her eyes dart to my face. I have a big smile plastered there and wink at her.

"Oh s-s-sorry. I forgot something." She turns and practically runs out of the room. The Evs roll around on the bed, laughing hysterically.

"Dad, you're so mean. She liked looking at your muscles. Like all the ladies do when you don't have a top on," Evelina says rolling her eyes at me and falling back on the bed. I laugh at her then remember her surgery yesterday.

"Evelina, please be careful of your cut. You don't want it coming open." I go to make sure it's not bleeding while grabbing my t-shirt and fastening my jeans. It's a good job I didn't have morning wood. That poor nurse would have run out screaming. I laugh to myself — not the thoughts I should be having now.

"How do you feel this morning, poppet?"

"Ok, I think. I have a little pain in my tummy, but not much. I'm just a little scared about my surgery today, Daddy. Will it be all right? Will you be here when I wake up? Will it hurt? Like really hurt, afterward?"

"Oh, poppet, don't be scared. I will be here in this room waiting for you. I'm not going anywhere. I'm not going to lie to you, it will be sore afterward, and you will have to take it really easy. No running around for a few weeks or jumping on beds or fighting with Evander. You have to be very careful. You will stay here for maybe a week, then I can take you home to look after you. When you are healed from surgery, that's when you will need the other medicine to make you better."

"But I'm confused."

"What about?"

"If they are taking the poorly thing from me because it can't be fixed and that will make me better, why do I need another medicine that's going to make me poorly to make me better?" . It's very confusing all this being poorly?" I laugh at her and kiss her forehead.

"I know it's confusing. The thing that has made your kidney broken is called a tumor, and some might still be in your body. They take the kidney out because it can't be fixed. Then, when you are healed, they give you the medicine to make sure the tumor is gone completely. The medicine makes you poorly because it kills any tumor still in your body. Does that make sense?" She nods and shrugs.

"I think so. So I have a tumor in my kidney, and they take my kidney out, but give me medicine to kill any tumor that might want to stay in my body?"

"You, Miss Evelina, are one smart little girl and your daddy tells you perfectly. Smart, beautiful, and brave. What more could anyone want?" Dr. Cassidy says from the door. She was obviously listening and didn't want to interrupt.

"Morning, Doctor," the three of us say at the same time.

"Good morning, Tourney family. How is my patient this morning? I heard your daddy gave my nurse a bit of a start just now?" She smiles and winks at Evelina before looking at me. I just shrug.

"I had my boxers on." I smile and wink back. She actually blushes a bit. The Evs snigger.

"Here we go again," Evander says rolling his eyes. We all look at him as if to say 'what?' but the Doctor quickly turns the subject to Evelina.

"The nurse will come and do your observations." She leans in close to Evelina. "Maybe when your daddy uses the bathroom," she whispers.

"Then they will get you ready for surgery. Mr. Al Syed will do the surgery. He is one of our best doctors, and I will be there in theatre with you all the time. Not that you will know because you'll be dreaming about your turtle and Stitch here," she says picking them both up.

"Are you ready for this, sweetie? Do you have anything you want to ask me?" Evelina shakes her head.

"No, Daddy told me everything." She takes the teddies from the doctor and cuddles them.

Just like yesterday, I go with her, holding her hand as far as they will let me.

"I love you, Evelina. I will see you really soon. Make sure you have some nice dreams in there. Love you to the moon and back, poppet."

"Love you back from the moon to us forever. See you soon." They whip her through the doors quickly. I just crouch down where I am, with my head in my hands, praying everything goes well. I look up to the ceiling asking Evelyn to watch over her and bring her back safe to me. I can feel the tears rolling down my cheek. There's a hand on my shoulder. I turn, and it's the young nurse who flew out of the room earlier.

"She will be fine, Mr. Tourney. She's in the best hands in there."

I get up. "Thank you, nurse, and sorry about earlier."

She shrugs, goes a bit red, and then leaves through the theatre doors.

Evander and I go for breakfast at the hospital restaurant.

"You okay, buddy? You've been very quiet. You know she's going to be okay, right?"

"Yeah, Dad, I know. I'm still worried though. Will they get all the cancer from her? My friend at school lost his mum to cancer. She had surgery to get rid of it, but it came back, and she died. Will that happen to Lina?"

"Nothing is certain in this world, son. We have to get on as best we can no matter what life throws at us. Evelina's cancer is at the lowest stage, which is really good and means it shouldn't have spread. They are almost sure the surgery will get rid of it, and the chemo is a precaution to make sure it's gone. We just have to hope and pray that it is the end."

"I hope so. I would be so sad if anything happened to Lina. We know you miss mom every day, and I think I kind of understand that now. You always say mom was your life — your other half, but Lina actually is half of me." Wow. Ten years old and he talks like he's my age.

"You know, buddy, you make me so damn proud to be your dad. You are the smartest ten-year-old I know. Except me when I was ten, of course." We both laugh. It's what we need to lighten the mood.

I'm back in Evelina's room with Evander when Sonia arrives with clean clothes for us. She brought my PJ bottoms so I don't scare any more nurses after Evander told her about the incident with the nurse this morning when she phoned. I'm sitting on a chair with my leg jumping when Sonia puts her hand on my knee to stop it.

"It's always been your telltale that you're nervous." I didn't even know I was doing it.

"It's been four hours now. Something must be wrong. The doctor said it should be two to three hours." Panic is setting in big time. I get up and go to the door to look down the corridor. Nothing, no sign of her, but I do see Alana, the lady I met yesterday, standing there, leaning against the wall. She has her head back on the wall, and her eyes closed. I decide to walk to her and see if she's okay. If I stay in the corridor, I won't miss Evelina coming back.

She hears me approach and looks at me. I can see she's been crying again. I hope her daughter Caroline is okay.

"Hi, Alana, are you okay? Is Caroline okay?" I ask when I get near her. She nods and wipes under her eyes.

"Yeah, she's okay, or as okay as she can be. It just gets hard you know. I needed a minute. I refuse to let her see me upset — she has enough to worry about. I usually sneak off when she's sleeping to have a cry." She shrugs. I know what she means though.

"Yeah, I get it. I'm the same. I don't want either of them knowing I'm upset to the extent I am. It's hard trying to be upbeat when your heart is breaking for your child. How's Caroline doing?

"Just the same really. Just before I met you yesterday, the doctor gave me the biopsy results. It wasn't good news. She has liver cancer, and she's pretext three, which means she will need major surgery to remove the tumor, but she may need a liver transplant as well." She starts crying again, and I'm not sure what to do. I don't know if I should comfort her. Shit, what do I do? I step closer and lightly touch her arm.

"Oh, Alana. I'm so sorry. I really know how hard this is. Is your husband with her?"

She shakes her head no and takes a deep breath. "No, he died seven years ago — the same cancer that Caroline's got. I can't believe I'm going through this again." Shit, she's sobbing now. I just pull her into me and hold her. I don't know if she has a partner or not, but I can't just let her stand there crying like this. She puts her arms around my waist and cries into my chest. I hug her.

"Let it out, Alana. Just let it go." We stay like that for a good ten minutes while she slowly calms down. She pulls away and looks up at me.

"I'm sorry, Theon. I've wet all your t-shirt now. I didn't mean to do that but thank you. Thank you, so much. You have no idea how much I needed that. I … I feel so helpless, and I don't have anyone to release it on."

"Believe me, Alana. I do know how it feels. I've been the same with Evelina. I lost my wife ten years ago in childbirth. I don't have anyone except my mother-in-law. She's looking at me with such sorrow on her face, but there's no pity. She's been there she knows what it's like.

"What a pair we are." She smiles at me. "The similarities are bizarre."

Yes, they are when I think about it. Both single parents with twins, both lost our partners, and both have a child with cancer. Wow.

Just then I hear the door at the end of the corridor and see Doctor Cassidy with the porters pushing a bed.

"Thank fuck for that."

"Are you okay, Theon?"

"Did I say that out loud? Yeah, sorry. It's Evelina. She's back from surgery. She's been gone longer than I expected and panic set in. I was looking in the corridor for any sign of her when I spotted you."

"Oh, I'm so sorry. You're comforting me when you're in a panic yourself. Go. Go to Evelina. She will need her daddy. No doubt I will bump into you again as we're on the same floor. Thank you, Theon. Thank you for being my shoulder to cry on. I really needed that."

"Anytime you need my shoulder or chest to wet again just let me know. Here she is. I best get going. Take care, Alana."

I'm at the door of Evelina's room just as they get there. My baby is all groggy, but she opens her eyes and sees me smiling down at her.

"Hi, my big brave girl. Daddy's here. Go to sleep, poppet." She smiles at me, and I hear her whisper, "Daddy," then she closes her eyes and sleeps. Evander is up and by her side, holding her hand while they sort her bed out.

"I missed you, Lina. I'm so glad you're back. I love you." I'm welling up again. He's being brave and really holding it together, but I know it's cutting him up inside. He is so sensitive, just like me. I look at the doctor.

"How did it go? I have to say I've been in a panic she was gone for so long?"

"It was a little longer than normal but nothing to worry about. It went perfectly. There was a slight bleed, which they had to stem before closing her up. That's not unusual, so don't worry. She's been out of surgery for a good forty minutes, in recovery. Mr. Al Syed said the tumor looked small from what he could see. Her kidney will go to the lab now for tests, and they should be able to tell if it penetrated the wall of the kidney. That's where chemo comes in, just in case some cells escaped. But surgery was a success." That's what I need to know. It was a success. I let out a huge sigh and run my hand over my head. I look up to the ceiling saying a silent thank you to Evelyn.

"She will be groggy for the rest of the day now with the amount of aesthetic she had. I don't know if you want to leave and get some rest or you're more than welcome to stay with her. If you stay and she wakes, just try and get her to have sips of water. Her throat and mouth will be dry. As you can see she has drips. One bag is fluids to keep her hydrated. The other is a painkiller, and then we will administer antibiotics intravenously. She's in good hands, Mr. Tourney."

"Thank you, Doctor. For everything." I can actually smile properly with relief.

Now the surgery is over, and Evander has seen Evelina with his own eyes, and he knows she's going to be fine, I manage to persuade him to go home with Sonia and get a good night's sleep. He reluctantly leaves. I'm sitting next to Evelina's bed holding her hand. I put the turtle under her other arm. It's her comfort. I sit, watching her breathing.

"Evelyn, I wish you were here, beautiful. I need you so badly right now. I'm glad you're there though, my angel, looking out for our baby girl," I whisper to myself.

Chapter 14

Business is booming. Evelyn and I are flat out with work. We now have fifteen people working for us, and we are looking at hiring more. We're enjoying married life. It's nearly a year since we got married and we still can't get enough of each other, but I don't think that will ever change. No matter how busy we are, we leave the office and have dinner together every night. We've also said no working weekends. That was a rule we made at the beginning, and we've stuck to it, no matter what deadlines are looming.

We enjoy our weekends, and we make sure we do things together. One weekend Evelyn picks what we do, the next I pick. We go to the beach, out to restaurants, travel: Vegas, New York, Atlanta, Nashville. We have been everywhere. We are very rich, and our only real indulgence is we fly privately, and we stay in the top hotels. That's at my insistence because I want her to have the best of everything.

I've also have Grandma staying with us on some weekends when we're just relaxing, or going to a museum or shopping. She still works her one job so she doesn't go stir crazy on her own she tells me. I've been worried about her though. When I spoke to her last weekend to see if she wanted to come and stay, she turned me down for the first time ever. I was surprised and asked what was wrong. She said she was feeling under the weather and it was nothing to worry about, but I am worried. I've phoned her every day this week. She's not been in work, so Evelyn and I are on our way to see her now. It's Friday evening. I stop at a deli and grab a couple of wraps for us and a lovely chicken broth for Grandma. She's told me before she loves the broth from here.

I have a key, so let myself into her house. It's quiet. Too quiet. I look at Evelyn. "There's no TV or radio on. Do you think she's out? Her car was in the drive though?"

"Maybe a friend picked her up and took her out somewhere." Hmm maybe. We head into the kitchen, and I stop, frozen. Evelyn slams into my back. Fuck. I run. Grandma is on the floor. I hear Evelyn say something, but I've no idea what it is.

"Grandma, Grandma, can you hear me? Grandma, it's me, Theon?" She moves slightly. I'm trying to check to see if she's hurt anywhere without moving her. Evelyn is next to her head stroking her hair.

"Grandma, it's Evelyn. Can you hear me?"

"Hmm, Susan is that you?" Oh no, Susan is my mother.

"Do you think she's banged her head?" I ask Evelyn.

"I don't think so. There are no cuts or bumps that I can see on this side?"

"We need the medics, Evelyn."

"They're on the way, baby." I look at her puzzled then it registers she was talking on the phone when we got to the kitchen. I thought she was talking to me. I sit on the floor next to Grandma, holding her hand and with my thumb stroking the back of it, the other hand gently stroking her cheek. It's fucking killing me, her being on the floor, but I can't move her. I'm talking to her constantly, she's mumbling back, but I can't make out her words. My first instinct was that she'd been attacked, but she looks okay, and I can't see any signs of a break in. It must be a stroke or a heart attack. I look up to the ceiling. Please don't take her from me. She's the only family I have, I say in my head.

"How long did they say they would be?" I ask Evelyn who's sitting on the other side of Grandma. She got a blanket and covered her to keep her warm. Why didn't I think of that? "What would I do without you, Evelyn?" She furrows her brow.

"They just said they are on the way." We suddenly hear doors shutting and running. Evelyn gets up to open the door, and two paramedics come rushing in.

"I don't know what happened, or how long she has been like this. We just found her. Please help her." I get in before they speak. I can feel the tears running down my face. Evelyn is in front of me in a flash and hugging me.

"Theon, they will look after her. Stay strong for her, okay? She needs us to be strong right now, baby." I nod and bury my head in her neck.

"I'm trying. She's all I've got, Evelyn. If she goes, I have no family. What's wrong with me? Why are all my family gone? Why, Evelyn?" I whisper in her neck while the paramedics attend to Grandma.

"Oh, baby. Shhh, don't say that. Let's get to the hospital and find out what happened. Come on, Theon. Be strong, baby."

One of them is wheeling in a gurney to put Grandma on. I look up. She looks lifeless. They gently put her onto a backboard then lift her up. They wheel her out to the ambulance.

"I'm going with her." I look at Evelyn

"Ok, baby, you stay with Grandma. I'll grab some of her stuff real quick and lock up. Then I will follow you. What hospital are you taking her to?" she asks the paramedics.

We arrive at Cedar-Sinai. They take her straight to the emergency room to see what is going on. I go to the desk and give them all Grandma's details. It's only just hit me how old Grandma is. You never think of your parents getting old, and you always see them as they were when you were a kid. She's sixty-nine. It's her seventieth birthday in three months. Where did that time go? She's worked so hard holding down three jobs to look after me when she should have been winding down for retirement. This is all my fault. If I hadn't been born, she wouldn't have had to work so hard. Oh god, what have I done? I somehow walk to a seat and sit down, leaning forward with my elbows on my knee with my head in my hands. I can feel the tears trickling down my cheeks.

I sense her before I feel her sit next to me. My rock, the most beautiful person I know. She hugs me to her. She always knows what to do.

"Baby, are you okay? Have they told you anything yet?" I shake my head no. I have a lump in my throat.

"It's all my fault," I whisper so low, but Evelyn hears me I feel her stop breathing just for a second.

"Oh, Theon, why would you say that? None of this is your fault, baby." She squeezes me to her harder.

"If I hadn't born she wouldn't have worked three jobs to look after me, to make sure I had what I needed. She's my grandma. It's not her job to raise me. That's my fucking mother's job, the useless, selfish bitch that she was. Grandma should have been winding down, not working so much. It's all my fault, Evelyn." I break down. Sobbing into her.

"Theon, look at me." She lifts my face up under my chin to look at her.

"This is NOT. YOUR. FAULT!" she says sternly emphasizing each word. She's looking me in the eyes.

"If anyone is at fault, it's Susan and your father. Not you. You didn't ask for this life, and if Grandma hears you talking like that, I know damn well she will clip you round the ears. You couldn't possibly be to blame for any illness your grandma has. It was also her choice to bring you up and love you unconditionally. It's life, Theon. We get sick. No one is to blame. Do you hear what I'm saying?" I look at her in awe. This woman in front of me, chastising me, is my life. I nod slightly, then lean in to kiss her lips. She pulls away.

"And another thing that upsets me. I know Grandma is your last blood relative, but, baby, I'm your family too, and you're stuck with me for infinity, remember? Your first and last forever. You're not getting rid of me ever, do you hear me, Theon? E.V.E.R!" She spells out to me. I hold her to me tight and just let her love pour into me. I love this woman with all that I am.

"I know you're my family, beautiful. I love you for infinity. You know that. I'm sorry. This is the last thing you need, me falling apart, but I'm scared, Evelyn, so fucking scared of losing her. In fact, I'm terrified." She squeezes me harder.

"No matter what, baby, just remember, I'm here for you, okay?"

We wait for what feels like hours, but when I look at the clock, it's only been just over an hour. Every time the door goes, I'm looking to see if it's a doctor or nurse looking for me but nothing yet.

"What's taking so damn long?" I say to Evelyn. I'm going out of my mind here. I keep getting up and pacing or sitting shaking my leg, which I do a lot when I'm anxious or nervous.

"Mr. Tourney, do we have a Mr. Tourney?" I'm stopped mid-conversation by a nurse shouting my name. I jump out of my seat.

"Yes," I say, walking towards her, dragging Evelyn by the hand with me.

"Can you follow me, sir?" she says and walks out of the waiting room. I follow her down the corridor. She stands at a room and knocks. We walk in, and there's a doctor behind a desk. This isn't good. I thought they were taking me to see Grandma.

"Please, Mr. Tourney, Mrs. Tourney, take a seat

"Where's my grandmother? I thought I was being taken to see her. I need to see her. Is she okay? What's going on?"

"My name is Dr. McDonald. I'm a heart specialist. I've examined your grandmother, and I'm sorry to say she's had a major heart attack." I freeze. Is he saying she's dead? I can't speak. I'm squeezing Evelyn's hand hard. She puts her other hand over mine and rubs.

"Dr. McDonald, what are you saying? Has Theon's grandmother not made it?" Oh god, she's asked what I couldn't. I just stare at him.

"She's alive, Mrs. Tourney, but I have to tell you, it's not good. The heart attack has caused a heart rupture. She's stable, but ..."

"What does that mean? A heart rupture?" I interrupt him.

"A heart rupture can appear if the heart's muscles, walls, or valves are severely damaged during the heart attack."

"What can you do to fix it?" Evelyn asks.

"The only thing is open heart surgery to try and repair the rupture, but at your grandmother's age, this is very high risk. It also depends on the extent of the damage to the heart. I have to give you the facts as they are and ... I have to tell you, she may not make it through surgery."

"What is her survival rate?" I interrupt

"I would say with surgery there's a 30% chance of survival. Without surgery, it's just a waiting game I'm afraid. It could be days or weeks. I'm so sorry, Mr. Tourney. It's a difficult decision you need to make. She is comfortable at the moment and stable. I will take you to her now, but I will have to press you for a decision on surgery. If you decide you want her to have surgery, we need to get her to theatre as soon as we can. Do you understand, Mr. Tourney?" Does he think I'm fucking stupid? Of course I understand.

"Yeah, basically, leave her to die on her own or take a very slim chance she survives with surgery. What will her quality of life be like if she survives surgery?"

"That's hard to say. Until we see the extent of the damage, she's going to be bedridden for fear of another rupture. Once the heart has been damaged and ruptured it makes it very weak. She could be okay to get in and out of bed assisted and wheeled around on a chair. She will need assistance with everything, probably with a home carer or in a hospice."

"No fucking way is she going in a home!" I shout at him. He doesn't even flinch. Evelyn puts her hand on my shoulder and squeezes to calm me. It works.

"Sorry, Doctor. If she needs care, she moves in with me, and I will hire nurses to look after her round the clock." I look at Evelyn, not for her acceptance of this decision, but for her approval of Grandma's surgery. She nods slightly.

"I would like to proceed with surgery, doctor. I want to give her a chance. There is no way I can sit by her bedside watching every breath she takes thinking is this her last. She's a fighter, and I want to give her a fighting chance. Can we see her now?"

"Yes, of course. I will take you to her room, and I will get everything prepped for surgery." We get up and follow him down a couple of corridors. Evelyn has hold of my hand, and she squeezes it, making me look at her.

"Be prepared, baby. Grandma will probably be full of tubes. You made the right decision. She can't fight it verbally, you have to do that for her, and let her fight physically." I lean over and kiss the top of her head.

We stop outside a room, and Dr. McDonald turns to us

"There are lots of tubes and monitors attached to her. She is also very pale and looks very frail, but she's breathing on her own which is a good sign. My team will be back soon to take her to surgery and also with a consent form for you to sign."

"Thank you, Doctor. Please do what you can for her." He holds out his hand to shake mine, then Evelyn's.

"I will, Mr. Tourney. Mrs. Tourney."

We enter her room, and I am shocked. I fall to my knees just inside the door, and I cry hard with my head in my hands.

"Oh god, Grandma, what happened? Why you? You've been healthy and active, why you?" I'm sobbing. Evelyn crouches down in front of me taking my hands from my face.

"Oh, baby, I'm so sorry." She kisses my eyelids that are closed, then my mouth. She wipes my tears as they fall. I gain some strength from her touch. I manage to get up, and Evelyn stands in front of me, looking up. She cups my cheeks, making me look at her and not Grandma.

"Theon, you are my strong, beautiful husband, we can do this, okay? Together we can be strong for Grandma and give her the fight she needs. If she comes through surgery, we will look after her at home, but we have to prepare ourselves that she might be too tired to come out of the other end, but we are here together, stronger — united. Okay, baby?"

She reaches up and kisses me on the lips. What did I ever do to deserve this beautiful woman in my life? We walk over to Grandma's bedside together. We stand either side of her and both have hold of her hands. We talk to her hoping she can hear. We reminisce about the wedding and all the trips we've been on together, and I remind her of things when I was growing up. We keep talking until the team arrives to take her to surgery. I sign the forms and kiss her for a long time on her forehead.

"I love you, Grandma." They wheel her away. I look up, asking whoever is up there to look after her, and bring her back to me. But they don't. She passes away on the operating table.

I'm twenty-two with no living blood relatives. I'm a broken man. Even with Evelyn by my side, it takes me a long time to get over losing my hero.

Chapter 15

THE DAY AFTER EVELINA'S surgery I wake up with a start again. It's the same nurse coming in to take Evelina's vitals. I'm in the tiny cot that has given me a terrible backache. The covers are hanging off me, and although I have a naked chest, I have my PJ bottoms on this morning. She's standing, staring at my chest, again. I cough to let her know I've caught her ogling me, and she looks at me startled. She's all flushed. I just smile and raise my eyebrows at her. She quickly moves over to Evelina who is still sleeping.

She's slept all night. I've woken up and checked on her several times throughout the night. She still sleeps as the nurse takes her blood pressure and temperature.

"Is this normal?" I gesture to Evelina as I stand on the other side of the bed.

"Is what normal?"

"Sleeping as much as this. She hasn't woken up at all." She goes to Evelina's chart and looks through it.

"Dr. Cassidy has her on a mild sedative to keep her asleep. It's so she doesn't move for the first twenty-four hours and also to help with the pain."

"Oh right, she never mentioned that, but it makes sense. How are her vitals?"

"Very good. All normal. The wound is looking good as well — no sign of infection." That's great news. I head to get a quick shower and change. No time to shave, in fact, I've got quite a growth going on, I haven't shaved for a few days. Evelyn used to love it when it was soft on her skin. It used to tickle her.

Evelina's still asleep. The nurse said they are not giving her any more sedatives, so she should wake soon. I need to grab some breakfast before she wakes. I hate leaving her. I hurry down to the restaurant. I'll grab and go. I'm at the cash register paying, and when I turn to leave, I see Alana, sitting at a table, in a world of her own, nursing a coffee in her hands. I can't ignore her. I move over to her table, but she doesn't even notice me standing there.

"Hey, good morning." I lean down to get in her line of sight. She blinks and startles.

"Oh, I'm sorry. I was miles away. Good morning, Theon."

"How's Caroline doing?"

She shrugs. "The same. It kills me. I feel so useless, helpless, and hopeless. She's starting chemo this afternoon to try and shrink the tumor. I'm not looking forward to that. The twins are coming in to see her before she has it. They are lost without her at home. How's Evelina doing this morning? How was surgery?"

"She's been sleeping. They gave her a sedative so she doesn't move around or pull the tubes, and to keep her pain free. She'll be coming round soon. I need to head back in case she wakes." I hold up my to-go food.

"I'll eat this in her room. I hope the chemo goes well, Alana." I leave her there. I feel shitty, but I need to be there when Evelina wakes up.

It's a couple of hours before she starts to wake. I'm so relieved. I'm at her side, stroking her head when her eyes flutter open.

"Well hello, sleepy head. Nice of you to join me. I've been sitting here watching you sleep. How are you feeling, poppet? Can you speak? Do you need a sip of water?" She nods her head. I get the beaker of water and put the straw to her mouth. She takes small sips.

"Hi, Daddy," she says softly smiling at me. I stroke her hair off her face. I can't stop smiling. I'm so relieved she's okay. These last few days have taken their toll on me, and I know we've still got a way to go.

"Evander will be here to see you soon, along with Grandma. Do you have any pain?"

"A little, Daddy. Was I a big brave girl?"

"You, my sweet baby girl, have been the bravest big girl I know. I am so proud of you." My stroking her head is sending her back to sleep. She needs to sleep to help her heal.

The day passes slowly as usual. Evander arrives with Sonia, and they stay for a few hours. He is so relieved to see Evelina sitting up and awake when he arrives. I'm reading to her. She's mad on Harry Potter, and I've been reading the books to her. I promise once she is home we will watch all the films. Evander goes back home with Sonia. I'm staying the night again. Evelina falls into a deep sleep. It's only just after seven, but I think that's her for the night. She did really well today. The wound is all clean, no sign of infection, and she hardly moaned about pain. God love her. I decide to go to the restaurant and get a coffee and something to eat and maybe go for a walk to get some fresh air.

I'm at the counter, deciding what to have when I feel someone behind me. I know who it is without turning around.

"Hi, Theon," she says as she comes to the side of me.

"Hi, Alana, how are you holding up?" She looks down. "Hey, did everything go all right this afternoon with the chemo?"

"Yeah, that was fine. It's knocked her for six; bless her. She's out cold, so I thought I'd come and grab a bite to eat and a coffee."

"Yeah, me too. Evelina is the same. She went out like a light. She's slept a lot today, but that's to be expected with the anesthetic and the sedative.

Then Evander and Sonia were with her all afternoon so that wore her out. I'm glad she's sleeping. It helps to heal."

"Yeah, I know the sleeping is good. I just worry so much, you know?" She looks tired and totally worn out. I feel for her. I know exactly what she means.

"Do I ever. Let's get a seat, and we can have a chat. It might help to have someone to talk to."

We find a table near a window. It's so busy in here because if the kids are sleeping, the parents come for a bit of a break. Looking around, you wonder why they are here — why is their child here? It's a children's hospital, but it's not all cancer-related.

"Are you okay, Theon, you look like you're miles away?"

"Yeah, just looking around. There are so many people here, which means there are so many sick kids. It's sad."

"How was Evelina's operation?"

"It went really well." I smile for the first time since I got here.

"Dr, Cassidy was very pleased. We now wait for her to heal, then she starts on chemo for six weeks to make sure no stray cells escaped. After that, providing all is okay, she leads a pretty normal life. You have no idea the relief that was to hear." She looks away with tears in her eyes. Oh, shit. I just realized what I said. Stupid man.

"Oh crap, I'm so sorry, Alana, what a stupid thing to say." She looks up at me and smiles. Then she grabs my hand that's on the table near my coffee.

"No, Theon. You are far from stupid. I'm truly happy, really. Why shouldn't you be relieved? God, I know I would be. Never apologize for Evelina pulling through this. I wish her the healthy and happiest life. I wish you all that." She squeezes my hand, and I look up at her.

"I wish it was the same for Caroline. In a way, I feel a bit guilty that Evelina is going to get through this, yet all the while, you're still none the wiser. I hate that for you, Alana." I put my other hand on top of hers and squeeze.

"I wish more than anything she pulls through. I know you said you lost your husband with liver cancer. Is it the same? Medicine has advanced so much in the seven years he's been gone?"

"Caroline's isn't as advanced as Gary's. We didn't find his 'til the latter stages, and it was too late by then. The stubborn fool refused to go to the doctor. He told me after his diagnosis that he had been sick for a while. I'm his wife! How could I have not known or seen the signs? It tore me up for a very long time — the guilt. He told me not to blame myself. I was running around after three kids. He said it was his fault. He knew there was something seriously wrong, but he couldn't face the truth. I still to this day feel I'm to blame in some way."

"Oh, Alana, love, you shouldn't feel guilty. He was a grown man who could look after himself. If he didn't tell you he was not feeling well, how could you know there was a problem? Liver cancer is not visible. It's not like he was cut or broken. It seems to me he was a silent sufferer. Is that right?" She looks so pained. We still have our hands on top of each other.

"Yes, Theon, he was. Gary was a hard-working man who would do anything for his family, which meant he suffered in silence until it was too late."

I pull my hands away. "I think we need to eat our food. It's getting cold," I say, hoping not to offend her. She smiles, then lets out a small laugh. It's nice she's smiling.

"I was thinking; we've only met a couple of times over the last couple of days, and every time the conversation gets heavy. It must be this place."

"The situations we're in doesn't help. But seriously, Alana, anytime you need to talk, just find me. So, tell me about you then. I know you have three kids. Do you have a partner? Who's looking after the twins?" I start to eat my food.

"No, I don't have a partner. It's just the kids and me. That's all I have time for. I used to work part-time in a florist. I loved that job, and I always wanted to open my own shop."

"That's very creative, so why didn't you do it?"

"Well, life really. I did that part-time and my other passion I did part-time, but from home."

"Which was?"

"No, you'll laugh. I never tell anyone. It's something I did growing up. I was a bit of a loner and spent a lot of time at home in my room and, well, it was my escape back then."

I raise my eyebrows at her. "You gonna keep me waiting?" I smile at her. She has a couple of mouthfuls of her food, as do I while watching each other. I'm waiting for her to tell me.

"You're not gonna leave this until I tell you, are you?"

"Not a chance. I'm intrigued now. I can't imagine what it is." She puts her fork down and grabs her water and takes a sip.

"It started, like I said, as an escape, but I found I was good at it. I turned it into a bit of a profession and made some good money." I raise my brow again.

"Do I need to guess?"

"Have a go, yes. One guess."

"I can't think of many things you could do from your bedroom that you found you were good at and made money. Unless?" Oh no, did she perform sexual acts to paying perverts? Please no.

"Unless what?"

Oh shit, what do I say? "You didn't run a website for paying perverts, did you?" She stares at me, opened-mouthed before she bursts out laughing. Really laughing, laughing so much she's crying. People around are starting to watch us. I'm laughing at her laughing. She looks so carefree right at this moment, and it strikes me just how beautiful she is. I've never really noticed before. We've been so consumed with why we're here in this place. But she's stunning. This is not the time or place to find someone I'm actually attracted to. I've never been attracted to anyone but Evelyn. It's only ever been her. Your first and last forever. Those words make me stop laughing all of a sudden. She's my first and last. There can't be anyone else. My last.

"Oh, Theon. Thank you, so much. I have not laughed in a really long time. I needed that. Thank you." She squeezes my hand again, and I get tingles running up my arm from her touch. Does she feel it? The way she's looking at me makes me wonder.

"No, I wasn't a website call girl, god no. I was short and dumpy or as they used to say fat."

"Who would say?"

"That's what I was escaping from. I was bullied at school. You couldn't go to a Beverley Hills school and be fat. Oh no, that was taboo. After all, this is L.A. right, the land of the beautiful and skinny people. I didn't get that memo in time. I was short and fat. They called me Augustus Gloop all the time. I used to get tricks played on me, things in my locker and pushed over to see if I rolled. That kind of stuff. I never had any friends, and my only sister was the opposite of me. She was embarrassed by me. She was taller than me and slim. She was a popular girl."

"Wow, that sucks, Alana. I'm so sorry you went through that."

"Well, it all turned out for the best. The thing I did in my bedroom was play games. Computer games like Warcraft, Final Fantasy, Legend of Zelda, and I was good; very good. I became a gamer. It started with Warcraft, then went from there. No one knew me behind the console or computer, and I was in my own little bubble with it all. I became popular in that world — who would have thought, me, popular? I then signed up to a gaming company and started testing games for them, which is where I made money. It was a win, win." She shrugs. Wow, another thing we have in common. There is no way all these coincidences are real. They can't be. Does she know who I am and is making this up? I'm terrible at trusting people, but there is no way she is a gamer. There is no way she belongs in my world.

"My kids are really good at gaming now. They give me a run for my money, that's for sure. Bailee, bless her, is better than Bryan, and that gets his back up. He thinks because he is the boy he should be better. We spend many a Saturday night having gaming competitions between us. It's our family time. Rather than have a film night with popcorn, we have gaming nights with chips. Caroline is good as well, although, she has no interest lately, with not being well. It's hard for her to concentrate, you know."

"I can imagine her concentration levels are low. But that's great you're a gamer. I would never laugh at that. I like the odd game myself, and Evander is a talented player. Evelina has never shown any interest. She likes her dolls and all that girly stuff too much. The little tinker had me buy a whole set of Monster dolls last week because she was good for Dr. Cassidy. That one has me wrapped around her little finger, that's for sure." I laugh at the thought.

"Do you have anyone else in your life, Theon?" I shake my head no and stab at the bit of food left on my plate.

"No, I have never found anyone else. But then I have never looked for anyone else. The twins have taken up all my time, which I'm more than happy about. I do worry sometimes about Evelina and her needing a mother figure. Sonia helps me out a lot, that's my mother in law. I couldn't have survived the loss without her help." I hang my head again. Alana reaches for my hand and squeezes it. I get feelings just from her touch, and I pull my hand back suddenly. I don't want these strange feelings. I don't need them, not now. Shit, Alana looks down at her plate sadly. I must have offended her by pulling my hand away. I'm not good at this. I need to get out of here and go for that walk. I can see if she wants to join me, that way there is no touching.

"Hey, do you fancy a little walk in the grounds, I could do with some fresh air before heading back to Evelina?"

"Yeah sure. I could do with some myself." I hope I've diverted the awkwardness.

We walk out of the main doors to the hospital in silence. It isn't an awkward silence. At least I don't think it is. We head to the hospital gardens where I first met Alana.

"It's great to get some air finally. It's so stuffy when you're cooped up in there all the time," I say to make conversation.

"Yes, it is."

"So, who is looking after the twins while you're here with Caroline?"

"My sister is staying at my house. Although she hated me when we were younger, we are really close now. Our parents are both gone, so we only have each other. She doesn't live far from me. She moved back from New York a few years ago to be near me. I couldn't do any of this without her. She adores the kids and would do anything for them. She found out she couldn't have children, which in turn split her marriage up, so it's just us now."

"Wow, sounds like you have a great sister there. I'm an only child, and so was Evelyn. I was brought up by my grandma, but she passed away a few years before we had the twins. On my side of the family, I have no one apart from the Evs. They are my entire life." We sit on the bench Alana was on the first time I saw her upset.

"The Evs?"

"Yes, that's what I call them sometimes Evelina and Evander."

"Ah, maybe I should call my two the B's." She laughs. It's nice we can have a little laugh when our lives are in such turmoil.

I remember every detail about the Evs from them being born, except the four weeks I was out of it after I lost Evelyn. I remember when we found out we were having a baby.

Chapter 16

We've been working non-stop. We haven't even had much time to get away at the weekends, which is what we love to do. Since Grandma passed, we have concentrated on building up the business. We ended up buying the building we had the offices in because of the growth of our company. The floors we don't currently occupy, we rent out to other companies. We now employ nearly three hundred people. We have a youth program to help any potential game creators out there. The way gaming has tripled over the years, this is definitely the future.

A few years back, we even employed gamers to work from home, testing out some of our games for us. It was great they gave us real feedback, and they got paid for it, so it was a win-win for everyone. We got to improve our games and they got paid for playing at home. The growth in our company was rapid, and it stunned us both. We decided at the grand old age of twenty-five, we would now make more time for ourselves. We had a fantastic management team that Patrick was now capable of running. It was a well-oiled wheel.

Six months ago, we decided to take more holidays to get away from it all. We had been working seven days a week, even though neither of us left the office without the other. We were always together, still choosing to spend our office hours with each other even though we had separate offices. We just worked well together. We loved each other more every day if that was possible. The problem was, we were so tired by the time we got back home each evening, we would have dinner then collapse into bed and half the time just fall asleep cuddling. We were intimate when we could be and tried to make the time, but we were burnt out, which is why we decided enough was enough. We hadn't built the company up like this to not have a life. In all honesty, with the money we both made, we could step back entirely if we wanted to and let our team run it, but that wasn't for us.

We'd visited nearly every state in the US now, and wanted somewhere a bit different and relaxing so I could enjoy my wife. I booked a private island in the Maldives, just for the two of us with no one to interrupt us. We were in heaven. Our house on the island was right on the beach, and every morning we could step outside and straight into the ocean. What an amazing place. Neither of us had ever been so relaxed. We had staff that would come over to the island each day to bring fresh food and prepare our meals. We spent so much time with me just buried in Evelyn. Now that was heaven. We were discovering ourselves all over again. We stayed for three weeks and didn't want to leave. We thought as we were there we would go to Asia and check out all the gaming that was going on there. We didn't work or have meetings as we were still on holiday. After a week in Asia, we headed back home and decided to just enjoy ourselves back in our own environment before venturing back to work.

We have been home for four weeks and have only been into the offices for occasional visits. A couple of weeks ago, Evelyn started to feel tired and wanted to sleep a lot, and I began to get a bit worried.

"Baby, do you think you should go to see the doctor? You may have picked something up while we were away?"

"Theon, stop worrying. I'm just tired that's all. I feel fine other than that. You don't mind if I go to my mother's tomorrow, do you? I said we would do a bit of shopping and have lunch, but I just wanted to check we didn't have anything on first?"

"No, nothing planned. You go and have some girly time with your mother, and I will go into the office for a bit and catch up on anything that needs our attention there."

"Great, I'll ring her and let her know." She walks off to the living room. I stay by the pool, to do some reading, trying to find the next big thing in the gaming industry. There are so many new things coming out. I've been working on a concept for a new game, which I want to run past Evelyn, but it will wait for a couple of days.

I spend a couple of hours in the office then head home. I'm surprised Evelyn's car is there as I thought she would still be with Sonia. I head inside and to the kitchen, but can't see Evelyn. I can't hear her either.

"Evelyn," I shout out and stand still, waiting. Nothing. Maybe Sonia picked her up. I look out the back to see if she's by the pool. Nothing. I go through the house and head upstairs to see if she's in the shower. Nothing. Why's this house so big?

"Evelyn!" I shout again coming down the stairs. I can hear music coming from the cinema room in the basement. I head down there.

The screen is lit up, but it's not a film. I read it: 'Sit down baby before you fall down.' Okaaaay, I take one of the recliners and wait.

A cartoon starts playing. It's Evelyn and me, a recreation of our life so far, from meeting, to going out, the proposal, our wedding, our honeymoon, and our work. All the while the music playing is my favorite band *Creed*. The song is 'with arms wide open'. Just as the lyrics get to the part about creating life, the image shows Evelyn holding a pregnancy stick in her hand. The cartoon Evelyn is smiling with happy tears, and I know what she's telling me. I'm stunned, tears streaming down my face. I close my eyes, and when I open them, she's there in front of me, tears falling down her face. The music's still playing. She looks nervous, apprehensive, maybe not sure of my reaction. I stand up and take her head in my hands, and I rest my forehead on hers.

"Is this real, baby, are we pregnant?" She nods yes holding my wrists. I breathe out, the tears just flowing now.

"Are you happy, Theon?" I smile down at her looking her in the eyes.

"I have no words, Evelyn," I whisper with a lump the size of a golf ball in my throat.

"I'm .... Shit. I'm numb, shocked, speechless but abso-fucking-lutely ecstatic." She lets out a breath I don't think she realized she was holding.

"Evelyn, I love you more than life, baby. But now this is the best day of my life, again. That tells you it all."

"Oh, Theon. I was scared you were going to say you weren't ready yet. We've been enjoying ourselves these past few months."

"When did you find out? How far along are you? When did you do this? I say pointing to the screen." I sit down and pull her onto my lap and wrap my arms around her.

"I had an idea I was pregnant just over a week ago. I went this morning, and they confirmed I'm eight weeks along."

"So we did this in the Maldives?" She nods yes.

"Guess we just must have been so relaxed and it just happened."

"How did you do this though?" I say nodding to the screen.

"I've been working on that for a long time for when it finally happened. I wanted to try to replicate your proposal to me. Did you like it?"

"Loved it, Evelyn. It's something to treasure along with the proposal — something to show our kids. I love you so much, baby. How are you feeling now?"

"I love you so much, Theon. Surprisingly, I'm fine for being eight weeks, barely any nausea but there's still time for that."

"Well, in that case —" I stand up with Evelyn in my arms. She laughs and clings to me. I head for the stairs.

"What are you doing?"

"Going to celebrate in you!" I shrug

"Is that okay, Mrs. Tourney?" She laughs

"Do you need to ask? Take me to your lair, my lord," she says then plants a kiss on my lips. It doesn't take long to escalate. I am the happiest man alive right now. I have the woman of my dreams clinging to me, and she's carrying my baby. Best day of my life by far.

Chapter 17

I TALK WITH ALANA FOR A few more minutes, but we both get a bit agitated wanting to get back to our girls. I look at my watch, and I've been gone from Evelina for fifty minutes — longer than I wanted.

"I'm going to head back and check on Evelina. I didn't realize I had been away from her that long."

"Oh gosh, yes, me too. I'll walk back with you." We head back, still talking, but when we reach our floor and the elevator doors open there is a flurry of activity. I don't like it. I have a terrible sick feeling in my gut. All the activity is at Evelina's room. I start to walk quickly, then start to run. I can hear Alana right behind me. Oh god, no, they are in Evelina's room. Too many nurses coming and going, then I see her bed being wheeled out and Dr. Cassidy following

"Doctor, what's happened? What's wrong with Evelina? Where are you taking her?"

"Mr. Tourney. I tried to phone you, but it went straight to voicemail.

The nurse was doing routine checks on Evelina, and her stats were low, her blood pressure very low. She didn't wake up when I tried. I'm almost sure she is hemorrhaging from the surgery. We need to get her back to theatre now to stop the blood loss."

"Fuck. Is she going to be okay? Can you stop the bleeding? Please, doc, tell me she's going to be okay?" My hands are in my hair, pulling at it, my voice quivering. I have a lump in my throat, and I feel the tears start to fall down my cheeks. I fall to the floor on my knees and hold my head in my hands

"Please, someone tell me she's going to be okay. She was fine earlier. Why is this happening?" Alana is beside me and pulls my head to her chest to hug me.

"Theon. She's going to be fine. It happens after surgery sometimes?" I look up; everyone apart from one nurse has gone, including Dr. Cassidy. A nurse comes to me to help me up with Alana "Sir, this can happen after surgery. They are taking her back to theatre to stop the bleeding. Dr. Cassidy will come and find you when she knows what's happening. Come on, let's get you into Evelina's room." They walk me into the room and sit me in the chair. I hear them talk, but I don't hear what they are saying. It's like white noise in my head. Like my brain is fuzzy and doesn't want to comprehend what's going on. I feel a hand on my arm and look at it. I don't look up. I just look at the hand. I know whose hand it is from the feelings I get.

"Theon. Theon. Look at me, Theon." I raise my head slowly. She's bending down to look me in the eyes. She hands me a tissue. I must look a mess, crying and snot dribbling from my nose. I think I'm having a breakdown. The last time I felt like this was when I lost Evelyn. I feel like I'm not here. I'm in my body, but my mind is not in here. I feel like my head is empty, there are no emotions or feelings. She squeezes my arm.

"Theon, come back to me. Evelina needs you. Come on, sweetie. You're her strong daddy. You have to be strong for your little girl. Here, drink this." She takes my hand, puts a cup in it, and slowly puts it to my lips. I take a sip. It's cold, really cold water. I gulp it down. I didn't know I was thirsty, but I'm starting to take in my surroundings. She said be strong. I'm a strong daddy for Evelina. Evelina! Oh fuck where is she. I start looking around then try to get up. I start to panic.

"Evelina, where is she? Evelina!" I shout, "where the fuck is she. Where's her bed?" Then it hits me, they wheeled her out. Dr Cassidy, she said something about hemorrhaging, theatre. I need to find her

"I need to find Evelina, where is she?"

"Shhh, Theon, calm down, she's in theatre with Dr Cassidy. They will bring her back as soon as they have fixed her."

Alana is stopping me getting up. She's hugging me. She knows something's wrong. Something is very wrong.

"What's wrong with her? Is she going to be okay? Will she die? I can't lose her as well. No, no, no, no, no, no —" I'm rocking back and forth. Alana is trying to hold me and stop me.

"Shhh, it's okay, Theon, you're not going to lose her. They are fixing her right now. Internal bleeding happens a lot after surgery. She's going to be okay."

"How do you know? How can you sit there and say that? You have no idea? None of us do." I get up and start pacing. I'm pulling my hair, chanting, no, no, no, no, over and over. It feels like I've been in here for ages, but when I look at the clock, it's not even been ten minutes. I'm going crazy. I need to get out of this room. Be near the theatre where she is. I head out in that direction. I walk on autopilot, not even knowing where I'm heading, but I end up near the locked doors that lead to where the theatres are. I pace and pace. A few doctors in scrubs come and go, as do some nurses. They all make sure the doors lock after them so I can't get through.

I'm still pacing when I see Dr. Cassidy through the glass. She's talking to someone in scrubs. She looks up and sees me. That look on her face. No, that's not good.

"Take it back," I shout through the glass

"Please take that look back." I start to cry. I can see pity, sorrow, and compassion on her face. That's for me. That's because she's going to tell me bad news. She's stalling. She doesn't want to come out. I fall to the floor. I'm on my hands and knees. My chest is heaving. I can't breathe. I can't see, and my eyes are full of tears. I can feel it. That feeling all over again. That emptiness. That hole in my heart. The feeling of loss again. The feeling of dread — hopelessness — of despair at my life shattering all over again. I roll onto my side and curl up into the fetal position. This can't happen again. How many times does one man have to go through this? Why me? Why do I lose everyone I love? This feeling is my life being sucked away. Just like when I lost Evelyn.

Chapter 18

PREGNANCY WAS REALLY STARTING to suit Evelyn. She was glowing and looked more beautiful with every day that passed. We loved everything to do with the pregnancy and Evelyn barely had any morning sickness. The doctors said she was very lucky. The best thing was her appetite for me. She couldn't get enough of me, and I was not complaining one little bit, no way.

It's approaching her twelve-week scan, and we are both a bit nervous, but neither of us know why. Although Evelyn is quite small, she already has a baby bump. Only visible because we know about it, but it's there. I've insisted on the best OB-GYN in LA. She doesn't come cheap, but when my wife and child are involved, I don't care what it costs.

We arrive at the prenatal clinic, and we have only just finished filling in the paperwork when a nurse calls us straight in. She asks Evelyn to do a urine sample and takes some bloods, then asks her to get onto the bed and tells us that the doctor will be in shortly. We are like two giddy school kids, smiling and laughing at each other. I'm sitting next to the bed, holding her hand.

"Do you think they can tell us if it's a boy or a girl, at this stage?" I asked Evelyn.

She frowns at me. "Do you want to know what we're having?"

I hadn't really given it much thought. It just seemed to be what people did all the time. I was pondering this when the doctor walked in.

"Hello, Mr. & Mrs. Tourney. I'm Doctor Zelda. It's a pleasure to meet you both," she says, shaking both our hands. Evelyn and I look at each other, and both burst out laughing. It's the doctor's name. We both love a game called, 'The Legend of Zelda'.

"Doctor Zelda, please forgive us, we are both giddy and nervous. It's lovely to meet you." Evelyn, ever the diplomatic one, digs us out of a hole. "Call me Evelyn, and this is Theon."

"Is this your first child?" she asks us both.

"Yes, and I'm terrified," Evelyn admits.

"Don't worry. Today I'm going to check you out and make sure everything looks okay with you and the baby. We will also do a scan and print you off some amazing 3D images of baby Tourney, providing the little one wants to be seen, that is."

I've been reading up, and the little bean is now quite well formed at this stage and looks like a baby. It's amazing. I've been fascinated by it all. Doctor Zelda asks Evelyn lots of questions about herself and how she's been feeling. Then she examines Evelyn while I'm still holding her hand. Then it's the fun bit. She gets some gel and spreads it on Evelyn's tummy, gets a probe thing and slowly moves it around. She's watching the monitor in front of her all the time. She's back and forth, back and forth, stopping, pressing buttons, stopping. We can't actually see the screen yet, so I'm watching her face. She looks puzzled, and it's scaring me. "Is everything okay, Doctor?" I ask, worried.

"Yes, here we are." She turns the monitor for us to see and we can't believe how clear the image is. We look at each other, and we just cry. Then look at the monitor.

"Wow, the baby looks quite big there," I say.

"Well, that's because there are two, one hiding behind the other. See, here you can make out the second one behind, which makes it look like one big baby." What the fuck! Did she say two? As in twins.

"Theon. Theon, are you okay, baby? Theon, answer me. You're very pale. Are you okay?" I think I'm in shock.

"We're having twins?" I whisper. I look at Evelyn. She's crying. I stand up and hug her.

"Two, Evelyn. Two! Can you believe it? We're having twins, baby." I kiss her nose, her cheek, her eyes, and her forehead. I'm ecstatic.

"Best day of my life, baby. Best day ever. Two babies."

"Oh, Theon. I can't believe that. I don't think we have twins in our family. It must be from your side. Oh god, I can't believe it. Oh god, my body is going to get huge." She cries some more.

The Doctor goes over all the dos and don'ts. The results all look good, except her sugar level is very slightly raised, which needs monitoring because it could be diabetes. She prints off a few 3D images for us, and we leave the doctor's office — both in shock.

"Twins, Evelyn. I can't believe it. It hasn't sunk in yet. I don't know if I have twins on my side. I know nothing about my father, so have no idea. But I don't care. We're having two babies baby. Double trouble! Oh no," I say laughing. As we hit the sidewalk, I lift her up and spin us around, both of us laughing.

"Theon, I'm gonna be sick if you carry on doing that," she says laughing.

"Oh shit, I need to be gentle with you now, mamma. Precious cargo on board. Quick, let's get to the drugstore and buy up all the cotton wool we can get." She stands and looks at me as I'm trying to grab her hand. The look on her face is priceless.

"What on earth do you want lots of cotton wool for?"

"To wrap you up in, of course. What do you think? Got three of you to protect now," I say all serious, but I'm failing to keep a straight face. She slaps my arm.

"Theon! You had me going then. Come on. We need to go and see mom and dad and break the news to them. This should be fun." We head off down the sidewalk swinging our joined hands between us. I'm not sure we will ever grow up.

Chapter 19

Present

I CAN FEEL A HAND RUBBING on my back — someone speaking softly to me. The voice is gentle and trying to coax me up. Trying to bring me to the here and now when all I want to do is stay in the past, inside my head. I don't want the now. It will bring me pain and devastation. I try to shrug off the hand. I'm still curled up on the floor.

"Mr. Tourney. Come on, let's get you up. Let's get you in a chair. There's a room we can go and sit in."

"NO!" I shout. I know what she's going to do. Get me in a room so she can tell me Evelina's gone. That it's my fault my baby girl is gone because I didn't stay with her. Her strong daddy wasn't there to watch over her — to notice she wasn't right. It's all my fucking fault she's gone. It's all on me. Evelyn will never forgive me. I'm not going in a room to be told that, no way.

Mr. Tourney, come on. Let's get you some water and tissues."

"NO, I'm not going. You don't need to tell me. I know it's my fault. It's all my fault." She's still rubbing my back.

"What's your fault? What did you do?" I look up at her. Is she mad? What does she mean, what did I do? She knows it's my fault. Stupid woman.

"I left her. I wasn't watching my baby girl. It's my fault she's gone."

"Gone, oh no, no, Mr. Tourney. Evelina hasn't gone. She's out of surgery and in the recovery room. Mr. Tourney, do you hear what I'm saying?"

"She's not gone? She's okay?" I'm looking up at her, pleading for her to repeat it just in case I only thought I heard it. She shakes her head no.

"She's not gone. She's in recovery. Come on, let's get back to Evelina's room, and I can explain it there." She helps me up, and we walk in silence to the room. She's not gone? But I felt it. I don't understand. I felt my baby girl had gone.

Back in Evelina's room, I sit in the chair, and Dr. Cassidy pulls a chair in front of me.

"Mr. Tourney, Evelina is not out of the woods yet. She was hemorrhaging, but they managed to stop the bleeding, and she's had to have a blood transfusion to replace the loss of blood. This is a complication after any surgery, Mr. Tourney, not just from the nephrectomy that Evelina's had. The surgeon thinks they stopped it in time. This was a reactive bleed, meaning it wouldn't be found during surgery and only shows itself once the blood pressure is back to normal after surgery.

"With a hemorrhage, if too much blood is lost, it can cause damage to the surrounding organs by compressing them. The surgeon doesn't think this has happened. Evelina did lose a lot of blood, and this can cause hemorrhagic shock, which can lead to brain damage. Again, the surgeon doesn't think this happened, We don't think Evelina has any complications, but she will stay in recovery for a while so she can be closely monitored. She may be moved to ICU depending on her recovery. Did you understand all that, Mr. Tourney?" I nod

"I think so. She's alive, right?" That's all I heard.

Chapter 20

10 years earlier

WE ARE IN THE SEVENTH MONTH OF pregnancy, into the third trimester. Evelyn is huge and growing each day. I'm worried she's going to burst if the babies keep growing like this. I've read all the books, and I don't think she's going to make it to the end. I'm convinced she's going to have them early. She's started to struggle, and if she thought I was being protective at first, then that's nothing compared to now. I don't leave her at all. She either comes into the office with me for a few hours, or we work from the home office. I love looking after her more than anything. I cook, clean, run her baths, bathe her, rub her swollen feet and legs, and massage her shoulders, head, and neck. I love it, and I love her even more.

The doctor has been monitoring her more than usual with it being twins, which I'm grateful for. She's had a few bouts of high blood pressure and had to have bedrest. I just worked on my laptop next to her on the bed during these times.

The day we found out about having twins we went straight to Sonia's and Arnold's to break the news to them. We planned out what we were going to do on our way over there. We were being mean. We were both sour-faced when we arrived and, of course, Sonia was worried, which was cruel of us because she knew we had our doctor's appointment that morning. Evelyn handed over the one scan picture, which made the baby look huge.

"Oh, Mom, look at the size of it. I'm having a giant. The doctor said she's never seen a baby as big as this at twelve weeks. It's going to be so big in the next few months that Theon is going to be rolling me everywhere." Sonia was looking at the scan.

"Oh, Evelyn, you must be further along than you thought, for it to be this big." She was looking worried.

"No, Mom. I'm not. The development, apart from the size, is all spot on for twelve weeks. It's a giant." Sonia was lost for words, but you could see the joy on her face, examining the scan. I couldn't keep my face straight. I burst out laughing, and of course, Evelyn followed.

"Ok, you two. What's going on? Did you mess with the picture on your computer and blow it up to wind us up?" We couldn't talk through laughing.

"No, mom. Here, look at this picture. Both of you, really look at it." She said to her parents. We watched the quizzical looks on their faces, the creased brows, and then the raised brows from Sonia when the penny dropped. She gasped and put her hand over her mouth. Arnold hadn't got it yet, so was looking worriedly at Sonia.

"What, Sonia? What is it?" She looked at us, smiling like Cheshire cats with our arms around each other.

"Twins. You're having twins? But how? I mean, I know how, but twins?"

"Yes, Grandma and Granddad. Two little terrors for you."

"Oh, Arnold, can you imagine two of them running around? I can't wait." She hugged us both, nearly squeezing us to death.

"You say that now, Sonia, just you wait till they are the terrible two's and you don't know which way to run after which one." We all laugh. Who am I kidding though? That will be me all over.

"Do you have twins in your family, Theon?" Sonia asks me. She knows about my past, but I still feel like shit admitting I have no idea.

"I don't know. I have no idea about my father. I don't know who he is, so will never know if there is a history of twins." I hang my head.

"Who cares?" Evelyn says grabbing my hand and squeezing it tight.

"All that matters is these babies and us, right, baby?" I smile the biggest smile at her. She's right, who cares.

That was a great day. The best day of my life.

Chapter 21

Present

I'M IN EVELINA'S ROOM. I'VE BEEN sitting in here for hours, just waiting for any bit of news, but I've heard nothing. I don't want to move from here, but I need to pee. I nip to the bathroom just down the hall and try to be quick. I walk back towards Evelina's room, and as I'm passing one of the open doors, I hear singing. I stop. It's beautiful. I recognize the song. It's one of Evelyn's favorites, 'Don't give up' by Peter Gabriel and Kate Bush. I stand there, next to the open door with my back against the wall. I'm crying, listening, thinking of Evelyn but also thinking of Evelina. I look up at the ceiling. "Evelyn, baby, please bring Evelina back to us. Evander will be so lost without his other half. We both need her," I whisper. I don't realize the singing has stopped, and as I turn to head back to Evelina's room, I freeze. There, in the open doorway is Alana. She looks really tired and sad.

"Hey," I say quietly.

"Hey," she says back.

"Was that you singing just now?" She nods and looks at the floor.

"It was beautiful, Alana. It stopped me from walking on. I love that song. It was one of Evelyn's favorites." It's my turn to look down now.

"Thank you, Theon. How's Evelina?" I shrug my shoulders but don't look up.

"I don't know. She was hemorrhaging. They managed to stop it and gave her a blood transfusion, but that's all I know. I've been waiting in her room. Dr. Cassidy said she would come and let me know what was going on and if they were going to take her to ICU. She was still in recovery, which is why I've not seen her yet." I look up and into Alana's eyes.

"I'm so scared, Alana. So fucking terrified. I can't lose her as well." Now I'm crying hard. She moves so quickly, and before I know it she's hugging me with my head on her shoulder. I let it out. I can do this with Alana. I can't in front of the kids. I have to be strong, positive, and their daddy. "Thank you. I needed that." I laugh, although it comes out a little more like a huff. "I'm not sure who's worse, you or me, but I'm grateful, Alana. So grateful to have an outlet."

"Same here, Theon. We're a right pair. At our most vulnerable but so grateful."

"How's Caroline doing?"

"Not very good. I know chemo makes you poorly, but it terrifies me as well. She's suffering, the poor little thing, and I feel so useless."

"Yeah, I know that feeling. I'm supposed to protect her. My baby girl. How can I do that against this? I thought this afternoon she was over the worse, but then this. When does it stop?"

"No idea, Theon. Life can be so cruel."

"I'm going to head back to her room and wait. It's killing me, not knowing. I'll see you later, and thanks again, Alana."

Back in Evelina's room, I'm pacing. I phoned Sonia to update her on what's happening, and I managed to do it without breaking down. I'm still waiting, my leg jumping with nerves.

Dr. Cassidy arrives. Thank God. I jump up. "What's happening, Doctor. I'm going out of my mind here?"

"I'm sorry, Mr. Tourney. I had another emergency. I've been and checked in on Evelina. Can we sit?" Oh shit, that's not good.

"What's wrong?"

"She's okay. We seem to have stopped the hemorrhaging, which is good news. They are taking her to ICU as we speak. I will take you up there in a few minutes once she's settled. Mr. Tourney, Evelina hasn't come round yet."

"Wait, what, come round from surgery?"

She nods at me. "She's slipped into a coma, Mr. Tourney."

I jump out of my chair. "What, why? What's wrong? Why is she in a coma? What does that mean?"

"Please, Mr. Tourney, it just means she's shut down for a little while. We are optimistic. It's just her body's way of healing. To be honest, it's not a bad thing with all that she's gone through. We are monitoring her 24/7. Do you have any questions?"

"Will she wake up? Tell me she will wake up?"

"I have faith that she will wake up, Mr. Tourney. She's a very strong little girl. What I can't tell you is when that will be. I have to tell you, it could be hours, days, weeks, months or, in extreme cases, years. We need to take each day as it comes. All the while, she is healing from her nephrectomy procedure, which is a good thing. We'll keep monitoring her and making sure there is no more hemorrhaging and if, and it's a big if, she doesn't wake up for a few weeks, we can still go ahead with the chemo while she's in a coma. Now, are you ready to go up and see her? I have to warn you, there are lots of monitors and tubes?"

"God, yes, please. It's killing me down here waiting."

We walk up to the ICU in silence. I'm trying to ready myself for what I will see. We walk in. Each room has floor-to-ceiling glass windows. We pass the nurses station and stop by a room almost opposite them. I see her. My baby girl is lying there, very still with monitors all behind the bed and to the side. I can't hold it in. I put the back of my hand to my mouth and bite it, trying to stifle the noise as tears stream down my face. Dr. Cassidy rubs my arm.

"I know, Mr. Tourney, this is one of the hardest things a parent has to witness. It's okay, you know. Let it all out, and then go and be with her. Talk to her, read to her — whatever brings you both comfort. Let Evander and her family come and see her and talk to her. It's well documented that coma patients hear what's going on around them. They remember conversations that went on while they slept. Play her favorite music or bring her favorite movie in. We encourage it, Mr. Tourney. Now, when you're ready, go in and sit with her. Try not to be upset in there. You're her strong daddy, remember." I nod wiping my eyes and nose on my sleeve. A nurse brings me some tissues.

"Here you go, Mr. Tourney. I'm Josie, I'm Evelina's nurse, and I promise to take good care of her. Anything you need or need to know, ask me. When I'm not on duty, it will be Margaret taking care of her."

"Thank you, Josie." I blow my nose, wipe my face, straighten up and compose myself. I walk straight into the room, confident and strong on the outside, but shattered and in pieces on the inside. I lean over and kiss her forehead.

"How's my baby girl doing? Are you sleeping on your daddy, huh? Well, that's fine, poppet. You sleep all you want to. Daddy will be right here for you when you wake up. In the meantime, I'm going to go and get your Harry Potter books so I can carry on reading them to you. I won't be long." I lean down and give her a lingering kiss on the forehead and stroke her hair. I look up to the ceiling.

"Come on, Evelyn. You owe me this. Look after her," I whisper.

I'm in her room, and I've been packing up her things to take up to ICU. I'm sitting on the chair next to the bed with my elbows on my knees and my head in my hands.

"I don't know if I'm strong enough for this, Evelyn. I don't know what to do. I won't survive if she's taken as well. The Evs are the only reason I'm even here at all after losing you. I'm telling you now, if it weren't for them, I'd be with you up there. Please don't let them take her, Evelyn. I'm begging you, baby." I'm crying again.

I feel Alana's presence before I hear her. I look up and see her standing at the door, wondering if she should come in or leave me to my pity party. I don't wonder for long, she rushes to me, kneeling on the floor in front of me, and grabs my hands.

"Theon, what's happened? Where's Evelina?" She looks at the empty bed and back to me with tears in her eyes. Oh god, she thinks she's gone. I shake my head.

"Oh no, she's in ICU, Alana. She's in a coma. She hasn't woken up from them fixing the hemorrhage. I don't know what to do here. I don't know if I'm strong enough."

"Oh Theon, come on, sweetie, none of this! You're not strong enough. You don't have a choice. You have to be strong because that little girl depends on you — her daddy. You're her hero. You have to be her superhero to get her through this. No wallowing. She's not gone. She's alive, and she needs you. Do you hear me?" She raises my head, so we're eye level. She hands me a tissue, and I wipe my eyes. She leans in and kisses my cheek. I feel it every time she touches me. I feel the connection, the sparks. I've never felt like that about anyone since Evelyn. Evelyn was my first and last, but she left me. I look at Alana — really look at her — thinking if we weren't in this place, in the situation we are in now, I would most definitely kiss her. It's just a case of the wrong time and the wrong place. I smile at her

"Thank you again, that's all we seem to do, thank each other. I'm starting to rely on you, Alana. You're my support through this. I don't have anyone else other than my in-laws."

"You're mine too, Theon. I have my sister, but that's it, and she's looking after the B's." She laughs at that, and I laugh with her.

"I'm glad we found each other to support at this horrendous time in our lives. Now, you get yourself sorted out and go and see your little girl. I need to get back to Caroline; she's not very good still. You know, Theon, the hardest part of being a parent is watching your child go through something really bad and not be able to fix it for them. We feel hopeless, but we have to stay strong for them. They rely on us. They only have us to look up to and show them how to be strong, and that alone should make us stronger. Yes, we're allowed meltdowns out of their sight, which is where you and I are good for each other, but to them we're invincible, we are their superheroes. Now go. I'll see you later." This time, I lean in and kiss her cheek. I linger slightly longer than I should.

"Thank you," I whisper.

I get up, grab Evelina's things and head out to see my little girl. I've got a lot of talking ahead of me, which will be hard enough without a smart, sassy ten-year-old back chatting me. I can't wait for that to happen again.

Chapter 22

10 years earlier

EIGHT MONTHS PREGNANT and ready to burst — Evelyn is on complete bedrest. Her blood pressure is through the roof. We have a nurse monitoring her constantly. The doctor wanted her to stay in hospital, but Evelyn wanted to be at home. So the compromise is we have round the clock nurses in the house. I've been so worried about her. She's very pale. I've made an appointment to see Dr. Zelda today, and I'm going to ask if we can get Evelyn induced because this pregnancy is now making her too poorly. She's drained, with no energy at all. She's barely eating, and that's not good for the babies.

Evelyn doesn't know I'm seeing the doctor. I don't want her to see how worried I actually am.

"Doctor, please can you consider inducing Evelyn? I'm fearful for her health. She is so uncomfortable, mostly bedridden, struggling to sleep, and she barely eats. I have to help her to the bathroom because walking is a struggle. I'm going out of my mind with worry for her and the babies."

"Mr. Tourney, I completely understand your concerns, as you know Mrs. Tourney refused the bedrest in hospital, but until her water's break or she and the babies are in any kind of distress, I'm afraid I can't enforce her going into hospital to be induced." Fuck, that is not what I want to hear. I rub my hands over my face. She can see how anxious and agitated I am.

"Mr. Tourney, how about I come and do a house visit this afternoon and see how Mrs. Tourney and the babies are doing? I can make the decision then or at least try to talk Mrs. Tourney into going into the hospital?"

"Yes, please, Doctor. That would be great, and hopefully, we can both talk her into it." I leave the office deflated.

I'm on my way home, thinking about Evelyn and how this last month has been a nightmare for her. My phone rings through the car system, and I connect the call. I can hear screaming. Shit! "Hello, Evelyn. Is that you, baby?"

"Theon, it's Louise. Evelyn has gone into labor. I've called the paramedics, and they will be here in a few minutes. Do you want to try to get home or meet us at the hospital?"

"Shit, how is she? Is she okay? I'm almost home. I'll be there in a couple of minutes?"

"She's not good, Theon. I'm keeping her comfortable. Got to go." She hangs up. I put my foot down. Please, traffic, don't stop me.

I throw the car into park on the drive just as the paramedics arrive. I rush into the house and up the stairs, shouting for them to follow me.

I run into our room and straight to Evelyn on the bed. She looks terrible. Oh god, please be okay, please be okay.

"Hey baby, how are you feeling? The paramedics are here to take us to have these babies. Are you ready?" She nods very gently at me. Tears streaming down her face into her ears. I wipe them away and kiss her lightly on the lips.

"I love you so damn much, baby. Never forget that." I move aside while the paramedics see to her. I'm watching everything they do.

"Sir, we need to get going now. Her blood pressure is very low, and she's drifting in and out of consciousness. The babies will start to get distressed if we don't move now." I nod. I can see Evelyn's eyes close. She suddenly screams out loud. It's a terrifying blood-curdling scream that scares the shit out of me. Then she goes still.

"Is she okay?" I'm freaking out. She doesn't look like she's moving. I watch her chest and can just make out it rising slowly. She's shuddering. Oh god, please no.

I follow the paramedics down the stairs, and I jump into the back with one. I don't give him a choice. There's no way I'm leaving her. She's bad. I know she is, and I'm scared out of my fucking mind. This isn't how having a baby is supposed to be. It's supposed to be her cursing me and digging her nails in me, but us being deliriously happy. There hasn't been any of that. She's been on bedrest for a month. Not feeling well at all. I've hated every minute of it. Just lately, I've hated her being pregnant at times. I've wished on so many occasions she wasn't and that it was just us again. I've felt guilty having those thoughts, but as I sit here, now holding her hand, watching her almost lifeless, I don't feel guilt. I want the babies out of her now. I wish we'd had them induced weeks back, but Evelyn refused. She wanted to go as long as she could. Stubborn fucking woman.

We arrive at the hospital and are taken straight to the trauma room. A doctor enters, who I've met twice, he works with Dr. Zelda.

"Mr. Tourney, I'm Dr. Frost. I'll be delivering the babies for you. Dr. Zelda is in an emergency, but she will be here as soon as she can. Evelyn has very low blood pressure. I'm going to have to do a C-section to get the babies out, as she cannot push. Can you consent to this?" What's he talking about? Didn't we already consent?

"Just do what you have to do. We already consented to this?"

"No. Evelyn withdrew the consent. She wanted to deliver them naturally."

"Just do it. Make her better. Get the fucking babies out, NOW!" I scream. Evelyn is not moving. I'm terrified. She's not moved since her last contraction. This can't be right. There's lots of action, they're prepping her, and I'm asked to leave. No fucking way. I refuse point blank. I have Evelyn's hand in mine, and I'm stroking her head and kissing her forehead. A nurse has an apron on me, but I won't move. They put an oxygen mask on her. I can feel the tears rolling down my face.

"Baby, we're having our babies today. Can you believe it? They're coming to greet us finally. They want to see their mommy and daddy. Let's get them out, and you can cuddle them. I love you, baby. My first, my last, forever and infinity."

There's a hive of activity around me, but I don't notice anything. There are monitors beeping. I faintly hear crying, babies crying, but I can't pull myself away from Evelyn.

I'm stroking her head.

She's not breathing.

A long, screaming high-pitched noise causes me to look up. It's the cardiac machine. It's showing a long green line. I look at the doctors as they move me out of the way. They're pumping on Evelyn's chest so hard, I'm sure I hear a rib crack. I'm stood stunned, lifeless at what's unfolding around me. I feel like I'm not here. This isn't happening. It's all a dream, and I'll wake up any minute now.

I feel like it's not my body standing here.

I can't breathe.

There is shouting, again. Someone shouting, "clear." Didn't they shout that already?

What's he doing now? Oh no. No fucking way, what's he trying to do, I grab at him. "What the fuck are you doing? Why are you covering her?" I'm still trying to grab at him. "Don't you fucking dare try to cover my beautiful wife! Don't you dare." I grab the sheet he's got in his hands to stop him.

"She won't be able to see the babies or me if you do that, you fucking dipshit."

What's he thinking? She'll be awake soon. Won't she.

Oh god, I can't breathe.

She's gone.

My life is gone with her.

This was supposed to be the best fucking day of my life.

It's turned into the worst nightmare of my life.

This can't be real.

I have to wake up.

I'll find her sprawled out beside me like she is every morning. Me cursing as I'm hanging off the bed because she's taking up all the room. She says it's because of the size she is now, that she needs to spread out but it's not, she's always done it.

I love her.

Time to wake up.

Except I can't.

I'm standing here in the emergency room. I can hear babies crying, but she's just lying there. They haven't covered her up — I wouldn't let them. I remember screaming at them when they called time on her.

I screamed when they try to cover her.

"What the fuck are you doing? Why are you covering her?"

The doctor tries to put a hand on my arm, but I shrug him off.

"Fix her!" I cry

"Just fix her…" I fall to my knees on the floor, my head in my hands. Trying to wake up from this nightmare.

My wife is gone.

I can't fathom what happened. It was a birth. They do this day in and day out, multiple times a day, so why did my wife die?

"What happened? Why is she gone? She was giving birth. You do this all the time. WHAT THE FUCK HAPPENED?" I scream at them.

The doctor crouches down to be eye level with me.

"I'm sorry, Mr. Tourney. Your wife had eclampsia and went into cardiac arrest. We did all we could for her, but, unfortunately, we couldn't save her. It's not common to have deaths in childbirth these days, but especially with twins, eclampsia can be a complication." I just stare at him, not quite understanding

"She had a heart attack? She's only 27. How the fuck could she have a heart attack?"

He winces slightly at my outburst. "Mr. Tourney. I'm so sorry. I know this is hard for you but you have two healthy babies over there." He nods his head in the direction of the crying babies

"They could probably do with meeting their daddy. Being born is stressful enough, but they've lost their mother. I believe they'll know that they've lost a connection. Would you like to meet your son and daughter?"

Would I?

Do I want to?

Did they kill her?

What the fuck do I do now?

I can't look after two babies on my own. They need their mother.

"Bring her back, doctor. Just bring her the fuck back. They need their Mommy. I need her. She's my life."

I break, collapsing backward on the floor. I'm curled up tight, tucking my legs into my chest as tight as I can get them. I start rocking and wailing. How pathetic must I look? A grown man curled up on a delivery room floor …

Not something they see every day.

I'm rocking back and forth, back and forth

"Evelyn, baby, don't leave me, please come back to me, please don't leave me. I can't live without you." I scramble to my knees and shuffle to her bed. There's blood on the floor. I'm kneeling in her blood. Fuck. I grab her hand. It's cold. I'm kissing her hand and sobbing so hard I can't breathe properly. I'm trying to take in gulps of air.

"Evelyn, please wake up. Baby, I need you. WAKE UP?" I scream at her. I start to get up using the bed to lever myself up. I feel arms under me trying to help me. I slip in the blood on the floor and fall to my knees Evelyn's hand rests against my face as my head rests on the bed.

"She's awake. Doctor, quick, she's awake. Baby, I love you. Baby, we'll get you better." More arms are helping me get up, so I don't slip this time, but when I look at Evelyn, she's not awake.

She's not breathing.

She's dead.

Turning blue, dead.

I collapse again, this time I must have passed out.

I wake suddenly. I hear someone moving around.

"Evelyn, is that you, baby? Evelyn, are you okay?"

"Theon, how are you feeling, sweetie?" Sonia murmurs. I feel a hand on my hair, stroking my head. I open my eyes. It's not my bedroom.

Fuck, what's happening?

Where am I?

Where's Evelyn?

Evelyn. Babies. Labor. Dying. Screaming Babies. It hits me. I scream; thrashing about, wanting to get up, there's a horrible noise and crying. I realize I'm making the noise. I'm wailing and crying. I can hear Sonia crying. She's thrown herself over me to keep me down, but she's hugging me and crying. I can't breathe. I start hyperventilating, gulping for breath.

"Shhh, Theon." She's trying to calm me down. I start to breathe easier.

"Where is she, Sonia? I need to see her. Where is she?"

"Oh, Theon, sweetie, she's gone. They couldn't save her. Do you remember? She went into cardiac arrest." She's crying into my chest. I wrap my arms around her, and we cry together for our loss. The images flash into my head. Evelyn lying on the bed — still. I remember blood on the floor, me slipping in her blood. Evelyn — blue and cold. They shut her eyes. She looked like she was sleeping. My beautiful angel laying there. I remember babies wailing, but I not seeing them.

"And the babies, Sonia?"

"They are beautiful, Theon. They are healthy and being looked after by the nurses. You have a son and a daughter. They are the most amazing little things. Do you think you can walk to go and see them?"

"NO!" I shout and startle her.

"No, it's their fault she's dead. It's all on them, Sonia. I can't look at them knowing they killed my Evelyn. They took my wife and my life from me." I turn my head away from her.

"No, Theon, it's not the babies' fault, sweetie. Please don't blame them. They have lost their mommy. They can't lose their daddy as well."

Chapter 23

Evelina has been in a coma for eight days now. I'm with her practically twenty-four seven, apart from going to the bathroom and having a quick shower, and I only do that when Sonia and Evander are reading and talking to her.

I'm going silently out of my mind.

Every day I pray she wakes up.

I stay strong on the outside for Evelina and Evander, but I know Sonia can see the turmoil in me just as I see it in her. I sometimes forget she lost her daughter and now her granddaughter is in a coma. I have to remember it's not just me, but it's hard. Evander is being a trooper. He seems so strong and just keeps saying she will wake up when she's ready.

I know she will.

Evander is at school, and Sonia has dropped in to see Evelina. She tells me to get a shower and go for some fresh air while she sits with her. I have my shower then head outside to go and sit in the garden area for a little while. I decide to phone the office and make sure everything is okay with Aggie and Patrick. It's been a couple of days since I've spoken to either of them. Luckily, they have everything under control. I'm sitting, staring up into the sky when I feel Alana approach. I always sense when she's near. I look to my right and watch her.

"Hi, Theon."

"Hi, Alana, how are you?"

"Holding on." She shrugs. "And you?"

"The same." I give her a small smile.

"Do you mind if I join you or would you prefer to be alone?"

"No, please sit."

"How is Evelina?"

"She's just the same, still in a coma. It's scaring the life out of me, you know? The longer it goes on, the scarier it gets. I keep thinking she isn't going to wake up." I breathe out.

"How is Caroline doing?"

"The chemo has been hard, but they did an x-ray this morning, and the tumor is shrinking. They think they may be able to operate on her next week if it continues to shrink. I'm just praying it does."

"That's great news, Alana. I hope they can operate on her." We sit in silence, with our own thoughts.

"God, Alana, why is life like this? Why is it so fucking hard?" I rub my hands over my face.

"I try to understand. I try to think, what have I done that was so bad to deserve this?"

"Me too. I think I must have been wicked in my previous life, you know, for all this to keep happening. I don't think it's fair. Life is not fair."

"You know Evelyn was a firm believer that everything happened for a reason. She said we just didn't know what that reason was straight away. That it sometimes took a while for us to realize why. I still do not know the reason she was taken from me or the reason Evelina is so poorly. Life is so shit sometimes." I lean my head back and look up to the sky, rubbing my hands over my face again. Then I rest them on my thighs and take in a deep sigh. Alana puts her hand on top of mine.

"You know, Theon. Evelyn sounds like my kind of person. I too believe things happen for a reason. I believe I lost Gary to help me notice the signs when Caroline became ill. If he hadn't had the same cancer, I probably wouldn't have noticed the symptoms in Caroline. That's my theory at the moment; it may change depending on the outcome. I know life is shit, and we are sent these curveballs to try us, and it's how we deal with them that makes us who we are."

"Now you even sound like Evelyn." I look down and smile.

"We always seem to have these pity talks, don't we?" I say looking at her.

"But I'm glad we do, Alana. I know we keep saying this, but I'm glad I have you to talk to. It helps me so much." I rest my other hand on top of hers and squeeze it, feeling that spark again. I wonder if she feels it too.

"Me too, Theon. It helps me so much, knowing I can come and find you and speak to you about things." We sit in silence for a bit longer, still holding hands. It's a comfortable, supportive silence.

"I worry she isn't going to wake up, Alana. I read to her all the time. I put her favorite shows on the TV so she can hear them. Why won't she wake up? I've been reading about coma patients and how there is no rhyme or reason to it. That they can just one day all of a sudden wake as though nothing has happened."

"What has Doctor Cassidy said about it?"

"That she could wake up at any time. It could be days, weeks or months. She said I shouldn't worry too much as she's convinced Evelina will wake up soon, although she can't say for sure. In young patients the chances of being in a coma for an extended period of time are minimal, but that doesn't mean it doesn't happen.

They've done tests on her brain, and they say everything looks normal — no sign of swelling and the bleeding has stopped. They don't think there is any brain damage but won't know for sure until she wakes up. Evander is being so strong. He says she will wake up when she's good and ready and not before. I wish I had his optimism. It just terrifies me. Doc said that if she is still in a coma next week, they will still go ahead with the chemo. In one respect, her being asleep helps her recovery from the surgery, helps heal faster, and if she's asleep when she has chemo, she won't feel all the side effects. I'm going to ask the doc if they can start the chemo now, while she is out, to try and alleviate all that sickness."

"If they could do that, Theon it would be better. Seeing what Caroline has gone through with her chemo has been soul destroying. She's been so poorly with it, and now because of the high dose they've been giving her to shrink the tumor her hair is falling out, and she cries all the time. I don't know what to do to comfort her. The only time she has a bit of life in her is when Bailee and Bryan come to see her. They just seem to perk her up. Like Evander, they stay strong. They amaze me."

We sit for a while longer, still holding hands. I feel a bit guilty — like I'm betraying Evelyn. I'm asking her to look out for Evelina, yet I'm sitting, holding another woman's hand. But then I seem to crave the comfort from Alana.

After a while, I feel I need to get back to Evelina. I hate being away from her for any length of time, especially after what happened last week. Alana seems to sense my need. We release our hands, and both stand up.

"Time to get back. I've been away longer than I like already." I've been checking my phone while here just making sure I wasn't missing any calls. I know if anything had happened Sonia would phone me straight away.

"Yes, I need to get back to Caroline too and see if she has woken up yet. She has chemo again in the morning, the poor love." We walk back together, just talking about us, and what we like to do with the kids. It's always about the kids, but then they are the biggest part of both our lives. I know they all like to game, but I haven't told her who I am, and she hasn't asked what I do yet. I will tell her when she asks.

I arrive back at Evelina's room after saying goodbye to Alana at Caroline's room with a kiss to the cheek. Every time I walk in here, I hold my breath in anticipation of her being awake. Every time, I'm deflated. This time is no different. Sonia is sitting next to her reading.

"Hey, how's she been? Any change?" I'm asking, but I know there will be nothing different, she would have told me.

"No, this little angel is just the same. Evelina, daddy's back. I told you he wouldn't be long, sweetie. Grandma has to get going now to go and pick Evander up from school. I'll bring him here, and I'm sure he will tell you all about school and what's been going on." She leans over and kisses her on the forehead. Nothing. No movement at all. I run my hand over my face. I just wish she would move, even a finger, I would be happy for anything.

Pull yourself together.

"Hey poppet, my little sleepy head. I'm back. Let's put a new Monster High DVD on when Grandma leaves. What do you say, baby?" I lean over and kiss her forehead. It kills me. I need this spunky little girl of mine to wake and give me her sass like I'm used to.

"See you in a while with Evander, Theon. Is there anything you need me to bring in for you? I've got your dirty laundry here, and I'll bring you the clean laundry I did yesterday. Are you okay for everything else?"

"God, Sonia, I'm sorry you're lumbered with my laundry. I really appreciate it. You know that right? Thank you. I couldn't get through this without you and Arnold?" She scowls at me and looks at Evelina. She nods, not wanting to say anything in front of her and it's her way of scolding me for just saying what I did, but in truth, I don't say it enough to her. She leaves us, and I get up to put the DVD on for Evelina. I sit back down on the bed next to her where I spend a lot of my time cuddling her, so she knows I'm there with her all the time. I would hate for her to think she was on her own. I start to drift off to sleep as I usually do when I sit here. I talk to Evelyn in my head, and I pray Evelina will wake up soon.

Chapter 24

10 Years Earlier

The day I lost Evelyn and ended up in my own hospital room was the hardest day of my life. I hadn't been admitted, so I could leave at any time, which is what I did. Sonia left me after I refused to see the babies. She wanted to go and check on them. I took this as my opportunity to leave. I was still in my blood-soaked jeans and t-shirt, and I needed to get out of them. I was going to throw up. I had Evelyn's blood all over me. I ran out of the room and ran to the entrance of the hospital. I started walking out of the doors and out of the hospital grounds onto the street. There were clothes shops over the other side, so I headed to the nearest one that sold men's stuff. I didn't care what I got just as long as I got changed. I got some sweatpants and a new top. I put them on in the changing room, and at the cash register, I asked for a bag for my bloodied clothes. I was going to burn them once I got home. I was retching again just thinking of Evelyn's blood. I flagged down a cab to take me home.

Once at my front door, I froze. I couldn't go inside. I still had the bag in my hand with my bloodied clothes in, and I headed around the back instead, to the burner out there to get rid of them. I just stood and watched them burn, I watched the flames get higher, engulfing the offending objects, flickering around. I glared into those flames. I was numb. I couldn't move. I couldn't think what to do next. What did I do without Evelyn? She's gone! I knew deep down she wasn't coming back. I fell to my knees, and I cried so hard in front of that burner. I didn't want to live without her. I couldn't live without her. She was my whole reason for living. I had no one else, just Evelyn, and now I had no one. I was alone.

"Oh god, Evelyn, please come back to me, baby. Please don't leave me like this. Why did you have to go? Why didn't you go to the hospital to be induced weeks ago? Why would you do this to us, to me? WHY, WHY, WHY?" I screamed up to the sky. My throat was hoarse, gravelly and scratchy. I couldn't believe she was gone.

I stayed like that while the clothes burned, trying to process, trying to think what to do. I got up and walked straight into my pool. I wanted to submerge under the water and never come up. I moved down the steps, one by one, getting in deeper and deeper. I took a big breath just as my head went under the water. My eyes were open, and I was standing there, anchoring myself down, trying not to float up. I could feel a burning sensation in my lungs. I wanted to open my mouth to gulp, but I couldn't, not yet. My body started to spasm, and my eyes were bulging out of my head. The burning was getting worse. I needed to breathe. I needed air. I suddenly saw Evelyn in front of me, telling me to float up, telling me the babies needed their daddy, telling me not to give up. I reached for her, and she rose. I followed, trying to reach her. I broke the surface of the pool, attempting to breathe. I gulped to get air into my burning lungs and started to panic and flap my arms, but I was dragged down by the weight of my clothes. I tried to take air before I went back under, but it was no good— this was it. I couldn't breathe. My lungs were cooling now with the water that was starting to flood them. This was what I wanted, wasn't it? I couldn't go on without her, so I just accepted it.

All of a sudden, I felt myself being pulled and turned over. I felt someone blowing into my mouth. I felt hard edges on my back, then pressure, so much pressure on my chest. I started to cough, the water pouring out of my mouth. I was in pain: my lungs, my chest, my back, all hurt. I was coughing, my throat burning. I opened my eyes, and I saw Arnold, soaking wet, looking down at me.

He pulled me out of the pool. He stopped me from drowning.

"Why, why the fuck did you do that? Why, Arnold, why pull me out?" He looked at me in fury.

"Fuck, Theon, you almost died, you ass. Don't you think it's bad enough we lost our fucking daughter today without losing you as well, you selfish prick? Who would look after your babies then? How fucking selfish can you be? Your babies just lost their fucking mother, and you were gonna let them lose their daddy as well." At that moment, him shouting at me, I felt so ashamed of myself. Ashamed I could do something like that. Ashamed I was so weak. But I couldn't live without her.

"I'm so sorry. I'm so sorry, I'm, I'm —" I couldn't take in breath quickly enough, the burning in my throat and lungs hurts so bad, "so, sorry. I'm sorry," I chant, over and over still trying to take in air. I coughed more and held my head in my hands.

"I wasn't thinking about anyone else," I sobbed and gulped in air. "I can't live without her ..." He grabbed me and pulled me to him. He was sitting on the top step of the pool, submerged in water, crying, hugging my head to his chest and rocking me back and forth like I'd done to Evelyn.

"Oh god, Theon. I know son, I know. That's my little girl. She's gone." He's sniffling and crying into my head. It's a comfort for us both. We'd both lost her. It hurt so much. I couldn't feel any physical pain because of the broken heart in my chest. We stayed like that for a while, rocking on the top step of the pool, both soaking wet, shivering and both heaving, trying to catch our breath.

"Come on, son, let's get inside and get dry. I think we both need a stiff drink." He helped me inside through the back. I stood in the kitchen, just frozen, Evelyn was everywhere.

"I can't do it, Arnold, she's everywhere I look."

"You can, son, let's get dry. With dry clothes on, you can pack a bag and come to stay with us for a bit while we work out what to do." He had his hand on my shoulder, and he had stooped to look me in the eyes, but I had my head down.

"We can do this, son. We have to. You have two babies that need you."

"NO!" I shout. I hadn't even thought of them. He leaned back, startled at my reaction.

"What do you mean, no?"

"No, I can't look after them. This is their fault. She died because of them, Arnold. I can't look at them without thinking what they did to her. THEY.FUCKING.KILLED.HER!" I shouted right in his face. He slapped my face hard. I didn't feel it, but my head jerked to the side.

"Stop with that shit. Theon. They didn't kill her. It's not their fault. They just lost their fucking mother. You can't blame them for this."

"Watch me," I said and stormed up the stairs to our room. I froze at the door to our bedroom. It was a mess from the paramedics being here earlier. Earlier … it seemed like fucking years ago. I moved slowly into the room and to my wardrobe to grab some dry clothes. I didn't even look at what I got. I just grabbed a bag and shoved what I could inside it. I wandered slowly over to the bathroom, trying not to look at the bed, but my eyes drifted there — to Evelyn lying there in pain. I stood and stared at the bed. I needed to picture us, and all the love that we shared in that bed. I needed the good images not the bad. I fell to my knees again, crying. I heard Arnold moving downstairs, and it made me get up and go into the bathroom where I stripped my wet clothes off and toweled myself dry before dressing in fresh clothes. I grabbed my toiletries and threw them into the bag. I literally ran out of the bedroom and down the stairs. I at the front door before I knew it. Arnold opened the door.

"Theon, you ready to go, son?" I nodded my head.

"Give me a minute while I just lock the house up and make it secure."

I just nodded again. A few minutes later, he came out. I heard the alarm setting in the house. I was standing in the same spot, bag on the ground and bent over with my hands on my knees just staring at nothing in front of me.

In the car, on the way to his house, it was silent. My head leaned on the window to the side of me; I was looking but not seeing. I felt numb. In fact, I didn't feel.

"Why did you go to the house?" I asked Arnold not looking at him

"Sonia phoned me. She told me to get here as soon as I could. She was on her way back to your room at the hospital when she saw you running out of the doors. She called to you, Theon, she doesn't think you heard her." I could see he had turned his head to look at me. Was that a question? Who knows?

"I was on my way back to the hospital when she phoned. She's staying there for a while. She's sorting out things with the coroner and with the babies." I sigh. I don't want to know.

"I can't deal with this." We traveled the rest of the way in silence. I wasn't prepared to talk about any of this yet.

Once at Arnold's, I followed him inside.

"Do you want a room upstairs or in the guesthouse?"

"Guesthouse," is all I say. I walked out to the back of the house through the kitchen, grabbing the key from the hook and heading to the guesthouse. I couldn't be around anyone right now. I wanted to be alone. I wanted to wallow in pity. Alone.

Chapter 25

They are going to give Evelina her first dose of chemo this morning. In one respect, I'm glad she hasn't woken up now, that way she won't suffer with this, but then, on the other hand, I am fucking terrified she is not going to wake up or that when she does, she won't be herself. Arnold is on his way in to sit with her for a bit, and I'll go and shower. He likes to sit and do math and English for her, reciting the times tables. I joke with him, saying no wonder she doesn't wake up being subjected to that. Evander has taken to playing her favorite board game with her, The Game of Life, only he does the moves for Evelina, and he lets her win because she can't see. She loves us all playing that game when we have game night at home, and she usually cheats. She loves getting married and having twins like mommy and daddy.

An hour later, I'm in the restaurant after my shower, just grabbing a quick bite. I haven't spoken to Alana for a few days, and when I looked in on Caroline yesterday, I didn't see Alana around. I hope she's okay. I shovel my bacon, eggs, and sausage down, eager to get back to Evelina. I have an hour before they come for her. I'm walking past Caroline's room on my way to get something from Evelina's other room to take up to her in ICU, and I hear crying. I don't want to intrude, but it sounds like Alana. The door is slightly ajar, so I peak through the crack and see Alana sitting on a chair in an empty room. I walk in and kneel in front of her. I grab her hands.

"Hey, What's wrong? Where's Caroline?" She looks up at me with the saddest look on her face. Shit. What's happened? My heart drops, and I'm holding my breath.

"They've just taken her to theatre. They said they need to go in now and remove the tumor. Yesterday's scan showed it had grown slightly and they are concerned it will just keep growing now, even with the chemo. They said it's now or never. Oh, Theon. I'm so scared for my baby. Will she be all right?" She throws herself into my arms, crying into my chest and gripping tightly onto my t-shirt. I wrap my arms around her to comfort her.

"Shhh, baby, I'm sure they know what they're doing. Hey, look at me." She lifts her head slightly and looks me in the eyes.

"You know you keep telling me how strong she has been throughout all the chemo?" She nods at me

"Well, we have to believe she will stay strong and she will pull through this, Alana. We have to believe. If we don't, we lose all hope, and without hope, we have nothing. I can't tell you she will be all right, just like I can't tell you Evelina will be all right, but I have hope and belief and love, and that's all I can count on right now. You have to do the same and no matter what, I'm here for you, okay, baby?" She clings to me and cries. I let her because she needs this. I'm just sorry I can't stay with her longer to comfort her while Caroline is in theatre. The waiting is the worst bit. I pull Alana up and sit where she was, then let her sit on my lap. She curls into me and cries silently. I rub her back gently to comfort her, and I kiss the top of her head letting her know I'm here for her. Forty minutes pass, I need to go so I can go with Evelina to chemo.

"Hey, baby, I hate to do this, but I have to leave. Evelina is going for her chemo in twenty minutes, and I'm going with her. I promise I will be right back as soon as Sonia gets here after the chemo. Is that okay?"

"Oh god, Theon. I'm so sorry. I don't want to keep you from Evelina. You must go. Never mind me. I will be fine. I will wait here until Dr. Cassidy comes to give me an update." She sits up and starts to scramble from my lap. I hold her tight for a minute, not wanting to let her go. It's comforting to me as much as it is to her. She sighs into my chest, realizing I'm not pushing her from me. A few minutes pass, and she gets off me, and I stand. She sits back on the chair, and I lean down and kiss the top of her head.

"I'll be back as soon as I can. You stay strong until I get back, okay?" I say, tilting her chin up, so she looks at me. She nods and just mouths 'thank you' to me. She grabs my hand and kisses my palm before letting it go.

They come for Evelina at 10 a.m. We head to a part of the hospital I haven't been to before, — the cancer treatment center. We are allocated an oncology nurse, Daisy, who will administer the chemo through an IV. Daisy gets Evelina all set up and dispenses the chemo through a port they inserted into her arm when she was in theatre. This will take about twenty minutes and then she can go back to ICU. I sit, holding Evelina's hand throughout the process and talk to her.

I'm a bit worried about Alana and want to make sure she's okay. When Sonia arrives, I explain what they did and about the port in Evelina's arm.

"Oh, the poor love."

"Do you mind if I go for a little while, Sonia? They took Caroline into theatre earlier, and I hate that Alana is on her own?"

"No of course not, Theon. I'm more than happy to stay here with my angel. Arnold is picking Evander up from school and bringing him in, so don't worry."

"Give me a ring if you need me. I shouldn't be too long." I lean over and kiss Evelina's forehead and then kiss Sonia on the top of her head.

"Thank you, Sonia. For everything." She squeezes my hand and nods.

At Caroline's door, which is fully open this time, I see Alana sitting where I left her. Her head is back, and her eyes are closed. I don't want to disturb her if she's sleeping.

"It's okay, Theon. I'm not asleep." I walk in and crouch down in front of her, grabbing her hand.

"How did you know I was there?" She looks at me and gives me a very slight smile.

"I always know when you're near. I feel you. Is that weird?"

I laugh a little. "Actually, no. I feel you when you enter the room, even when it's busy like the restaurant. I just know you're there. I wondered if it was weird, as well." I frown slightly at that.

"Any news on Caroline yet?"

"No, nothing. It's the not knowing that kills you. The waiting is like a lifetime. There is no concept of time. The clock never seems to move no matter how often you look at it. It feels like an hour has passed, but you look and its only been ten minutes.

I hate the feeling.

I hate the not knowing.

I hate being so useless.

I hate that I can't help her or fix her. But,

I know you understand exactly how I'm feeling."

I do, only I wished I didn't.

"I hate all those things as well.

I wish I didn't understand your feelings.

I wish that none of this ever happened.

I wish that Evelina would wake up and get better.

I wish for Caroline to get through her surgery and recover.

I wish we had met under better circumstances." I pull her head down toward me, and I kiss her forehead. She smiles at me when I look at her.

"Have you been okay in here waiting? Have you managed to get out to get a coffee or for a bathroom break?"

"No, neither."

"How about you go for a quick bathroom break, and I will wait here, then when you get back, I will go and get us coffee. I could really do with one myself," I say running my hand through my messed-up hair. It's grown a lot since we've been in here. I think I need to tie it back. Alana looks at me with a funny look.

"What? My hair's grown. I need to tie it back into a man bun." I laugh.

Alana goes for her bathroom break, and when she comes back, I go and get us coffee. When I return and I enter the room Dr. Cassidy follows me in not a minute later.

"Oh, hello, Mr. Tourney, are you in the wrong room?" She smiles at me, but it makes me feel bad. I hand Alana the coffee and head for the door without saying a word. Is she implying I shouldn't be away from Evelina?

"Theon, wait, where are you going?"

"Back to Evelina. I'll leave you to talk to the doctor." I say not looking at Dr. Cassidy.

"No, please, can you stay with me? I need you." The plea on her face and in her eyes has me heading back to her and crouching down in front of her. I look at Dr. Cassidy.

"Is it okay with you, if I stay?"

"Of course. It's up to Mrs. Tudrow." I look at Alana and nod I will stay.

"Ok, Caroline is out of theatre and in recovery. She's just coming round from the anesthetic. I spoke to the surgeon, and he said although the tumor had shrunk there were three sections of the liver infected by the tumor. As I explained to you, with pretext three that means three sections, or two separate sections not connected that are affected. One part of the liver was badly damaged, and he thinks she will need a liver transplant. Now, before you panic, he says he doesn't think it's urgent. She can survive with what she has, but it will need doing within the next six to twelve months."

"Oh, god, so what happens now?" I squeeze Alana's hand and rub my thumb over the back of it to let her know she's not alone. Dr. Cassidy continues.

"We are putting her on the liver transplant list, and we wait for a suitable liver to become available. If one were to become available sooner rather than later, we would do the transplant straight away rather than wait. He has done more biopsies to check it hasn't spread. At this stage, he can't be certain this isn't the case."

"Oh, god no, please, no." She's pleading to Dr. Cassidy. I feel so helpless, crouched here in front of her. I pull her to me and let her cry into my chest. I look at the doctor, just asking for a moment, then I stand, pulling Alana up with me, before sitting and putting her on my lap like she was earlier. I nod to Dr. Cassidy to tell her to continue.

"We should know the results later on today or tomorrow. There are three ways that cancer could have spread: through the tissue, the lymph system or the blood, so he wants to make sure. They are going to put her in ICU maybe just for a night or two to monitor her. When you're ready, I can take you up there to the room you can wait in until she comes out of recovery.

"Oh, yes, please, Doctor."

"I'll walk up with you. Evelina's in ICU," I say, and we all get up.

I leave Alana in Caroline's room in ICU, so she can wait for Caroline, and I head back to Evelina. I feel guilty for being away for so long, but I just couldn't leave Alana on her own. I know how bad I was when waiting for Evelina to get out of theatre. Plus, I know Sonia would phone me if there were any change.

I walk into Evelina's room, and Sonia is holding her hand with the TV on. I watch them for a few minutes wishing she would wake up, and I could get her home. I'm going out of my mind with the worry that she's never going to wake or if she does she will have some brain damage.

"Hey, Sonia, thanks for sitting with her. Sorry I was longer than I thought."

"It's fine, Theon. How is Alana? Any news on Caroline?"

"She's just come out of theatre and is in recovery. Then they are putting her just over the hallway for the night to monitor her. They said the surgery went well, but they are not sure if it's spread or not, so have done more biopsies. Alana is having a hard time, and she doesn't have anyone. Her sister has the twins, and they come to visit, but she has to stay strong for them all."

"Oh, the poor thing. I'm glad you're there to help her, Theon. You're a good man. It's good you can both relate." I just nod and move nearer to kiss first Evelina on the forehead and then Sonia.

"Do you need anything, Sonia?"

"No, thank you, sweetie. I have my flask of coffee. That's all I need. Arnold will be here soon with Evander." I sit on the chair on the other side of Evelina, holding her hand, and I watch the TV without seeing what's actually on it. I can't concentrate on anything. It's a good job they don't need me at the office. I would be a waste of space. I rest my head back and close my eyes.

"Evelyn, you must be there, baby, watching this play out. Please, is there anything you can do for our little angel? I don't know how long I can keep up this façade. I just want to let loose and destroy things — get all my frustrations out. I'm hurting here, baby. If anything happens to our little angel, I swear, I will not survive. I know I said that when I lost you, and I very nearly didn't survive, but I can't do it again. I'm begging you. I love you, baby." That's the daily conversation I have in my head with Evelyn. I don't know if she's there, but it helps me to speak to her. What it also does is remind me of the darkest time of my life.

Chapter 26

10 Years Earlier

ONCE IN THE GUESTHOUSE, I just stand there. Not moving, my bag still in my hand. What now? What the fuck am I supposed to do now? I've been with Evelyn almost every day for the last eight years. What do I do without her in my life by my side? I can't bring up two kids who killed her. I can't even go to see them. How can Sonia and Arnold say it wasn't their fault? Who's fucking fault was it? I drop the bag and collapse to my knees. I sit back on my haunches with my hands resting on my thighs, and I cry. I cry hard. The tears and snot are just running off my face, and I don't give a shit.

My life is over.

Finished.

Ended with the last breath she took.

Why did Arnold pull me from the pool? Then I remember. I remember Evelyn in the pool. I was trying to reach her, and she floated to the surface making me float up too. She was saving me. She didn't want me to drown or die. I'm crazy — simple as — out of my mind. I fall to the side and curl up into a ball, wrapping my arms around my knees. I stay there, just crying.

I must have fallen asleep. It's dark out when I wake. Why did I wake? Then I hear a tap. It must have been the tapping that woke me. I get up. I'm freezing. I wipe my face on my t-shirt and open the door. Arnold is standing there.

"How are you, son? I didn't see any lights on, and wasn't sure if you'd gone out or not? Sonia has made some dinner, will you join us?"

I look at him like he's got four heads. He's talking about dinner when all I can think about is the fact that I've lost Evelyn: my wife, his daughter.

"Why? Why would I want to come and have dinner, Arnold? You think I can come in the house to sit and have dinner as though I haven't just lost my wife, your daughter? As if we can just play happy families when she isn't here?"

He holds his hand up before I can go any further. He can see the anger starting to build. I'm struggling to control it as it's building inside of me.

"Theon, son. We're hurting too. Believe me, we lost our only daughter today and how Sonia has even managed to cook anything is beyond me. But she's trying to act and be normal. I know for a fact, the minute she stops busying herself she is going to crack. It's like watching a tsunami heading for land. It keeps rolling in, and it could hit any minute now. I've got to be there to catch her when she falls, and I'm here for you too, son. I haven't told Sonia what happened in the pool, and I would prefer we kept it to ourselves right now. She's hanging on by a thread son. I think we all are." I know he's right.

"You are not alone in your grief. If you need to fall, I will catch you. I understand you don't want to sit and have dinner. In all honesty, it's the last thing I want to do. But if I can prolong that tsunami for a little while longer, then I will do. I will go and get you some food. You haven't eaten all day, and you need something. I suspect your lungs are still burning a little after what happened earlier, so I think some soup would help. Okay, son?"

I just nod, hang my head, then shut the door. Waiting where I am,

I don't move as I listen to the slow thud of Arnold's footsteps heading back to the house. I could see the turmoil in his face. He's trying to hold it together, for Sonia and probably for me. What a shitstorm this is. I hear his footsteps coming back, and I still haven't moved. I open the door just as he approaches. He hands me a tray with a bowl of soup and some bread.

"Thank you, Arnold, for everything. But tell me, who's going to catch you when you fall? If you're there to catch Sonia and me, then who the fuck is there to catch you?" I take the tray from him, step back, kick the door shut, turn and walk to the small kitchen area and put the tray down on the side. There's no way I can eat this.

I'm on the bed, still dressed. I look at the clock. It's 10.30 p.m. I didn't touch the soup. I just crawled onto the bed and curled into a ball, rocking. I must have gone to sleep, and I do feel a bit hungry now. I'm also thirsty. I get up with a banging headache. I put the soup into the microwave to heat up, and I nibble on the bread while I wait. There's a small fridge in here, and when I open it, I see bottles of water, but also some cans of Budweiser. That will do! I'm not a big beer drinker. I prefer wine. Evelyn loved wine, and it was what we always drank when we went out.

I look in the other cupboards, and I find bottles of spirits, all lined up just waiting for me: Jack Daniels, Jim Beam, Vodka, Gin, Hennessey Whiskey, Fireball, just a whole lot of bottles. Hmm, maybe I could have a drink or two. I fancy trying this fireball. I grab a tall glass and fill it with the bright orange liquid. I take a sip. It's not too bad, so I take some more sips. My soup is ready, and I eat it with the stale bread. When I've finished, I put the dishes in the sink, then sit on the bed with my glass of fireball. I finish it, then fill my glass up again. I decide to go and sit by the pool. I'm still in the same clothes. It's freezing out, but the Fireball is making me warmer. Still, I grab a towel to wrap around me and sit on a lounger. It's so quiet out here. I start to drift off to sleep again. I think it's the drink. I feel all warm and fuzzy. I'm lightheaded. I feel kind of relaxed, strange but peaceful.

I wake with a start; the sun is shining in my eyes. I can't open them much, it hurts — it's too bright. My head is banging I feel like I've been in a boxing ring. Arnold is standing over me.

"Theon, you okay? Did you sleep out here all night, son?"

"Eh, guess I did, yeah. I managed to sleep, as well."

"Must have been something to do with this?" he says, holding up the empty Fireball bottle. Shit, did I drink it all? No wonder my head is killing me.

"Maybe. Did I drink the bottle?"

"Looks like it, apart from what was left in the glass that you dropped." I look down and see the glass on its side. Luckily, it's not broken. I lean to pick it up.

"Shit, that hurts," I say grabbing my head. Arnold disappears back to the house. I manage to turn on the lounger and just sit there with my elbows on my knees holding my head up. I think if I let go, it will fall off. I hear Arnold come back out of the house. I don't look up. He stands in front of me.

"Here, son, take these." I manage to look up a little and see he is holding out a glass of water and some painkillers. I take them from him, muttering, 'thanks,' and wash the tablets down with the full glass of water. So thirsty. I hear him chuckle to himself.

"It's not funny. I feel like shit," I say to him.

"Sonia is making some bacon and eggs. Do you think you could manage some and an orange juice?" I'm starving, so I nod.

"Do you want to come into the house, or would you prefer I bring it out to you?"

"I'll come in. I'm gonna get a quick shower first though."

"Ok, see you in a few minutes." He walks back to the house, taking the glass with him as I head to the shower.

Ten minutes later, I'm entering the main house. I stop at the door. Sonia is just finishing plating the food. She turns to me, and I can see the strain on her face. One look is all it takes, and we both cry. Me, silently with the tears falling down my cheeks. Her, sobbing. She walks over to me and grabs me. We cling to each other, both feeling the devastation. She has her head in my chest, and I have my arms wrapped around her, leaning my chin on her head. We stand like that for what feels like ages. I hear Arnold come into the kitchen, and I look at him. He freezes.

"Tsunami," is all he says, and I nod. Sonia turns slightly at the sound of his voice, and she runs over to him. She is full on heaving now, into his chest. He is holding her tightly and rubbing her back. He too is now crying. I walk over to them both, and all three of us stand there, hugging and crying, feeling the loss of Evelyn together. I know I'm not alone in this, and I'm grateful to have them. It doesn't lessen the pain any though. My heart has been ripped out. I don't think it will ever mend after this.

We pull apart, wiping our eyes, and Arnold grabs some tissues for us.

"Well I think that was the tidal wave and the tsunami is still to come." He says to me patting my shoulder as he passes me.

"What are you talking about tsunamis for Arnold?" Sonia asks him, and I just look at them both. Sonia brings the filled plates over to the table, putting them down next to the jug of orange juice. I sit and start to eat. I don't wait. I brace myself because I know Sonia is going to talk about the babies, which is one of the reasons I didn't want to come in last night. She brings over coffee and cups then sits down. We all eat in silence until …

"Theon, the babies need to come home." I drop my fork with a clang as it hits the plate, and I stare at her. I never gave any thought to them coming out of hospital.

"Theon, what's wrong?"

What's wrong? Is she for real? I'm still staring at her, trying to fathom out if she has any idea they killed Evelyn. I shake my head at the bewildered look on her face.

"Are you for real?" I ask her. She looks hurt and confused.

"What do you mean?"

"Home? Where and when?" I glare at her as I ask. They are not coming to me, that's for fucking sure. No way. She recoils at the venom in my voice.

"Theon," Arnold warns.

"Well, they need to leave hospital today. The doctors say they are both fit and healthy."

I snort, stopping her from carrying on. Arnold grabs her hand and squeezes, I think possibly as a warning not to push me, but she carries on.

"They are fit and healthy and ready to come home. You can take them home to your house. You have the nursery set up there for them."

"NO!" I shout at her, banging my hand on the table and making her and Arnold jump.

"Enough, Theon!" he growls at me and scowls.

"No, fucking way. They are not going to my house," I say through gritted teeth.

"Then we'll get some cots delivered here today, and they'll stay here with us all."

I stand up, quickly pushing my chair back, which then falls onto the tiled floor with a bang, making Sonia jump again.

"You can fucking have them," I shout. "I'm outta here."

I leave them and head for the guesthouse. It's not even 10 a.m., but I don't give a shit as I head straight for the cupboard and pull the first bottle I get my hands on. I pour a big glass of amber liquid, not caring what it is. I down the lot. It burns my throat, and I start to cough. I pour another glass.

I hear the door open. I don't turn around. I know it's Arnold coming to say his piece.

"Come on, get it over with. Give me the sermon," I say.

He sighs.

I know, if I turn around, I will see disappointment written all over his face. I don't need them judging me.

"Look, son. I know this is hard for you. It is for us all, But the babies need to be home; preferably with their daddy. We will help in any way we can, but Theon, you have got two little cherubs there that need you, son. They have lost one parent and —"

"NO!" I shout, swinging around with the glass in my hand. I down half of it. I'm starting to get a buzz. This is what I need to numb my feelings. This makes me forget the hurt. I take another swig, nearly finishing this glass.

"That's not going to help you, son." He nods to the glass in my hand.

"Yeah, actually it is," I say finishing the rest and turning to refill the glass.

"Theon, we'll bring the babies back here. Sonia is getting everything we need, and we will set them up in one of the rooms upstairs. Do you mind if I go to your house and bring back some things you've already bought?"

I shrug my shoulders.

"Knock yourself out. Do what you need to do." I start to head to the bathroom.

"Wait, Theon. Will you come with us to bring them home?"

"NO!" I shout. "I'm going out."

I storm off to the bathroom, hoping he gets the message and leaves. I hate being mean to Sonia and Arnold, but there is no way I can see the babies.

About an hour later, I'm at Santa Monica Pier. I have no idea what I'm doing here. We used to love coming here when we had some free time. We would walk on the pier, holding hands, swinging our arms like teenagers in love. So many memories — why am I torturing myself? We would walk under the pier. I remember one time we were chasing each other around the pier stilts when I caught her and wrestled her to the ground. We were in the water, but luckily it wasn't too deep. We got into some heavy petting — it's a good job Evelyn was the sensible one, or we may have been arrested for indecent exposure and lewd acts in a public place.

It's going to be like this all the time. No matter where I go in LA, there are going to be so many reminders of Evelyn. We did everything together. Until Evelyn, I had never been anywhere. Grandma couldn't afford it, so every experience I had outside of Mission Hills was with Evelyn. How am I going to get through this? Memories everywhere are going to kill me.

I call at a drug store and buy a bottle of Fireball. I sit under the pier alone, watching people mill around. Just to my right, I can see how crowded the beach is with kids playing with kites or digging holes in the sand. I see one family and the kids have buried a man in the sand — he's probably their dad. The little girl is giggling hard because her daddy can't get up and her brother, who looks older than her, just poured a bucket of water over his head. There is a woman lying on a towel next to them, she's watching them all adoringly. The little girl runs to her mom and sits on her legs. The mom sits up and cuddles her, both of them laughing together while the dad makes funny spluttering noises. It makes me sad watching them. This family all having so much fun at the beach, knowing it's something I will never have.

What the fuck is my life going to be like now? I unscrew the lid off my bottle, keeping it in

the brown paper bag it came in so no one can see what it is. I take a big gulp and almost choke at the burn in my throat. My coughing catches the attention of some young teenagers that are milling around. They move farther away from me. What must I look like?

Sometime later, I hear someone or something near me. I must have fallen asleep after finishing the bottle. It's a dog sniffing around my head.

"Heyyy boyyy, wotcha doing," I'm slurring my words. I feel good though. Happy almost. Who would have thought? It looks like it's getting dark. Not the best place to be in the dark. I must have been here for hours. I start to move, and the dog runs away over to his owner. Looking around, the beach is almost empty now.

I think I should head back if I can, see if I can get a cab. I try to get up, then fall over. Oh shit, I'm drunk. Maybe if I can get to the road, I can find a bar or restaurant, some food would be good. I manage to get up again and stay up this time but on very wobbly legs. I make my way towards the beach, stumbling a few times, trying to dodge the holes in the sand under the pier and the rocks lying around. I find my way up onto the street. I'm stumbling so much that if I saw someone looking like this, I would steer clear of them and cross over. I head to a restaurant that I spot over the road, and I get beeped at by a car that almost runs into me or did I run into it? I don't know. I just salute the driver, tapping the hood of the car. I walk into the restaurant, but the guy at the front stops me going in.

"I'm sorry, sir, do you have a reservation?"

"No, I'm hungry, though. I can pay," I tell him, pulling out my wallet from my jeans pocket. He looks at me wearily. Maybe he thinks I stole the wallet. I pull out my driver's license, so he can see it's mine. He takes the card from me. He moves away and taps on his computer.

"Hey, wacha doing with my carrdd?" I slur.

"Mr. Tourney. Yes, I thought it was you, sir."

"Huh, do you know who … do you know me?" I ask him.

"You have been in a few times with your lovely wife. How is she, sir? Will she be joining you tonight?" Fuck.

"No, no, not ever. She's dead." I see the shock on his face.

"I need a drink."

"Sir, I am so sorry, please accept my condolences. If you don't mind, may I take you to a room I have in the back to give you some privacy? I think it would be a good idea to have plenty of water with a good hearty steak. I can have that brought to you."

What's he saying?

"Don't you want me in your fanshy restaurant? Am I not good enough?"

"Sir, of course you are. It's just, well, you are a bit worse for wear if you don't mind me saying, and I would like to help you. Is there anyone I could call for you? Maybe have someone come and take you home? It's not safe being out on the streets after dark around here, sir, that is all." I nod at him, and he helps me through to the back to what looks like an employee room. He gets me some water and then sits at the table with me.

"Sir, Mr. Tourney. May I ask when Mrs. Tourney passed?" I glare at him. When was it? It feels like it was a long time ago. I know it wasn't. I think back, and I pinch the bridge of my nose. When was it? This morning, I had breakfast with Sonia and Arnold. Shit, it was yesterday.

"Yesterday," I say. My mind is a bit foggy. Yesterday! Was that all it was? It's only been a day. My life is shit, and it's only been a day.

"Oh no, I am so terribly sorry, Mr. Tourney. Can I get you something to eat and maybe call someone to come and get you?"

"I'm starving, yes, please. I haven't eaten since this morning. I have my phone here." I fumble in my pocket for my phone. I drop it as I pull it out. He picks it up for me. He hands it back looking at my screen. It's a picture of Evelyn and me. I can feel the tears running down my face. He stands and pats me on the shoulder.

"Let me get you something to eat. Then we can call someone to come and pick you up."

"Thank you," is all I can say.

I'm on my way home, to my house. I think I would rather stay there even with Evelyn all around me than go back to Sonia and Arnold's with the babies screaming. The same babies that killed my wife. No, I can't do it. I called a taxi from the restaurant. I tried to pay Stuart, the maître d, but he refused. I hugged him when I was leaving, thanking him for his generous hospitality, and for not throwing my drunken, dirty ass out on the street.

I get home to a dark, empty house. I look for what drink we have in. Neither of us really drank much, but we have plenty of wine. That will do. I take a couple of bottles upstairs with me. I can't bring myself to stay in our room, not yet. It's still all a mess from yesterday, so I go to one of the spare rooms with my bottles. I have a quick shower, put on my PJ bottoms, and lay on top of the bed.

I torture myself by looking at pictures of us from over the years. I have tears running down my face yet again. I'm going through the wine pretty quickly. I'm on my second bottle already. I really like the fuzzy feeling I'm getting. The numbness it brings is a relaxant. I fall asleep again, thinking of Evelyn. Putting what has happened, way back in my head for another day.

Chapter 27

Evelina has been in a coma for twelve days now. She's had two doses of chemo. Dr. Cassidy said they will administer two treatments a week while she's in a coma as long as her body can take it. That means she only has four shots left. I'm counting them down.

I haven't left the hospital in two weeks — since we brought her in for her biopsy. I want to go out this afternoon, for my own sanity as much as anything. I want to go to the toy store and get some things for Evelina. She has her beloved Stitch and her momma's sea turtle next to her pillow, and I put them under her arms at night when we sleep, but I want to get her something nice and new. She will never replace the turtle, that belonged to her momma. It's the one I gave her when I proposed, when Evelina was 2 she found it and it now sleeps with her every night. She cherishes that turtle, it's the only piece of her momma she has. Sonia is here today, and Arnold is bringing Evander in after school.

"Sonia, are you okay if I go out for a little while?" She looks at me startled.

"You mean out, as in leave the hospital, out?" I laugh a little

"Yes, I mean leave the hospital out, if I can remember my way out. I feel like I've been here for years." I laugh again and run my hand through my long hair. Which reminds me to pull out my band that Alana dropped in yesterday before they moved Caroline out of ICU and back down to her room.

I hadn't seen her much with us both being at our daughters' bedsides and only leaving for bathroom breaks, so I haven't had a chance to make sure she is coping okay or as okay as can be under the circumstances and there was a small knock at the door as I was reading to Evelina.

"Come in," I shout.

"Oh, hey, Theon, I hope you don't mind me popping in. Caroline wanted me to give you this band that she had. She saw you walk past her room and commented on how long your hair had gotten. I had to laugh, with us having that conversation the other day." She looks at Evelina. "How's she doing?"

"She's doing great. My little angel is just sleeping a lot." I laugh and then nod to the door to indicate we move out of the room.

"Won't be a minute, poppet, hold on for me." I kiss her forehead and head out of the room, keeping the door ajar slightly.

"Sorry, I don't like saying anything in front of her. I believe she can hear everything. She's just the same. Nothing has changed. How's Caroline doing?"

She looks down, and I see the anguish on her face.

"She seems fine in herself. She's awake and alert, and she is a lot better now than she was before the operation. I worry it's a case of the calm before the storm. I'm just waiting for something bad to happen, you know?" I know what she means.

"Oh, Alana, stay positive. I'm sure she will recover from her operation, and they will get a liver for her. Did you get the results from the biopsies they took during surgery?"

"They were inconclusive. They want to do more tests on her. The surgeon isn't convinced the cancer hasn't spread. It's another waiting game. They say it's possible a cell from the infected liver has strayed but can't be sure about it at this time and want to administer another course of chemo. I don't know what to think anymore, Theon. I'm just trying to get through one day at a time. Bailee and Bryan are coming later, and that always cheers Caroline up. It also means I must put on a brave face. They know about the liver transplant, but they don't know about the biopsies. I'll tell them if anything comes from it." I pull her into me and hug her to my chest. She sighs into me and wraps her arms around my waist. This feels so good, so comforting. Something I've missed for so long now.

"Thank you. This is just what I need. You always seem to know what I need." She looks up at me. God, I can't get over how beautiful she is. How I didn't see it straight away is beyond me, but then I didn't really look. The more time I spend with her, the more I'm falling for her. This is going to be hard. I have never thought of anyone in this way since Evelyn. What are the chances of falling for someone under such stressful circumstances? Is it the circumstances that are making me feel this way?

"As do you. I'm here for you, Alana." I kiss the top of her head. I love how she feels in my arms. I also feel guilty for feeling like this. Just then, Sonia walks around the corner. Our eyes meet, and I step away from Alana quickly. I feel like a kid who has just been caught kissing his girlfriend. I'm sure I blush. Sonia walks past us and into Evelina's room, smiling and saying hi to Alana. She is really cool about it when I walked back into the room, just asking how Caroline and Alana were doing.

I'm on my way to the toy store. I'm going to get Evander something as well, but that will be in the Apple store. He's been after an iMac laptop for a while now, and I think he deserves something for going through all this. I don't think I spoil them that much and they have to do chores at home for pocket money. I'm a firm believer in having them be able to fend for themselves. I have a housekeeper, and to be honest, I couldn't do without Mavis, and she adores the Evs, but they still have to do dishes and tidy their rooms. I also have Mavis teaching them how to cook simple stuff.

I pick up some new DVD's, and I go to the Monster High aisle and grab some bits there. I have no idea if what I have got is what she wants, but I'm sure she hasn't got them already. I get a Monster High pillow for her bed at the hospital, which I know she will love. Then, in the soft toy aisle, I get her a Sully from Monsters Inc. and a Lotso bear from Toy Story. I know she loves both of these characters. I then pick up a big Eeyore and a big Pooh Bear for Caroline. I want to put a smile on her face. She's younger than Evelina, so I'm sure she will love them. I seem to remember some Eeyore slippers in her room, so she must like him.

I head to the Apple store and get the iMac for Evander. He's getting to be a right whizz with computers. He loves spending time with me at the office when they are on school holidays. He really gets into the graphics side of creating games, which makes me so happy. He's definitely going to take after his mum and me. I have no idea where Evelina is heading. She lives in the clouds most of the time. I need to check in with Sonia. It's killing me being away for so long.

"Hey, how's she doing? Any change?"

"Hi, Theon. No, nothing. You know I would phone you if there were. Hey, don't worry. Have a bit of 'you' time. You need it. Stay out a bit longer and try not to worry. Go and treat yourself. Get a haircut. You've been saying for days that your hair is too long."

"Ok, but call me if anything changes. I hate being away. I feel I should be there."

"I know, but please don't worry. I don't think anything is going to happen today. See you soon." And she hangs up on me before I can say anymore.

I head to a barbershop, not to cut my hair because I kind of like it long, but a nice shave with a hot towel on my face is just what I need. I do just that. I get a tidy up of my hair, but he doesn't cut much length off it. He even gives me an Alice band to wear.

"Are you shitting me right now?" I ask him as he hands me the band. "My daughter wears these. She will say I look really silly with an Alice band in my hair. Please don't give me a purple sparkly one or she will pinch it off me," I say laughing at him.

"These are all the rage with the young men who have long hair. Here, let me show you some pictures. They look really good." He shows me pictures on his phone, and he's right, they do look good. He gives me a black one. It keeps my hair from my face, which is a good thing. I kind of like it.

I want to buy a gift for Alana. I have no idea what to get her. I know she's a gamer and she likes flowers. I don't want to get her any jewelry because I think that's a bit forward and personal. I'm passing a shop when I spot something in the window that I think she will love, just a little something to cheer her up and put a smile on her beautiful face, even if it's just for a minute. Then, I go into the florist that is near my parked car, and I get a lovely big floral display for Sonia, again to put a smile on her face.

Chapter 28

10 Years Earlier

I WAKE UP THE NEXT DAY IN THE SPARE bedroom. I have to think why I'm in here, lying on the bed with photos next to me and two bottles of wine on the bedside table. Then it hits me like a wrecking ball.

Evelyn.

Fuck.

She's gone, and I cry with the reality hitting me. No wonder I have a constant headache with all the crying. I need to get in touch with the hospital and see what has happened with her. I have no fucking idea where she is or even where to go from here, but burying my head in the sand or in a bottle isn't helping me. Well actually yes it is, it makes me forget for a few hours but then when that fucking wrecking ball or tsunami as Arnold says hits, then it's like losing her for the first time all over again.

I grab my phone from my bedside, and I see I have five missed calls from Arnold and Sonia and that it's also 11 a.m. I presume they got the babies yesterday and wanted me to help them. I can't, not yet. I don't know if I ever will. Can I really do this to them? Was it their fault? Maybe if I speak to the doctor, she can shed some light on why this happened, and I can ask if it was the babies that killed her. Dr. Zelda should be able to tell me. Am I ready to find out and speak about losing Evelyn? The simple answer is no, but I don't think I ever will be, and I know I've got to do it. I can't leave everything to Sonia and Arnold. She was their daughter, and I know they're hurting as much as I am.

I get up and go to the bathroom before heading downstairs. I need a coffee before I make any phone calls. Maybe some wine even. No, I can't do that. Not now. I need to be strong.

I shower, which I need badly — I still have sand in my hair and stink of the ocean. It all comes back to me. Santa Monica — and what a sight I must have looked to that poor guy in the restaurant. I must thank him.

I head into the babies' room to see if Arnold has been and taken what he needs. It feels strange coming into the room. It should make me feel ecstatic, knowing we have two little mini-me's as we referred to them, but as it is, I don't feel anything as I stand here. Numb.

I'd loved this room, the way we had both decorated it ready for the twins to arrive. Now, not so much.

It certainly looks like stuff has been taken and moved around. The bath basins and romper baskets are gone, along with all the baby lotions, blankets, some baby toys, the bottles, and sterilizing units. I look where the sterilizing unit once stood, and there, on the side, is the breast milk pump. It breaks me, knowing there will be no breast milk for them, to help them grow. I collapse to the floor on my knees, and I cry, cry for my Evelyn, that she is gone and will never experience being a mother, and for me because I've lost her. I knew it was too soon to come into this room. I crawl out on my hands and knees making sure I shut the door closed with a bang. I don't want to go in there again.

Once I pull myself together, I head downstairs for some coffee before starting on my phone calls.

I speak to Arnold, who wants to make sure I'm okay as I haven't been back to the house. I tell him I need space, and that I came home last night. I don't once ask him how the babies are, and he never mentions them. The conversation goes okay until he puts Sonia on the phone to me. She's just finished feeding baby two, and baby one is crying.

"Theon, sweetie, are you going to come back?"

"No," is all I say.

She sighs down the phone. "They need their daddy, Theon. I know it's hard for you right now, but they need you. You need to come and see them, and they need proper names."

"They don't need me, and I don't need them. Call them what you want. Thing One and Thing Two would be appropriate."

"Theon Tourney, don't you dare say that about your babies. About Evelyn's babies. I will not have it. You and Evelyn had names ready, so you need to give your babies some names. Either use what you and Evelyn picked, or you come and see them and name them yourself. We have to get them registered." I don't like doing it, but I hang up on her. I didn't want to hear any of this shit. I grab a bottle of wine and pour myself a generous glass.

I didn't want to do this, but I need it.

My next phone call is to Dr. Zelda.

"Mr. Tourney, I am deeply sorry for your loss. I know you must have some questions for me?"

"Yes, I do. Can I come in to see you?"

"Yes, can you get here in the hour?"

"Yes, I will be there." I hang up. I take another gulp of wine but am going to drive so don't have any more. I get to Dr. Zelda's office in forty minutes, not caring if I get pulled over for speeding. I walk into the office and stand at the reception desk until Dr. Zelda comes out. I'm in no mood for shit off anyone. We walk into her office, and I don't even sit down.

"What happened? Why did she die? She had babies for fuck's sake. Hundreds and thousands of women have babies and don't die, so why the fuck did she die, doc?" I have to say, she doesn't look shocked at my outburst. She was obviously expecting it.

"Please have a seat, Mr. Tourney." I sit in front of her desk. My bouncing leg showing my agitation.

"Mr. Tourney, please accept my deepest condolences. I know you don't think this should happen in this day and age, but unfortunately, death in childbirth is a lot more common than you realize. Pre-Eclampsia is a common complication during pregnancy. We closely monitored Mrs. Tourney due to her high blood pressure, but, unfortunately, Mrs. Tourney developed eclampsia going into labor at home, which is why she was passing out and why she was non-responsive in theatre. She had gone into a coma, Mr. Tourney. This is why they had to do the C-section to get your babies out before something happened to them." She stops as if judging my reaction before carrying on.

"Mr. Tourney, there was no way of saving Mrs. Tourney. It all happened too fast."

"Did the babies kill her?"

"If you're asking me if Mrs. Tourney had not got pregnant then would she be alive today, then the answer is yes. But it wasn't the babies that killed her, Mr. Tourney. It was childbirth that took her away from you. It was being pregnant that killed her. It just seemed pregnancy wasn't for Mrs. Tourney. The babies did not kill your wife, Mr. Tourney."

I sigh with relief. They didn't kill her. I lean forward, rubbing my hands over my face and letting out a deep breath. Then it hits me hard. I get up stumbling to the door.

"It's me. I killed her. Fucking hell. I killed my wife by getting her pregnant. It's all my fault she isn't here — not the babies. It's me. I did it. I murdered my wife."

I grab for the door, falling to the floor in front of it before getting it open, my legs just turning to jelly. Dr. Zelda is trying to get me up, but I'm too big for her, and I shrug her off me. She's talking to me, but I have no idea what she's saying. I can hear her saying things like, no you didn't murder her, not your fault, no-one could know, it could happen at any pregnancy, but , I can't take it in. I don't look at her. I manage to get up and somehow walk out of the office.

I find myself in a bar. I have no idea how, and I don't care. I'm downing Fireball by the glass until the bartender refuses to give me any more, telling me I've had enough. Who the fuck is he to tell me I've had enough? I stumble from the bar and find a liquor store. I buy a bottle of Fireball then just walk, if you can call it that, staggering all over the place. I see the entrance to a storm drain. I don't care who is in there — it will do. I sit, and I drink the fireball. That's the last I remember.

I wake up not knowing where I am. My phone is buzzing, and I fumble for it. It's Arnold. I ignore it. Then it hits me, Dr. Zelda's office, and finding out I killed Evelyn. It was me. All my fault. My phone buzzed again in my hand. It's Arnold. I can't speak to him. I can't tell them I killed Evelyn. It's 2.30 a.m., shit, how long was I passed out? I need more drink. I need to forget and numb my feelings.

The bottle at the side of me is empty. I try to get up but fall back down and bang my head on the wall I've been slumped against. That fucking hurt. I rub it and see I have blood on my hand. Good. I want to bleed. I want to hurt. I manage to get up to go and look for a liquor store. I find one and get two bottles of Fireball this time. I head back to the storm drain and sit back down, taking long gulps from one of the bottles. It helps. I need the burn. I need it to numb everything I feel. I need it to carry on breathing. I pass out again.

I wake with a start. Someone is touching me. I swat in front of me, but I can't open my eyes.

"Getch ov me," I slur, but they don't say anything, and I don't have the strength to fight anyone. In fact, I don't want to. Let them do what they want to me. I don't fucking care. I deserve everything I get. I hear footsteps running away. I reach for my bottle and put it to my lips. I tilt my head back, but there's nothing in the bottle. I manage to crack my eyes open to search for a bottle with something in it, but there is nothing. I fall to the side and pass out again.

Someone is shaking me. "Sir, sir can you hear me, sir?"

"Huh, leave me alone."

"Sir, can you sit up for me?"

"No, leave me."

"I can't do that, sir. I need to get you to the hospital. I need you to sit up. Come on, let me help you?"

"No." I can hear talking, voices, then I feel myself being hauled up and put onto something. Then I'm moving. My head is throbbing. I feel sick.

"Shick," I manage then lean over and throw up.

"It's okay, sir, get it out." We've stopped. I open my eyes and see we are on a street, but I have no idea where we are. I retch again and again. Once I lay back down, we start moving. I feel like I'm being lifted. Then, there's movement again, and I pass out.

"Sir, Sir, can you hear me? Do you know where you are? Can you tell me your name?" The voice sounds miles away. I can feel someone touching my face, my eyes, but can't open them. Then there's a light. It's being shone in my eyes as someone is prying my lids open.

"Sir, you're in the hospital. You were found passed out. Do you know what happened?"

"No." That's all I can manage. Then nothing again.

I wake up wondering where I am. I'm in a room — a hospital room. Fuck what am I doing here? Oww my head hurts. My eyes hurt. The light is killing me. I reach up to my head, and there is a bandage wrapped around it. What happened? I don't remember anything. I don't know what day it is or what time it is. Just then a nurse comes in.

"Oh, you're awake. Welcome back. How are you feeling?"

"Honestly, like crap. How long have I been here?"

"Do you know where you are, sir?"

"Hospital, I take it, seems as though you're a nurse."

"Yes, you were brought in yesterday morning. You were unconscious, with a nasty gash on your head. Do you remember what happened?" I go to shake my head, but it kills.

"No."

"We couldn't find any ID or a phone. Looks like you were mugged?" Oh shit, no. My phone has so many pictures of us in it and recent ones too.

"Sir, can you remember your name?"

"Yes, Theon Tourney."

"Great Mr. Tourney, is there anyone I can phone. Your wife must be really worried about you." I freeze. My wife.

"Fuck!" I say out loud as it all comes flooding back. I put my hand over my eyes. The tears are starting to run down my cheeks. I can't stop them.

"Mr. Tourney. Are you okay, sir? Is it your head? I can get you some painkillers?" I can't speak. I start coughing from the lump in my throat, which in turn makes my head throb even more. God, kill me now. Why am I still here? Why.

"Mr. Tourney?" She puts her hand on my arm, and it makes me jump.

"I'm sorry, sir. But, are you okay?" I'm getting angry now, not at her, but myself. I remember seeing Dr. Zelda and the realization I killed Evelyn.

"No, I'm not fucking okay. I killed my fucking wife, so no there is no one to call. No one to worry about me, okay?" I say gritting my teeth. She steps back with a look of horror on her face.

"Yeah, that's right, I'm a monster."

She quickly exits the room.

Chapter 29

Present

I place Sully and Lotso on Evelina's bed along with the Monsters High pillow from my shopping trip, telling her that she has some new friends that want to meet her. Later on, I go to Caroline's room. The door is ajar, and I stand there for a minute until Alana turns and sees me. She sensed I was there. I knew she would.

"Hey, how are you feeling, Caroline?" She looks better than I've seen her before, which is a great sign. Alana smiles as soon as she sees me.

"I'm feeling okay thank you, Mr. Tourney."

"Do you mind if I come in?" Caroline shakes her head at the same time as Alana says, "Of course not, please have a seat." I walk in with the bag I have behind my back, and I sit down in the chair next to Alana.

"I have a little something for you," I say to Caroline. She looks at her mom and then to me. "For me?" I nod and open the bag. I pull out Eeyore and Pooh Bear. The look on her face is priceless

"Are they for me, Mr. Tourney?"

"They certainly are. I was passing the toy store when I heard a little voice. I stopped and leaned down to Pooh Bear, he said he and Eeyore needed looking after, and they thought Caroline would be the best person to do that. So here they are.

She laughs at me. "That's silly. They can't talk." I look shocked, then use Eeyore and Pooh Bear to mimic them talking to each other and put on a little show for Caroline, making her laugh. I pass her the teddies, and she squeezes them both to her.

"Oh, thank you so much, Mr. Tourney. I love them. I don't have Eeyore and he's my favorite." She's smiling so much, and when I look at Alana, she too is smiling, although her eyes are wet. I squeeze her hand to let her know it's all right. I don't stay too long. Caroline is worn out and falls asleep. As I get up to leave, Alana comes to the door with me. We stand in the hallway.

"Thank you so much, Theon. That was the sweetest thing to do. Making her smile and even giggle like that had my heart melting. It's been a while since she's been like that."

"It was my pleasure, honestly. Just to bring that little bit of relief to her was all I wanted. Here, I got this for you too." I pull out the little white cardboard box. She looks at me puzzled, takes the gift out and unwraps the tissue paper.

"Oh, Theon. That's beautiful, so intricate. How did you know I love turtles?" She's examining the little turtle trinket box I bought for her. It's a beautiful box made from different colored gems. I didn't know, but I love turtles. They are so majestic.

"Lucky guess. Do you like it?" I ask starting to feel silly that I bought her a gift.

"I love it. It's beautiful. Thank you." She rises on her tiptoes and kisses my cheek very gently but lingers. I turn into her, and our lips meet. Shit, what am I doing? She's shocked as am I about it, and we both step back.

"Oh, I'm so sorry, Alana. I shouldn't have done that. I don't know what came over me, I, I..." She stops me talking by placing her finger on my lips and shaking her head.

"Don't, Theon. Please don't apologize. There's no need. We both feel it but…" She sighs.

"It's the wrong time and the wrong place. I really appreciate you and your friendship. Let's just keep that for the time being. Is that okay?" I nod and pull her into me for a hug.

"Of course, Alana. Thank you."

"No, thank you, and I love my gift."

"I love turtles, they are my favorite animal, that's what made me pick it. They are such unassuming, gentle, graceful and majestic animals. They go about their business not bothering any other animals. I just love them. I have a colorful turtle tattoo on my back. I'll show you one day." I look down and smile at her. "Time for me to get back to Evelina."

"How is she?"

"Just the same," I lean down and kiss her cheek.

"See you soon," I say walking off.

"Hey, Theon," Alana shouts after me. I turn to see what she wants.

"I like the new look." She says pointing to the beard and the Alice band on my head. She winks at me then turns and walks back into Caroline's room. I laugh and walk back to Evelina's room with a big smile on my face.

It's the eighteenth day of Evelina's coma. I can't take much more of this. The only plus side is she's had two more doses of chemo and now only has two left, which is a relief. I still wish she would wake up.

Caroline has been doing great recovering after her surgery. I wish I could say the same about Evelina.

I haven't talked to Evelyn the last two days. I'm growing weary of it. I'm beginning to wonder if she is there looking out for our angel. Maybe it's also because of Alana. Maybe I feel guilty I have feelings for another woman. I'm breaking my promise to Evelyn that she's my first and last.

When I kissed her that day it was like she was stealing my breath. It was only a peck on the mouth, but I wanted more. So much more. I wanted to take her away at that moment, to take her pain away and just comfort her. I wanted this to all not be happening. I wanted our daughters to be healthy and playing like little girls should be. I wanted Alana so badly in those few seconds. Seconds was all it was, seconds and then the guilt and embarrassment hit me.

I've spent a bit more time with Alana. I find I'm seeking her out. I look forward to our talks, even if they get heavy sometimes. Since the kiss, we have tried to meet up at least once a day to catch up.

We talk a lot about our families. She's met Evander, and I've met Bailee and Bryan and her sister, who was wary of me. We all get on. I hope when Evelina wakes, we can all spend time getting to know each other. My biggest worry is Sonia, yet she has been the most supportive of Alana, calling in to see if she needs anything or any errands. She's said for a long time that I should move on, but I always tell her not to go there. Maybe she can see how much I like Alana.

Chapter 30

10 Years Earlier

I FELL ASLEEP AFTER THE NURSE left me and I don't know how long I was out, but I was woken up by a deep, gruff voice. I open my eyes to see two police officers standing next to my bed. Oh fuck, what now.

"Sir, can you tell me your full name?" I try to speak, but my throat is so dry. One of them hands me a glass of water, and I take a sip.

"Thank you. My name is Theon John Tourney. Is there a problem?"

"Mr. Tourney, I'm Officer Janson, and this is Officer Dillon, we had a report that you have confessed to killing your wife. Is this true, sir?"

Well, fuck me.

I merely nod.

"Sir, can you tell me your wife's full name and the circumstances?" I sigh and look up to the ceiling.

"Her name is Evelyn Tourney. She died —" I stop. I don't even know how long ago it was now. How long have I been here? I close my eyes and pinch the bridge of my nose.

"Are you okay, sir? Can you continue?" I don't open my eyes.

"What day are we on?"

"It's Friday today. You were brought into the hospital with a head injury yesterday morning, which was Thursday."

"Well, in that case, she died on Tuesday."

"How did she die, Mr. Tourney?"

"Giving birth to my babies." They both looked at me puzzled.

"But you said you killed her?"

"I did."

"I don't understand. Mr. Tourney. If she died in childbirth, then how did you kill her?"

"I got her pregnant. If I hadn't have gotten her pregnant, she would still be here. The OB-GYN, Dr. Zelda, said it was the pregnancy that killed her. Therefore, it's my fault. It's my fault she's dead, and I have two babies to bring up, which I can't because I blame them for killing her." I look at them, both with puzzled looks on their faces.

"Mr. Tourney, we are deeply sorry for your loss, sir, please accept our condolences. But, Mr. Tourney, you didn't kill your wife, sir. In childbirth, many complications can arise. Unfortunately, on this occasion, it sounds like there wasn't anything you or anyone could have done. Please don't blame yourself, sir. We are sorry to have troubled you, Mr. Tourney."

The one doing the talking pats my arm in sympathy, and they both start to leave the room. I didn't want sympathy. I killed my wife for fuck's sake. I needed to get out of here. I didn't even know which hospital this was. From what the nurse said, I don't have my wallet or phone, and she didn't mention my car keys, so I probably don't have a car.

"Officer?" I shout just before the door closes behind them. The one who talked turns and comes back in.

"The nurse said my wallet and phone are missing. I also had my car keys on me, so I'm not sure if the nurse has them or if they have been stolen as well. What do I do about this?" He goes to the door and asks the other officer to go and see if they had my car keys.

"I will take a report now, so we can file it, in case anything turns up and for your insurance. Can you tell me what you had in your wallet?"

"I had my credit cards, about $200 in cash, and a photo of my wife." I look at the window, biting back the tears again as I think of Evelyn.

"It's okay, take your time, Mr. Tourney."

"That was it, I think. I don't suppose I will see any of it again. I need the numbers for JP Morgan and Amex to put a stop on my cards. Do you know where I can get those from please?"

"I will go and get them for you now and ask the nurse to bring a phone in for you to use." Just then the door opens, and the other officer comes in.

"No keys, sir. Was it just your car keys? What about house keys? Did you have your address in your wallet?"

"Fuck, yes. My driving license was in there with my name and address."

"We will send someone over there now to check it out. Do you have anyone to contact that we can ask to meet us at the house? You said about your babies, sir? Where are they now?"

"With my wife's parents. I need to phone them. They have keys to my house. But, I need the police there before they get there?"

"Yes, we will do that now, sir. It's been over twenty-four hours since you were admitted to hospital. I don't like the odds here; I have to tell you."

"Well, it seems everything is going wrong in my life right now so why not this as well. I have a tracker on my car, in case they have taken that. If I give you the registration details, can you put a trace on it to find out where it is, please?"

"Yes, of course. We are really sorry all this has happened to you, on top of losing your wife, Mr. Tourney." I nod a thank you at them, then they both leave to sort out my shitstorm.

Not long after the officers leave the nurse comes in with a phone for me.

"Thank you, nurse, and I'm sorry about earlier."

"It's okay, sir. It was a misunderstanding. Here are the numbers for the credit cards that you asked for. The officers have sent someone over to your house now, to check on it. Is there anything else I can get for you?"

"I don't know my father in law's number, do you have a phone directory I could look him up on please. I have all my numbers programmed into my cell phone." I shrug.

"Tell me his name, and I will look online for you at the desk." I write the name down on the paper she brought me with the numbers I need. She leaves, and I make the calls to put a stop on my cards. It's easy enough, and they both say there had been no activity on the cards yet. Luckily. The nurse brings me Arnold's number while I'm on the phone, so that's my next call. I think I will withhold the truth about me being passed out and just tell him I got mugged.

"Hello."

"Hi Arnold, it's Theon."

"Oh, thank god. Where have you been? We have been worried sick about you. Why are you not ringing me on your cell? Is everything all right, Theon?"

"No, I'm in the hospital. Don't panic. I'm all right, but I got mugged and was brought in with a head injury. Shit, I don't even know which hospital it is. Anyway, I was brought in yesterday morning but had no ID or anything on me, so they couldn't identify me until I woke up, which was earlier today. My keys were taken as well with my car and house keys on. The police are concerned that whoever mugged me has my license with my address on and they think they may have broken into the house. They've sent a car over there now, but I need you to go over if you can please, Arnold. The locks will all need changing if you can arrange that for me. I'm not sure anyone will have broken in with all the security I have on the place, but you never know."

Arnold calls back a while later. I still have the hospital phone with me thankfully. "Theon is that you, son?"

"Yes Arnold, how is everything at the house?"

"No break-in." I sigh with relief. Thank god for that.

"I have a locksmith coming over now to change all the locks. I'm going to get the garage and pool house done as well just in case. The police were at the gates when I arrived, and they checked it all out first. I just wanted to let you know so you didn't worry. Do you need me to get you a new phone? I can bring it to you? Do you know where you are yet or when you will be home?"

"No, I haven't seen anyone for a while. I will ask as soon as the nurse comes back. Thank you, Arnold. I know you don't need this added pressure from me."

"Hey, nonsense. It's good to get out of the house. Between Sonia and two crying babies, it was driving me a bit batty." I feel so guilty. They are looking after them because I can't. I feel like the biggest failure ever. I just can't do it yet. I'm not ready to face them.

"I'm sorry you are looking after them. I will get there, I promise. Just not yet."

"I understand, son. I do understand. Ring me when you find anything out. I will grab you a new phone once the locksmith has finished."

"Yes, thank you, Arnold." I hang up. My life is just so crap at the moment. I'm just a burden to Sonia and Arnold. I'm no good for the babies. What use am I without Evelyn? I don't even want to live. I have no purpose here anymore. I fall asleep.

I'm woken up by the door again. It's the nurse from earlier. "How are you feeling Mr. Tourney?"

"Honestly? Like crap and not because of my head. When can I leave and where am I?"

"The doctor is coming to see you in a while to make sure your head is okay, and it's up to him to discharge you. I need you to fill out this form for me please, Mr. Tourney for your insurance. You do have medical insurance, don't you? You're in Cedars Sinai."

"Yes, I have medical insurance. I would like to leave today though."

"Like I said, the doctor will be here to assess you soon. If you can wait until then that would be great." She walks out, leaving me to fill in my form.

The doctor arrives sometime later. I still don't have any concept of time being in here, there is no clock on the wall, and I don't have my phone.

"Mr. Tourney, I'm Dr. Singh, pleased to meet you. I believe you were brought in yesterday with a concussion from a head injury, but you were also inebriated. You were found in a storm drain in downtown, is that right?"

"I have no idea, Doctor."

"Do you remember being attacked? Do you remember how you got the head injury? Did the attackers do that or did you do it yourself from being inebriated?"

"Doc, you just said yourself I was concussed. I didn't wake up until today. I don't remember anything. I couldn't even tell you where I parked my car or what I did the day before yesterday. All I can tell you is I lost my wife three days ago in childbirth. Everything else since then has been a blur." I hang my head in shame. I feel ashamed about what I've done. But I need to numb the pain.

"I'm sorry for your loss, Mr. Tourney, I know how hard it can be. Do you think talking will help you with your loss? I think if we can get you to see a counselor then it may stop you turning to substance abuse." Fuck, he has me pegged all right. Seeing a counselor won't numb the pain like alcohol does. I know it's wrong, and I have never been a drinker, I will never use drugs, I know that, but I need to forget, and the only way I know is the drink.

"No, I don't think talking to someone will numb the pain I have in here do you, Doctor?" I say banging my fist over my heart.

"I don't need any help. I'm fine, thank you. Now if you can just make sure my head is not going to fall off, then I can get out of here if that's okay with you?" He sighs because he can't do much else. He shines his light in my eyes asking me to follow it, then his finger, then look up and down and to the sides, and I do it all. He then asks me a lot of bullshit questions about my full name, date of birth, what year it is, who is the President and so on.

"Do you feel any nausea, Mr. Tourney?"

"Nope."

"Then I think you are fine to go home. I don't want you driving for at least 48 hours and stay away from alcohol please with the painkillers you are on. I don't want you to end up back in here."

"Can I ask did your baby survive?"

"Babies, yes they did. They are with my wife's parents at the moment." After a few tests he clears me to leave. I just want to get out of here.

Chapter 31

TWENTY-FIVE DAYS AND SHE STILL hasn't woken up. Over three weeks of waiting. I feel like I've been holding my breath all this time, waiting for her eyes to open, and for her to smile at me. I miss my little poppet smiling at me and acting like she's twenty and not ten and for her cheek, which I find so adorable. The only good news is that she has now finished her course of chemo. She has not had to go through all the sickness it brings, and that is the only blessing. I need her to wake up now, so we can all go home.

I'm stroking her hair, talking to her, when I sense Alana. I turn to the door and see her crying.

"Hey, what's wrong?" I rush to her, holding each side of her face and lifting it up so she looks at me. I wipe away tears that are rolling down her cheeks.

"Baby, what's wrong. You're scaring me here?"

"Sorry, Theon. I'm just having a bad day. Caroline isn't feeling well, and she's been sleeping too much. She was doing so well. Dr. Cassidy came, and they have taken her for an MRI scan to see if there is anything going on inside. I'm scared, Theon. Really scared. What if her liver is failing sooner than they thought and she needs a transplant now? What if she can't wait anymore? What if the cancer has spread and now it's started to make her sick again? Oh, Theon. I am so scared. I didn't know where else to go. I'm sorry for troubling you."

"Hey, come here." I pull her into my chest, hold her head and hug her. She hugs me back so tightly. She needs this comfort right now.

"You know you can come to me at any time, don't forget that. You are no trouble at all. Let's wait to see what Dr. Cassidy says before jumping to conclusions, Okay?" She nods her head. I keep hold of her. Hugging her. Comforting her as well as me taking some comfort from this. I kiss the top of her head as she continues to cry, and I see Sonia come into view. She stops when she sees us at the doorway to Evelina's room. She mouths, asking if everything is okay, I nod, letting her know its fine to carry on.

"Hey, Theon, Alana. Is Caroline okay?" Alana steps out of my arms looking a little embarrassed that Sonia saw that. She wipes her eyes. Sonia reaches into her purse and gives Alana a tissue to blow her nose.

"Thank you, Sonia. No, Caroline seems to be getting sick again. They've taken her for an MRI. I don't know what's happening yet. I'm scared." I pull her back into my chest. It's where she feels safest at the moment.

"Oh, Alana. I'm sorry, love. Let's hope they find out why she is poorly again. I'll nip in and sit with Evelina if you two want to go get a coffee." She nods at me, and I nod back, mouthing thank you. She rubs Alana's back and then steps around me into Evelina's room. I turn to Sonia. "Call me if you need me. Thank you."

We head outside to our bench for some fresh air. Alana's tucked into my side, but she's not crying now. I have my arm around her shoulder, and I'm rubbing it.

"I'm sure they will sort her out, Alana. Maybe they will get a liver very soon. I know what you're going through. I keep telling Evelina that it's time to wake up now so we can all go home. It's killing me. Even Dr. Cassidy said last week she was surprised how long she has been in a coma and that just made me panic."

"Oh, Theon, I'm sure she will wake up when she's ready. This may be just her way of not having to go through the sickness of the chemo. It's horrible." I know she's right.

Just then Alana's phone buzzes, she looks at it. "I need to go. Dr. Cassidy is looking for me. She's asked if I will go to her office. I'm scared, Theon. Will you come with me please?"

I don't hesitate. "Of course I will. Come on." I get up, holding my hand out to her. We walk back to Dr. Cassidy's office, and Alana taps gently on the door but doesn't wait for Dr. Cassidy to speak, she just walks in. I walk in with her and see the look of surprise on the Doc's face.

"Hi, Dr. Cassidy. I've brought Theon for support. I don't mind him hearing any of this."

"Ok, great, please take a seat both of you." She gestures to the chairs in front of her desk. I don't like this office. It's always brought bad news, and I don't like the look on her face right now either.

"Mrs. Tudrow. We've done an MRI and a CT scan on Caroline, and it's not good news, I'm afraid." Alana grabs my hand and squeezes hard as the doc is talking.

"Caroline's liver is failing. It's more damaged than the surgeon thought. She needs a liver transplant immediately. Her kidneys are also struggling, which is common with liver failure. I'm so sorry to tell you that if we don't get a liver for Caroline in the next day or two, she will not survive more than a few days."

"NO, please! No! Oh, god. No, please, no," Alana screams out then collapses on the floor. I catch her just before she hits her head on the desk. I pull her onto my knee and stroke her back.

"Shhh, Alana. Are you with me, baby? Can you hear me?" She looks up at me, and her face is pure agony.

"Dr. Cassidy, how can we expedite a liver for Caroline? Can I pay for one privately? Does it work like that?"

"No, it doesn't I'm afraid. Caroline will now go near the top of the waiting list, and if one becomes available that is a match for her, then she gets it. We can't buy a liver."

"Money can buy anything. I don't care how much it costs. Can I pay to get Caroline to the top of the list, not just near the top?" Alana is sobbing into my chest while I rub her back. I don't think she is with us at this point. I stare at the doc and raise my eyebrows at her?

"I'm sorry but no Mr. Tourney, the hospital will not do that. There are too many patients waiting for organs, as sad as that is, there is no way to expedite one." I know she's right. I know Caroline is not the only child in here waiting for an organ, I just feel so hopeless and want to be able to help.

She gets up from behind her desk. "Can you take Mrs. Tudrow back to Caroline's room? Caroline is in ICU at the moment. Once Mrs. Tudrow is ready, I will take you up there to see her. I am sorry, Mrs. Tudrow." I nod and carry Alana out and over to Caroline's room. I sit on the chair with her on my lap. I'm just comforting her while she sobs into my chest. She's clutching my t-shirt tightly. I can't say anything. All I can do is sit with her.

"Theon, I don't know what to do. I can't feel. I'm numb. I don't know if I took in what she said to me. All I heard was 'I'm so sorry'. Then I lost it. Did she say that if they don't get a liver in the next day or two, Caroline won't last the week? Was that it in a nutshell?"

I put my finger under her chin to look at me. "It was, Alana. They are putting Caroline on the transplant list. I asked if we could buy a liver..."

She shakes her head. "Theon, that has to be illegal, and there is no way on this earth I can throw money at this anyway? I don't have money to do that."

"It's okay Alana, Dr. Cassidy said no. I also asked if we could pay to put her top of the transplant list, she said the hospital wouldn't do that. There are too many children in the same boat, waiting for transplants. I just had to try and do something to help Alana. I can't stand not being able to help. I do have the money to at least try."

She looks at me, really looks at me "I don't really know you, do I,

Theon? I mean, we talk every day, and I have so many feelings for you, but I don't actually know you. I never asked you what you do. I'm a terrible person. So wrapped up in myself and what's going on in my life. I'm so sorry, Theon."

"Hey, shh, none of that. You are not a terrible person. God, Alana, you are so selfless. All you think about are your children. There is plenty of time for us to get to know each other, and I would love nothing more. I have strong feelings for you too, but we need to see if those feelings are real and not just because of our situation.

"Now, do you think you're ready to go and sit with Caroline? You know you have to be brave, baby. I understand that and how hard it is. If you need me to sit with her while you phone your sister, then I can do that as Sonia is with Evelina, okay? Ready?" She gets up off of my lap and holds her hand out for me.

"Will you walk up there with me, please?"

I grab her hand. "Of course I will." I put my arm around her, pulling her to me and that's how we walk to ICU. I stop at the door the nurse points us to, and I kiss Alana softly on the lips. The feelings I have for her are so strong. She kisses me back. Not a passionate kiss, but a loving, thank you, kiss.

"You know where I am if you need me anytime, okay, baby. If you need a cry, come over to me, if you need a hug, come over to me — if you need anything at all, come over and see me." I kiss her nose, and I head over to Evelina's room. Just before I enter, I turn and watch as Alana stands up straight, breathes out a couple of times to compose herself before entering Caroline's room. God love her. It's so fucking hard being a parent with a sick child. I never want to be in this position again in my life.

Chapter 32

10 Years Earlier

I PHONED ARNOLD FROM the hospital to let him know I was being discharged. He was coming for me within the hour, after the locksmith finished, and bringing me some clean clothes.

The more I sat in this bed, wallowing, the harder it got again. I couldn't remember much, but I did remember Dr. Zelda telling me that it was Evelyn being pregnant that eventually killed her, which made it all my fault. How did I tell Arnold and Sonia? Did I tell them? I can't do it just yet. I'm still blaming the babies. I know I shouldn't, but right now, I can't help it. If it weren't for them, Evelyn would be here.

I must have dropped back off to sleep, but I wake when I feel a shake to my shoulder. I open my eyes and Arnold is standing there.

"How are you feeling, son?"

Like fucking shit. "Not bad considering. I suppose. Got a banging headache."

"I have some clothes for you. Are you having a shower first?"

"If you don't mind waiting, yes. I will be quick."

"No problem. You go, and I will go and find somewhere to grab a coffee. Do you want one?"

"Yes, please, Arnold, that would be great." I rush off to the shower rooms down the hall and have the quickest shower of my life. When I get back to the room, Arnold is there with two take-out coffees. I don't have anything to take with me, so we leave.

We travel in slightly awkward silence until he starts talking about the babies. I knew he would at some point, even though I was hoping that he wouldn't. I try to stay courteous, but it's hard.

"Sonia is struggling with the babies, Theon. I know it's only been two days, but they are hard work. One baby is hard enough but two … It seems you settle one down and the other one starts, and it goes on like that nonstop."

Fuck! I knew this would happen. I'm not ready to see them. I can't, and I don't know if I ever will. Maybe I need to think about adoption. It's too much for Sonia and Arnold to take on twins in their retirement. I put my head in my hands, squeezing my eyes shut and rubbing them. I'm sure he looks over at me because his hand comes over and squeezes my arm.

"I'm sorry to push you, son, but we need to talk about this." I know we do, and I'm not being fair on them. I look up and over at him and nod. What I really want is to get out of this fucking car and run. Run away from everything. Bury my head in the sand as though it never happened. That life never happened. Or better still walk into the ocean and never come back out.

"I was thinking," I say, looking his way. "We should hire a nanny to look after them. Take the pressure off you and Sonia. It's not fair to you two. If we hire two nannies, then you can have round the clock care for them." I look out of my side window. I don't want to see the disappointment that I know will be on his face because I'm not facing up to my responsibilities. He doesn't speak, just carries on driving heading for home. We don't talk all the way. I'm resting my head back with my eyes shut, pretending to sleep. I'm not — the cogs will not switch off. I want a drink when Arnold goes. I want to get the numb feeling back to forget my life. This time, I will stay home though.

We get home, and Arnold heads straight into the kitchen. He stands at the island, sorting out the keys to all the doors in silence, and I can see he's tense.

"Arnold, I'm sorry, okay. I can't face them right now. I don't have any feelings towards them apart from loathing for taking Evelyn from me. I can phone Sonia and ask her to look for a couple of nannies to help. I'm sorry you are both lumbered with them, but until I decide what to do— I mean until I'm in the right frame of mind, I can't decide what to do with them."

"What does that mean, Theon? What to do with them? They are babies — you can't just throw them away because you don't want them. They are not disposable. They are human beings. Tiny human beings. They need their daddy. They are not going to have a mommy so I'll be damned if I'll let you stay away from them too long."

"It's my choice, Arnold. If I decide I never want to see them, then I will have them adopted, but it's my choice and no one else's."

"ADOPTED!" he shouts at me. I've never heard Arnold shout before. I step back, shocked at first.

"Over my dead body will I ever let you give them babies away like they are nothing. They are not dogs, Theon. You don't just give babies away. If you don't want them, then they stay with us. They are the last piece of Evelyn we have, and there is no way on this earth you are giving them away. Do you understand me?" I look at him for a beat. It hits me. They are the last piece of Evelyn that is left. Oh god, what the fuck am I doing? I hang my head in shame for suggesting it.

"I'm sorry, Arnold," I mumble with my head down. I feel the tears flowing down my cheeks and gathering on my chin until they are big enough to drop to the floor. I wipe my nose with my arm. The next thing I know, I'm in Arnold's arms, crying. My head is on his shoulder, and he's stroking my hair with his hand.

"Theon, you have always been like the son I never had. I know this is killing you inside because it's ripping my heart apart too. I get it. I do. I know you feel your life is not worth living, but when you see the two gorgeous babies that you and Evelyn created out of pure love, you'll understand. Look at me, son." I do. "I promise you, your world will swing back onto its correct axis. It will level you out and ground you more. They will never replace Evelyn but believe me when I say you will be smitten with them once you lay your eyes on them. Your daughter is the spitting image of Evelyn when she was born. It tore my heart to see her. I fell in love with both of them the minute I saw them. You will too, son, if you believe in the good that came out of this awful situation. I know you blame them, but, Theon, they are just tiny innocent babies. I'll be damned, while I live and breathe, they will get to know their amazing father though. Do you hear me?" I just nod. I can't speak. He hugs me harder now, and I cry more. My head feels like it's going to explode.

"I will give you a little more time, son. You need the time to grieve, and I will look for a nanny because it is far too much for Sonia and me to cope with. It's hard enough for us losing Evelyn. Sonia will say she loves it because well, it's a way of coping with the loss, but I can see just from two days how tired she is.. I'm also sorry, son, but we have Evelyn's funeral arrangements to sort out, and we need you for that. You're her next of kin, Theon, and we can't go ahead with anything without you. We will help you all we can. You're not on your own."

Oh, shit I hadn't even thought of a funeral. I can't even accept she's gone. How can I do this and what do I do? Arnold must feel me stiffen up. He pushes me back, so he can look at me.

"Look, Theon, we've got to do this. I'm not letting anyone but us sort this out. I want Evelyn to have the best send-off we can give her. You can't bury your head in the sand, son. Not on this. I will give you the time you need for the babies, but the funeral has to be sorted now." He's right. I know he is. Funerals can't wait.

"Has the coroner or ME signed off on her death yet?"

"I don't know. They won't tell us anything even though we're her parents. You are her next of kin, and it has to be you they give the death certificate to."

I nod. I have to do this. I grab the phone directory and search for the coroner, then dial the number.

"Hello, yes, my name is Mr. Tourney. Can you let me know if the coroner has signed off on my wife, Evelyn Tourney? I need to know if he has released her body yet, please?" I look at Arnold while I wait for whoever is on the phone to come back to me.

"Ok, yes, I see. Well, I can come down now." I look to Arnold for confirmation, and he nods yes.

"I can be there in about forty minutes. Okay, thank you." I hang up the phone.

"I have to go down with mine and Evelyn's ID, and they will let me know what is happening then. I know you're right, Arnold. I need to get this done. I need to find some courage, but only on this for now. I will see how it goes after the funeral and how I feel about the babies then." I reach in my back pocket for my wallet then realize I don't have it or my driver's license.

"I don't have my ID. It was stolen with my wallet. Shit." I rake my hand over my head forgetting I still have a bandage on, and I catch it and wince.

"Shit!" That hurt.

"You have your passports, don't you?"

"Yes, I do. I'll grab them from the safe. I won't be a minute." I head to our home office where the safe is, to retrieve our passports. I open Evelyn's. It floors me seeing her image there in my hands. I look up and see images of us together all over the wall. Evelyn insisted on a wall of photos of us in the different places we'd visited around the world. I haven't been in here and seen these since I lost her, and it guts me more. Seeing us together in all the places we visited, how happy we are, were — shit. Arnold comes in to see if I'm okay and sees me standing, staring at the wall, the tears streaming down my face. He stands next to me, and I hear him sniff. This is hard for him as well.

"God, Arnold, look at her. The most beautiful women in the world and she was all mine. I feel we didn't have long together — nine years, but it wasn't long enough. It wasn't a lifetime. We used to say to each other even a lifetime wouldn't be enough." I glance at Arnold, and I see the tears trickling down his cheeks as he looks at the pictures, but he's smiling at them.

"She was the light of my life, Theon. I used to see how happy she was with you and it would make me feel so warm knowing you'd found each other. I never doubted for a minute the love you both had for each other, and I knew you would never hurt her or upset her. I knew you were good for each other. Every time you looked at her, I could see it written all over your face. The love and adoration you had for her. I could see she was your entire life and you would do absolutely anything for her happiness. Let me tell you, that is all a father asks for.

I stare at him in horror ... but it was me that killed her. How did I protect her then? What will he think of me when I tell him? He won't be calling me son then, will he? God, how am I going to tell him?

"Theon, are you okay?" I can't answer.

"Theon, what's wrong, son? Are you okay? Is it your head?" The guilt is killing me. I have all these things going on in my head. I feel like I'm going to explode. I need to tell him.

"It was me as well, Arnold."

"What was you as well?"

I look away then back to him. "I killed her. You said all that about protecting her, but I fucking killed her," I shout at him.

He stares at me a bit dumbfounded. "Theon, what are you talking about? You didn't kill her."

"YES, I DID!" I scream at him.

"It was my fault she died. I got her pregnant, Arnold. If she weren't pregnant, she would still be alive. It was all my fault for getting her pregnant. I killed her. I'm so sorry. I didn't protect her like I should have done — like I was supposed to do."

"You silly, silly man. You did not kill her. No one could have known what was going to happen. We don't think of childbirth being a risk these days because millions of women give birth, but I was reading up about it and far more die from childbirth complications than I think anyone realizes. Childbirth is a risk for any woman. Evelyn just got unlucky. It wasn't meant to be, Theon. You both got pregnant. It wasn't one-sided, and neither of you could have predicted this happening. Theon, you cannot blame yourself. The world is full of 'what ifs' and 'if only's' but there is absolutely nothing we can do about it. If you hadn't have got pregnant together, then there wouldn't be the two tiny beautiful parts of you both back at my house. It doesn't take away that we lost Evelyn, but she left them behind for us to look after, and to cherish and always let them not know who their momma was."

I know he's right, deep down, I know it, but it's something I have to come to terms with on my own. He will never know just how grateful for his support I am. I love him as though he was my own father.

"Evelyn had the best parents in the world," I mutter into him.

We arrive at the coroner's office a bit later than I wanted after my meltdown. I have my shades on to hide my bloodshot eyes. The receptionist checks our ID's, then has us take a seat.

"Mr. Tourney," a voice calls, and I stand up and head to the man who is standing there in blue scrubs.

"Hi, Mr. Tourney. I'm Dr. Daniels. Please follow me."

"Can my father in law come with us? I ask, beckoning Arnold to come with us, not giving Dr. Daniels a chance to answer.

"Yes, of course." We head through some doors and into an office.

"Please take a seat." We both sit in front of his desk.

"Firstly, my sincerest apologies on your loss," he says nodding to us both. I just nod at him, removing my shades. "We are now happy to release the body to your chosen funeral home. If you could please let them know they can collect Mrs. Tourney that would be most helpful. I will give you a release form with the coroner's number on it that pertains to Mrs. Tourney. If you give the funeral home a copy of this, they can collect her."

"Oh, I don't have a funeral home picked out yet. Do you have a list of good funeral homes I could see please?" He pulls out some leaflets of funeral homes, and Arnold takes them from him.

"What happens now?"

"I understand there is a lot to do and take in, Mr. Tourney and it's the last thing you need during this time of grief. If you firstly find a funeral home they will help guide you through the procedure and alleviate as much as they can from you."

I nod at him taking the information he gives me, and thank him as we head out.

"God, Arnold, there's so much to do."

"Come on, let's get in the car and make some calls. We may as well sort out what we can today. I need to phone Sonia and make sure she's okay. She said she had a couple of friends going over to help her today." We both make phone calls.

We had talked about our funerals, we laughed because we thought it wouldn't be for many years to come, we picked the songs we wanted playing, she wanted one of her favorite songs which was Peter Gabriel and Kate Bush with Don't Give Up. I said I wanted something more upbeat like ZZ Top, Give me all your Lovin', and we laughed about that. Then we both said we would like to donate any organs we had if it could help save someone's life, we said we would both be too old and wrinkly by then as we had till infinity and beyond, so our organs may be too old to help anyone. How wrong we were, but Evelyn's will be of no use now as she's been gone for a few days.

"I've found a funeral home near where we live, Theon and it looks beautiful. They can take Evelyn, and they asked if we could go in now to see them and make the arrangements. Are you up to that?"

"Yes, sure, I'm on a roll. Don't stop me now or I may never do it. It's killing me but it's keeping me from wallowing, I suppose. How's Sonia?"

"Her friends are over all cooing over the babies and helping her. I told her about the nannies you suggested. She wasn't thrilled, but I think she understands it's what we need. She's asking for recommendations from her friends' daughters who have nannies."

"Great, thank you."

We head to the funeral home, we both agree on a lovely cedar wood casket lined in white silk. I pick her favorite flowers — multi-colored lilies. I didn't want just white. She was full of life, and she should have lots of color. I also told them the music to play. I give them the coroner's details, so they can collect her when she's ready.

The next thing I need to do is buy a plot at the cemetery near our home. I'm in luck, they have a couple of plots left, so I pick quite a big one out. I figure I have two kids to think about now, it may as well be a family Tourney plot.

On our way back home, I ask him to stop at the liquor store. He frowns at me.

"Drink doesn't solve anything, Theon. It only prolongs the situation. The more you bury it, the longer it takes to come to terms with it. You're a grown man, and I can't stop you, but please promise me you will be sensible about this."

"I know, but it helps me forget, and right now I need to forget everything. Please don't lecture me on it, Arnold. I appreciate everything you've done for me, but please leave me alone on this one." We stop off, and I buy a few bottles of Fireball. I don't let him see in the bag as I put it in the trunk, but you can hear the bottles chinking as we drive home. He stops at the gate to let me out. I get out but lean in before shutting the door.

"Thank you, Arnold, for everything. I couldn't do this without you, and I know you're suffering as much as I am. So, thank you."

"Anytime you need me, son, pick up the phone, no matter what time it is. If you need to talk or cry on my shoulder, you call me. Do you hear me, Theon?" I nod then close the door, get my bottles from the trunk and head to the empty, lonely house. With each step, I feel my heart getting heavier and heavier. Each step is getting harder and harder — it's like my shoes are made from concrete. I come to a stop. I don't want to go any farther, but I know I have to. I try again.

I enter the silent house and head to the kitchen with my bottles. I make some pasta with tuna and take it to the cinema room. I want to watch my proposal and also the cartoon she did to tell me she was pregnant, with my bottle of Fireball for company. After the food, I pour a very large glass, recline my seat and watch the two shorts play over and over again on a loop. I drink myself into oblivion and wake up the next day with two empty Fireball bottles beside me. There is vomit all down me, and I peed myself, but I don't care. It worked. I forgot it all, felt numb, and slept peacefully. And I did it all over again that day and the day after and the day after that.

Chapter 33

I COULDN'T SLEEP WELL LAST night. I kept thinking of Caroline, the poor kid, and also Alana and how she must be feeling. I need to speak to Dr. Cassidy just to make sure we can't get her to the top of the list. She didn't come to see me but then it's not my daughter I'm asking about, and I didn't see Alana again yesterday after I left her. The problem is that time is running out for Caroline.

I'm sitting with Evelina, hoping for a sign. Every morning, I wait, holding my breath to see if she moves a finger, a hand, or twitches an eye. Every morning is the same — nothing, and I turn away and let out the breath I hold and try not to show my disappointment. This morning is no different.

A little while later, Sonia arrives. As usual, she has her bag full of snacks and her flask because she doesn't want to leave Evelina's side.

"Good morning, Sonia. How are you today?"

"Oh, the same, sweetie. How are you and my little angel here?"

"The same, no change," I say with a shrug and a sorrowful look on my face.

"I have a feeling about today, Theon. I woke up with a start. Evelyn told me to get here and stay here. I know I sound like an old coot, but I swear it felt real."

I don't say anything. I'm not building my hopes up. I've been asking Evelyn for weeks now and got nothing, so I gave up.

"Do you mind if I go for my shower and some breakfast?"

"No, not at all. I have everything I need in here." She pats her big fabric bag.

She reminds me of Mary Poppins with that bag. I chuckle, and she looks at me quizzically.

"It's your bag — you always remind me of Mary Poppins, it just made me laugh. Evelina loves that film, but she says Nanny McPhee is her favorite." I bend down to kiss Sonia on the top of the head. "I also need to go and see Dr. Cassidy about Caroline and then speak to Alana. I'll try not to be too long so I can get back. But if something does happen, please phone me."

"You know I will. You go now."

After my shower and breakfast, I head to Dr. Cassidy's office. I knock and wait. She opens the door

"Mr. Tourney, please come in. I was just on my way to see Mrs. Tudrow."

"Good morning, Doc. I just wanted to see if there was anything at all we can do for Caroline?"

"No, Mr. Tourney, I'm sorry, I know it's not what you wanted to hear, and I'm holding onto hope that we can get a match. That is all we have, hope."

I rub my hand over my face. "I know, Doctor, and I'm sorry, I just feel helpless."

"I know Mr. Tourney. It's so hard, we can only wait and see. I'm on my way to see Mrs. Tudrow. Do you want to come with me and we can tell her together, she may need your support?"

"Yes, I was on my way to see her after here anyway." We head out of her office to make our way up to ICU.

"Still no change in Evelina this morning, Mr. Tourney?"

"No Doctor, still the same. I just pray every day this will be the day she wakes up but nothing. I hold my breath every morning, the minute I wake up hoping she says, good morning, Daddy, but nothing. I'm not gonna lie, it's scaring the shit out of me the longer it goes on."

"I'm sure she will wake up soon. I said you had a very brave and smart young lady there and I think the smart in her is showing."

I cock my eyebrow at her. "How so?"

"Well, she knew before her surgery that she was going to get sick with the medicine that's supposed to make her better. I think her brain told her not to wake up until it was over, so she didn't feel the sickness." She shrugs.

"Just my theory and I'm sticking to it," she says to me as we exit the elevator onto the ICU floor.

"I'm just going to pop my head in to make sure Sonia is okay and make sure there is no change with Evelina. I will be right back."

"No worries, I want to do some checks on Caroline anyway. I won't say anything until you come back about what we discussed." I nod and head to Evelina's room while she goes into Caroline's room.

"Hey, Sonia, how is my little poppet doing?"

"Just the same, sweetie. How is Caroline doing?"

"I'm just on my way in there now but wanted to check in here first. The doc said there is nothing we can do except hope a liver becomes available, so it's just a waiting game. I can't even imagine what's going through Alana's mind with all this. She must be on the edge of her seat, just waiting all the time. I hate seeing them like this, especially when she looked like she was getting better the other day." I tell her the doc's theory on Evelina as well, and she tends to agree. I head on over to Caroline's room, knock and wait for the door to open. It's the doctor.

"Sorry, I was just finishing up my exams on Caroline. You can come in now if that's okay with Mrs. Tudrow?" she says so Alana can hear.

"Yes, please come in, Theon." I walk in and over to Alana where she sits next to Caroline. Caroline is asleep, mildly sedated for the pain.

I lean down and kiss Alana on the top of her head. "Hey, how are you today, baby?"

She shrugs, not saying anything and just looks at Caroline. She reaches for my hand to hold, and I squeeze hers when she does to let her know I'm with her. I look at the doc and nod for her to speak. The doc explains to Alana what she told me. Alana has tears flowing down her cheeks. "I appreciate your honesty, Dr. Cassidy. What are the chances of getting a match in the next day?" I see the anguish on her face asking the question.

"Honestly, Mrs. Tudrow, they are very slim, maybe about 3%. I'm really sorry." Alana hangs her head down and puts it in both of her hands. I nod a thank you to the doctor and let her know I've got it from here. I pull Alana into my chest and let her cry. All I can do is hold her, I feel helpless yet again. I rub her back, whispering, trying to be encouraging, but not to give her false hope. We sit there for a while longer, not speaking until she looks at me.

"Thank you, Theon. You will never know how much your support has meant to me." She strokes my cheek, then leans in and kisses my lips. I can't help it — I react. I know I shouldn't, but she is so damn beautiful. I kiss her back, but I don't let the kiss deepen, pulling back. She looks a little hurt, but I smile at her.

"Baby, you have no idea what you do to me." I look at Caroline. "This isn't the time or the place. I'm here for you though, no matter what, okay?"

She nods, looks down and traces the logo on my t-shirt. I lift her chin with a finger, to make her look me in the eyes.

"This," I motion between us, "this can wait. We have two poorly girls that need us right now. We can explore this later. Please don't think it's a brush off. I haven't had feelings for anyone in the ten years since I lost Evelyn. Then here, in this godforsaken place, you hit me like a tsunami, and I'm not sure what to do about it. It's not the right time or place, but we will have the time once the girls are better. Do you hear me, baby?" She nods then leans in to gently kiss my lips again.

"Yes, Theon. I hear you, and I agree. I have never had feelings for anyone since I lost Gary. In fact," she hangs her head so she's not looking at me, "I have never even kissed anyone since I lost Gary. I've been too busy with three kids. They have been my life. It's just been the four of us." She shrugs then looks back into my eyes. "Until you came along. I have strong feelings for you, but I know I shouldn't because my sole reason for being here is Caroline. Your friendship has knocked me for six. The chemistry I feel when you're near me makes me feel like a teenager, so I do know in here —" she puts her hand over her heart and then over mine. "— I know that what I feel is real. You make my heart skip a beat when we are near. I know you are near because I sense you and I get butterflies every time you touch me. But you are right. We can explore this later." She kisses my lips again. "When we can do this properly. Thank you for being the sensible one, Theon. My head is all over the place at the moment. I'm scared, petrified, lost, and powerless in this situation. Having you here to support me means the world to me, and I'm grateful every day that our paths crossed." She leans her head on my shoulder, and I hug her tightly to me.

"Me too, Alana, me too."

Chapter 34

10 Years Earlier

I DON'T KNOW WHAT DAY IT IS, but I don't care. I hear my phone going somewhere in the house, but I can't be bothered. The last time I checked it, I had several missed calls from Arnold and Sonia. I lift my head up to see exactly where I am — the living room. The last I remember, I was in the cinema room, not sure how I got here. I remember hearing banging, but I didn't wake up and couldn't tell you when it was. Then I heard my phone, which is what I think just woke me up.

God my head hurts. I thud my head back on the couch and close my eyes, my head is banging, and that loud thudding is making it worse.

"Theon, Theon, are you in there?" Shit, who is that? I try to get up, but it proves too difficult. The banging continues, louder now, closer. I lift my head and see a figure at the French doors that lead to the garden. Who the fuck is it? I look around, and the floor is a mess. Littered with empty bottles and pizza boxes.

I edge off the couch and crawl to the French doors, knocking the rubbish out of my way as I go. Someone is trying to peer through the almost-closed curtains. I pull them back slightly to see my old friend and office manager, Patrick.

"Oh, Theon. Thank god for that. No one has been able to get hold of you. Your house phone just kept going to answer machine, and your cell went to answer service. We have been worried sick about you." He shouts through the glass. I close the curtain because the light is hurting my eyes. I manage to stand, using the chair at the side to lever myself up. I open the curtain again and unlock the door to let him in. I step to the side.

"Fuck, Theon, have you had a party? Look at the state of this place, and it stinks in here." He starts picking the shit up. Who asked him to come in here and start doing this? He works for me not the other way around.

"Theon, are you all right? I have to say, and I know you're my boss, but I hope you take this from a friend — you look like shit. You stink like a brewery, your clothes are filthy, you didn't manage to make it to the bathroom, the house looks trashed, and no one has heard from you for over a week." Great just what I fucking need to hear.

"Arnold called the office. He said he left the spare keys on the island in the kitchen when he was last here, so he couldn't get in, and he was getting worried about you too. He's ready to call the cops. I said I'd try here one more time before he did. You look like you're about to keel over. Theon. Theon?"

I know he's there, but I can't hear what he's saying. It feels like an out of body experience. Like I'm looking down at this playing out. I suddenly retch, and I see the floor getting closer and closer.

I think it's some time later, and I'm back on the couch. I smell; really smell. It's making me want to vomit. I put my hand up to cover my eyes because it's a bit bright in here. I pull a wet rag off my forehead. I don't have any clothes on apart from my boxers. A towel that's covering me falls away as I manage to pull myself to a sitting position using the back of the couch to help me. I try to look around, but my head is banging. I put my head in my hands trying to stop the room from spinning and making me feel sick.

I'm going to throw up. I lean to the side, and there is a trash can there. I grab it and vomit into it. I feel like crap. Just then, I hear movement near the door. I can't look. I remember Patrick coming but was I dreaming that? I don't care right now.

"Oh, hey. You're awake. Lost you there for a bit. How are you feeling? I've got some water and two Advil's for you here."

I look up. Yep, Patrick. It wasn't a dream. He puts the water on the table with the tablets, then sits on it.

"That's not a seat. It's a table."

He just shrugs at me. "You finished throwing up now?" He takes the bucket away from me and hands me the glass and tablets and watches me take them.

"How long have you been here?"

"About three hours. You went out cold. I had to take your filthy, vomit-covered clothes off, then haul your ass over to the couch. You're no lightweight you know, and who knew you looked like that under your clothes?" he says waving his hand down my body.

Yeah, no one except Evelyn has ever seen this. Shit Evelyn. Dead Evelyn. Here it comes again — the realization she's gone. I need to stop drinking myself into a coma. Every time I come to and realize Evelyn's dead it's like losing her all over again. I can't carry on doing this. I can't keep losing her again and again. It's going to kill me. I already want to be with her, but something deep down is stopping me.

The times when I've come to, I've gotten the sleeping pills out of the medicine cabinet, and gone to the bathroom to fill the tub. Five times that I remember, I filled the tub and sat in it. I had the pills in my hands ready to take. I could quite easily have taken them and then slipped under the water and drowned while in a deep sleep.

Each time something stopped me from doing it. Maybe I'm just a big fucking wimp and couldn't do it. God knows how many times thought about it. Maybe one of these times I will actually do it. Suicide isn't the fucking answer though, you big pussy. Maybe I need to talk to someone?

Get some help. I feel alone, and I know I'm not. Maybe I'm an alcoholic now. I know I do it to forget, but it is literally killing me every time I remember. Patrick is still sitting in front of me. Did he say something and is waiting for me to speak? I just look at him.

"I didn't know you worked out. You've got a body like Hercules hidden under those clothes, but then you look like Clarke Kent. You're not superman, are you?" I can't even smile at him and just shrug. "Do you feel up to a shower? I phoned Arnold while you were out to let him know you were here and he said he was going to come over. I'll clean up some more now you're awake. I didn't want to disturb you before. I figured you needed to sleep it off. Bet your head's banging now, judging by all the empty bottles around this place?"

"You could say that."

"Do me a favor, Patrick. If you find any bottles of booze will you toss them for me? I've got to stop. It's killing me." I try to get up but fall back down. Patrick jumps off the table to help me.

"Thank you, Patrick, I'm really sorry you had to see this."

"Hey, not a problem. Just know you have a lot of people worried about you. You are not on your own in this, no matter what you think. Now get your ass up and get a shower, you stink." I give him a slight smile and head for the shower.

There's a knock on the bathroom door. I don't know how long I've been in here. I washed then broke down on the shower floor. I've been curled up on the floor with the water pounding down on me. It's not hot now, in fact, it's going cold. Arnold comes rushing into the shower and turns off the water. He grabs a towel and throws it around me before helping me up, and walks me into the bedroom to sit on the bed.

"Theon, son. Look at me." My head is hanging in shame. They have their own grief to contend with, and they're looking after my babies; they don't need the burden of me as well. That's why I am better off not here. I'm a dead weight to them, and I can never be a dad to the babies.

"Look at me, son." His voice is firm and demanding. I look up instantly.

"Theon, being holed up here for over a week drinking yourself into oblivion is not the answer. You may forget while you're drunk, but then it all crashes down once you come off that high. This is not the answer. You need help, Theon. Someone to talk to."

I nod at him. "I know," I whisper to him.

He looks relieved. "The first step to getting help is admitting you need it, son. Sonia has a good friend who is a therapist, and she would be willing to talk to you. Will you do it, Theon? For you, for Evelyn, for your babies, and for Sonia and me?"

I nod. I need to do this. If I don't, then who knows how long I will live. I may be nothing, but I shouldn't put Arnold or Sonia through another loss.

"Patrick has cleaned up down there. He left about ten minutes ago and said he would phone you, but to make sure you answer the phone next time, or he will come banging again." He chuckles at that. "He's a good man and a good friend. I know you and Evelyn have been wrapped up with each other since being kids, but you need your friends at times like this, Theon." He stands and squeezes my shoulder. "Get dried, and dressed, and I'll make the coffee."

I nod at him.

I enter the kitchen where Arnold is sitting with his coffee in his hand and staring into space. He doesn't hear me come in, and he jumps, spilling a bit of his coffee on the island.

"Oh god, Theon, I didn't hear you."

"Sorry, Arnold." It was a loaded sorry. Not just for the scaring him but for everything. He nods at me, then nods to the coffee waiting for me. I sit down opposite him.

"I know it's hard, but we have got to discuss the funeral. I take it you haven't been in touch with the funeral home since we were last there sorting stuff out?"

I shake my head no. "Let me get my phone. I haven't checked any messages for god knows how long." I go to the living room, pick the phone up and check the missed calls and messages. There are calls from Arnold, Sonia, Patrick, and Aggie, and another number I don't recognize, which I presume is the funeral home.

"Hello, Mr. Tourney. This is the funeral home taking care of your wife, the late Mrs. Tourney. I just wanted to let you know we now have your wife resting with us. You are welcome to come and see her with your family if you would like to. Please can you give me a ring to confirm the details for the funeral? I have a few dates available for you." I stop the message. I put the phone on the side then lean over the island with my head in my hands, and I cry. It's all I ever seem to fucking do, is cry.

I hear Arnold moving. He's at my side and squeezing my shoulder. "Theon, are you okay, son?" I shake my head then wipe my eyes with my hand and look up at him.

"It was a message from the funeral home letting me know they had Evelyn there resting."

"It's okay, Theon, let it out, son. It's better out than stewing inside you. Now, tell me, what did they say?"

"We can go in and see her if we like. Oh, and visiting hours are two 'til four and only two visitors per bed." Sarcasm isn't really me, and I don't know why I'm so angry. I have all this anger inside me, and I feel like I want to hit something. I put my elbows on the island and put my chin in my hands.

"Sorry, Arnold. I just feel angry. If you and Sonia want to go and see her, you can. I can't do that. I want to remember her how she was, not have a picture of her dead in my head. It's bad enough that I can't shake the image of her in the ER covered in blood. I hope that will fade. They want me to call them to arrange the date of the funeral."

"Theon, don't apologize. There are several stages of grief and anger is one of them. I will see if Sonia wants to go and see Evelyn, and I will go along with whatever she wants. Do you want to phone them back now so we can sort out the date? We need to get this done sooner rather than later." He squeezes my shoulder again. I grab my phone and call the number for the funeral home. We decide on noon on Friday.

"Shit, Arnold, it's real isn't it? The funeral is booked, and, oh god, it's real. She's not coming back. She's gone for good. What do I do now? What do I do without her? Arnold, I don't think I can live without her. I don't think I can go on without her. She was my life. I breathed air because of her. I carried on living because of her. I had no one but Evelyn, you and Sonia."

"Hey…" he pulls me into him as I'm crying and starting to fall apart.

"You still have Sonia and me. We are here for you. You have us, Theon. Please don't forget that. You also have your two beautiful babies. You should see them. Hey, come home and have dinner with us. Come and meet your babies, Theon."

I shake my head vigorously. "No, Arnold, I can't. I'm sorry. I don't know if I ever will be able to. I know you think I'm a heartless bastard, but I can't do it." I step away out of his arms shaking my head.

"Ok, okay, Theon. I can't say I understand. Your babies are the last part of Evelyn, and I for one would be clinging to them. You have your reasons, and I hope seeing the therapist and talking it through with her will help you come around. Let me get some dinner for you, and I want to call Sonia to make that appointment for you. Is that okay?" I nod my head, and we cook some food together. He makes the call to Sonia and asks her to give the therapist my number, so she can call me to make the arrangements. I still don't know how I'm going to get through the next week.

Chapter 35

I DON'T EVEN KNOW WHAT DAY IT IS. It feels like it's been days since the doctor told Alana that Caroline had less than a 3% chance of survival, but it was only yesterday.

I take a quick bathroom break and risk leaving Evelina alone, which I hate, in case she wakes up with no one there.

When I get back, I stand at her door and stare. Alana is sitting there talking to Evelina. I hear her telling Evelina how much her daddy loves her before she stops, and I know she has sensed me at the door. She gets up and turns around.

"Hey," I say to her softly.

"Morning, Theon. Sorry, I was passing, and I saw you weren't here. I know you don't like Evelina being on her own, so I just thought I would talk to her until you came back. My sister just arrived and said she would sit with Caroline so I could get out of the room for a few minutes. I hope you don't mind?"

I tilt my head to the side and look at the beautiful, sad woman in front of me. I'm leaning against the doorframe with my arms folded and one leg crossed over the other, still in my PJ bottoms and a t-shirt. Alana looks down and fiddles with a button on her shirt. She looks so nervous. She reminds me a bit of Evelyn, but they have different hair. Evelyn's was mouse-brown whereas Alana's is blonde. But they are roughly the same height with the same frame. Evelyn had beautiful brown eyes while Alana has stunning pale blue eyes. It's some of Alana's mannerisms that remind me of Evelyn. She looks up at me, and I'm still standing with my head tilted, smiling at her.

I start to walk towards her, and as I approach, I clasp her face in my hands and lean down to kiss her very gently. Her breath hitches, and it makes me hard.

"Thank you," is all I say, pulling her up to me to kiss her again. She can feel how hard I am, but I can't help it. That's what she does to me. I know it's all kinds of wrong, here in my daughter's hospital room, but I have no control. She smiles at me and sheepishly looks down where she can't mistake the tent in my PJ's.

"Sorry. You did that to me. Purely looking at you sometimes does that to me. I don't have much control." I shrug, and she puts her hand to her mouth to stifle a giggle. I love that I can do that to her during this devastating time.

"I'm just going to get some coffee and a wrap. Do you want me to get you something? I know you won't leave until Sonia gets here?"

"Coffee would be great. Thank you. I'm not sure who's coming today or what time. How's Caroline this morning? I take it still no news on a donor?" She looks back at Evelina so she doesn't have to look at me. I know she wants to break down. I turn her and pull her into my chest. "It's okay, baby. Don't bottle it up. Let it out." I feel her crying into my chest.

I hear someone approaching the door and turn my head to see Arnold at the door. He's respecting us by hanging back. "Hey, Arnold is here now. I need to go and wash and change, and then I'll join you for some breakfast. Is that okay?

She wipes her eyes and looks around me to the door. "Hey, Arnold, sorry about that. Just one of my many meltdowns." She looks up at me.

"Caroline is still the same. There's no news on a transplant yet. Yes, I'd love for you to join me for breakfast. I need some light adult conversation. I'll meet you down there, Theon." I nod as she leaves the room saying bye to Arnold.

"How's she holding up?"

"By all accounts, she's doing amazing. She only seems to let her guard down with me. I hurt so bad for her."

"The poor woman. She's really going through it and to be in her own too."

I nod. "Do you mind if I go and grab some breakfast after I've changed?"

"Not at all. You go. Have a change of scenery. I'll call you if there is anything to report."

"Thanks, Arnold." He squeezes my shoulder like he always does as he passes.

I see Alana sitting at a table in the restaurant and head over there.

"Hey. Thanks for the coffee."

We talk about stuff — nothing in particular. She's still never asked me about my job, but I guess she will one day. Just then she gets a text, and I see the panic on her face.

"What is it, Alana?"

"I have to go. It's Susan. She said Caroline isn't good and she's called for Dr. Cassidy."

"Shit, let's go then." We both move quickly, leaving everything on the table. We take the stairs up to ICU rather than wait for a lift. When we reach Caroline's room, it's bedlam.

Alana rushes in. "Oh god, no. What's wrong? What's happening?" Susan rushes to Alana, and they cling to each other watching the doctors and nurses around Caroline. I stay at the door. I can't see what's going on, but I hear someone shout, 'clear' then they shock her. Fuck. I feel like I shouldn't be here, but I can't move. Please, don't let her die. Please don't. She's just a kid. I hear the heart monitoring her heartbeat again. Thank fuck for that. I let out the breath I was holding. Alana is wailing. I move to her. I can't help it. I want to hold her. Susan sees me and lets go of Alana who falls straight into me, clinging to me as I wrap her in my arms.

"Shhh, baby, she's back. Listen to her heart. Can you hear it beating? It's slow but steady. Listen, Alana. Music to our ears, baby." I kiss the top of her head. She stills to listen and stops crying.

"That's her heart beating?" I nod as I rest my chin on her head and watch. Some nurses have left — there's only one now and Dr. Cassidy.

"What happened, Dr.? Is she going to be okay?" I ask.

"She crashed. I'm afraid she's getting weaker. She's sedated, but her body is starting to shut down. I'm so sorry, Mrs. Tudrow. I don't think Caroline is going to be with us for much longer. I'm still praying we get a liver for her today. You might want to have the rest of your family around to say goodbye. I know her siblings are young and that is a decision you need to make." Alana is shaking her head, no. The doctor leaves, and it's just the three of us remaining.

Susan is looking at Caroline, crying. Alana is still clinging to me, crying. I'm holding her to me tightly. "Hey, baby, go and sit with your little angel and talk to her. Hold her hand and talk. Do you want Bailee and Bryan to come in and sit with her?" She shakes her head, no.

"I can't. She's not going yet. I won't give up." She leaves me and goes to sit with Caroline, where her and Susan talk to her.

"You know where I am if you need me." She looks at me and nods.

I walk into Evelina's room. I need to be with my baby. Arnold must see I've been crying

"Everything okay, son? I heard a lot of shouting and nurses rushing about. Was it Caroline?" I nod. "Yeah. The poor kid crashed, but they shocked her and brought her back. The doc said her body is failing now and she doesn't think it will be much longer. God, Arnold. It's so hard. She's a little girl. Why is life so cruel?"

"I don't know, son. Bad things happen to good people all the time. It makes no sense." If that was Evelina, after losing Evelyn, I think it would destroy me beyond repair. Poor Evander would lose his sister and then get a shell of a dad. It's not going to happen. No way. I sit holding her hand and get Harry Potter out to read. I need to steer my mind in another direction. I can't handle where it's heading. I look out of the window to the sky and ask Evelyn in my head to wake our angel up. Please wake her up.

Chapter 36

10 Years Earlier

IT'S THE DAY OF THE FUNERAL, AND I'm a mess. I can't function. I've been dreading this day since we arranged it last week. I've been like a zombie. I tried to stay off the drink, and I did for a few days, but the closer this day got, the worse I got. I drank, and I don't remember much. Arnold came to check on me two days after his last visit, and I was sitting in the cinema room with our stories playing over and over. I hadn't had a drink, but I also hadn't eaten or slept and looked like shit. I was merely existing. I didn't go to bed, get washed, or changed. I think the only time I moved was to use the bathroom. He made me go for a shower while he made me some scrambled eggs on toast.

The day after that I went to the liquor store and bought a box of a dozen bottles of Fireball. I went home and drank myself stupid. I don't know how long I was there, all I remembered was Arnold somehow putting me under the outdoor shower, as I was passed out near the pool. I know he thought that I'd tried to drown myself again. In all honesty, I probably did, but I don't remember anything. He said I was wet and cold, and my lips were turning blue. It has been three days since Arnold was last here.

Once I sobered up, he made me phone the therapist and arrange to see her, which I did yesterday. I did it for Arnold. I could see the toll this was taking on him. He not only had to help Sonia with two newborn babies, but he had to keep an eye on me.

He drove me to the therapist's office and waited for me. She was a nice lady. Probably about Sonia's age, very smart, her name was Deborah. She wanted to know about me, and my feelings. Was I angry, hurt, did I feel betrayed, because Evelyn had left me? She told me I was going through the Kübler-Ross model. I looked at her like she had two heads and she smiled. She explained it was the correct term for the five stages of grief:

Denial - definitely having this still.

Anger - definitely having this still.

Bargaining - no idea what that is.

Depression – probably.

Acceptance - nowhere near ready for this.

I said there was also a number six: guilt. I told her it was my fault for getting Evelyn pregnant. She tried to make me look at it from a different perspective, but I couldn't. Not yet. We seemed to talk for a long time, and when I left, after arranging to see her on Saturday after the funeral, I admitted to Arnold that I did actually feel a bit better having talked about how I was feeling. That is until I got home and broke down because I remembered it was the funeral the next day. Arnold, who I could tell was having a hard time himself, sat with me on the couch, hugging me.

I'm barely functioning at this point. I'm sick to death of people coming up to me and saying how sorry they are for my loss. I swear I'm going to punch someone soon.

Arnold and Sonia have been moving me around, sandwiched between them. They've both been crying and finding this extremely hard. Me, I can't feel anything. I need a drink. I know that much. I didn't hear what was said at the service. Arnold got up to speak and broke down. I didn't move. Now,

I'm standing around the graveside while someone is waffling on and on, and I'm just staring blankly at the casket in front of me.

My Evelyn is in that box. Oh my god, she's in there, in front of me, it's just hit me! I need to get her out.

"NO!" I suddenly shout and throw myself on the ground next to the casket. "I need to open it. Get her out. She won't be able to breathe. QUICK, GET HER OUT OF THE FUCKING THING!" I scream, clawing at the brass screws on the top of the box. I need a tool to open it.

"Quick, get her out. She can't breathe. Help me, someone. Help me get her out." I'm crying hard. I don't know if they understand me. Sonia is wailing, and I turn to the noise. Arnold is frozen, holding her, both looking at me like I've gone mad.

"Why are you just standing there? It's your fucking daughter —my wife, help me get her out. HELP ME" I scream again. I feel someone trying to get me up off the grass, and I look up at Patrick.

"Come on, Theon. Let's get you up. There's nothing you can do for Evelyn now. Look at me. She's gone. She's not coming back. This is your time to say goodbye to her. Theon, look at me. Do you hear me?" I nod slightly looking back at the casket.

"She's gone. It's time for her to rest in peace. It's why we are all here to say goodbye to her. Do you understand? Time to let go and say goodbye to Evelyn. Goodbye but never forgotten." I break as his words sink in. He holds me up stopping me from falling. I'm clinging to him, a broken man. I don't know if I ever will accept she's gone. My Evelyn.

"Why can't it be me in there? Why can't I be in there with her? Fuck, she's gone for good, hasn't she? She's never coming back. All this time I hoped it was a nightmare, but it's not is it?" I look at Patrick, at Sonia and Arnold, and Aggie and lots of other people from the office, then back to Patrick. "She's really gone?"

He nods at me with tears streaming down his face. I turn to the casket and drop to my knees. "I love you so much. You're my whole world, baby. To infinity and beyond, remember, Evelyn. We are our firsts and lasts, baby, our firsts and lasts. You've given me so many best days of my life, but you've also given me the worst day of my life. I will never have another best day of my life because you're not in my life to give it to me. I love you, Evelyn. Only ever you, baby. It's not goodbye. It will never be goodbye. This is until we meet again. Sleep tight, my angel. I love you." I sit on my haunches with my head bowed. The casket starts being lowered into the ground. I cry so hard that I can barely breathe, and I'm gulping for breath. I can't see through the tears. I hear movement. Arnold and Sonia are throwing roses onto the casket. Sonia hands me one. I kiss it and throw it down the hole. I can't see her anymore.

"See you soon, my angel. Infinity and beyond." I sit there for what seems like ages. Patrick helps me up, and when I look around everyone has gone. They all left me to say my goodbyes.

After the wake, at some hotel near the funeral home that I hate with a passion, Patrick takes me home. I didn't drink, and I just stayed out of everyone's way. I didn't want to hear, 'I'm sorry for your loss' one more time. Patrick is staying with me tonight. I don't think anyone trusts me to be alone. Maybe they are right not to.

I head outside and perch on a lounger by the pool. Evelyn used to love it when I was like this in just my trousers, my shirt undone at the top, my tie dangling loose down each side. She used to say I should be on the cover of Vogue or some big shot fashion magazine. I used to laugh at her and tell her she was just biased cause she was married to me.

I lay back on the lounger. I don't even know what time it is. The sun is still out although it's getting lower, which suggests it's evening. I hear Patrick come outside. He puts two cups on the table next to me then sits on the lounger next to the table.

It's black coffee. Black but very sweet, as I like it. Evelyn used to go mad at the four sugars I used to put in my coffee. Patrick makes it with four as he knows me.

"Thanks, Patrick. Not just for the coffee, but for being there for me."

"Anytime, Theon. Anytime." That's all he says. He grabs his coffee and sits back, mirroring me. We sit in a comfortable silence. The view we have from here is the L.A. skyline. It's one of the things Evelyn loved about the house. We could sit our here on an evening, cuddle on a lounger with wine, and just watch the sun setting behind L.A. It's an amazing view. It hurts so much thinking that we will never do stuff like that again. That we will never experience the little things like this that we took for granted. I feel the tears slowly trickle down my cheeks, but I'm smiling. Actually smiling for the first time in what feels like forever. Why, I have no fucking clue. I just buried my wife, and I'm sitting here smiling.

I think it may be relief that the day is over. Not because she's gone because that will hurt till the day I die, but because I said goodbye today, and I think I finally realize she's not coming back. That she's gone forever.

"You okay?" Patrick asks.

"I think so, Patrick. I think so." I wipe my cheeks with my hands, grab my coffee, and sip it slowly.

It's almost a week since I said bye to Evelyn, and I haven't had a drink of alcohol. I decided to get a tattoo. I found this perfect colorful sea turtle tattoo and I went and got that done on my back. It's my way of having a piece of Evelyn with me permanently. It's perfect.

I have more meetings with Deborah, my therapist. I have to admit She's been great, just being able to talk to her about Evelyn has helped me so much. I think I'm finally accepting that I wasn't to blame for losing Evelyn. We've been talking for about thirty minutes when she hits me with what I had subconsciously been waiting for.

"Have you thought any more about seeing your babies, Theon?" The question I was dreading, but I know I've got to do this. The truth is, I have been thinking about them. I don't feel hate like I did when it happened, which is an improvement. How could anyone really hate two babies they haven't even met? That are his own flesh and blood?

"I have actually, yes."

"What have you been thinking? Do you still hold them responsible?"

I shake my head no. "I stopped blaming them really when I started blaming myself. I knew deep down it wasn't their fault, but I couldn't bring myself to actually say it. I just wanted someone to blame. First, it was them, and then it was me. But I hated myself so much for causing them to lose their mother that I just thought they are better off without me."

"And now?"

I look at her and shrug. "The longer I stay away, the harder it is. Now I'm scared that if I see them, it will send me right back to loathing."

"Them or yourself?"

"Me, them, both. I don't know. I do know I don't want to feel like that again."

"You said you felt hatred for them. Is that still the case?"

I shake my head no. "No, what kind of man would that make me. How could I hate anything that Evelyn and I created out of love — my own flesh and blood?"

It suddenly hits me, like a lightning bolt. In the babies, I now have blood relations. I wasn't on my own. Not that I ever was with Evelyn, but I didn't have any blood relative left after losing my grandma. Now I had flesh and blood that was all mine. I burst into tears with this new revelation. Deborah passes me a tissue.

"What are you feeling, Theon?"

"Love, I think. I just realized they are my own flesh and blood. Until I said it to you, it never hit me before. It's what Arnold has been saying, but I didn't hear him. We created them. They are part Evelyn and me. But, I—" I stop.

Can I look after them?

"Go on."

"I'm scared."

"That's a natural reaction. You're scared of the unknown. What else are you scared of?"

I think about what I was going to say. "Being a dad. Looking after two babies on my own. Can I do it, would they be better off without me?"

"They have already lost their momma, Theon, why would they be better off with no daddy as well? Do you think every parent, every new mom and dad have the same worries? Of course they do. Tell me, Theon, you grew up with no mom or dad, and just your grandma. Didn't you ever wish you had a mom or dad as well?"

Could I do that to them? Knowing what I went through by not having a mom or a dad. They would be in the same boat as me, being brought up by grandparents. I don't think I can do that to them. I realize that I'm starting to feel something for our babies. They are a part of Evelyn — the last part of her. Oh god, what am I doing to them.

"Theon, are you okay? What are you thinking?"

"I need to see my babies. I need to go and meet them and tell them I'm their daddy. Tell them I'm sorry for abandoning them when they needed me. That I will look after them and love them unconditionally like a daddy should do."

I have to see my babies.

Chapter 37

Present

I WAKE UP WITH A START. It's only 5.30 a.m., so a noise must have woken me, but I'm not sure what it was. I close my eyes and try to sleep, then I hear it. I hear what I've been waiting for all this time.

"Daddy, are you there?" I dive out of my cot and over to Evelina's bedside. I look down, but she looks like she's asleep. Fuck is my mind playing tricks on me. I stroke her cheek — she looks so peaceful. I have hold of her hand, and she moves it slightly trying to grip my hand and slowly opens her eyes.

"Hey, poppet, my little angel. How are you feeling?" I'm about fit to burst inside, but I don't want to scare her.

"Can you speak, baby. Nod your head if it hurts." She nods. She fucking nods. She understands me. She is perfect. I'm so relieved, and I know there are tears falling down my cheeks.

"Daddy," she croaks. I get the jug of water and pour a beaker for her and put it to her lips. Her mouth must be so dry.

"Small sips, baby girl. Just wet your mouth and lips." I press the buzzer for the nurses.

"Daddy, why are you crying? Are you hurt, Daddy?"

"No, poppet, just so happy to see you awake, baby. You've been asleep for a very long time."

"Have I? Was that because the surgery was a long one? I don't think I hurt. Was I really brave?" She starts coughing. I lift her up slightly so I can rub her back.

"Shhh, baby, don't try to speak too much just yet. You've been the bravest big girl in the whole wide world. Daddy is so proud of you. I love you to the moon and back." I lean down and hug her face to me as I sit next to her on the bed. I can't believe she's woken up finally, and she's fine. No brain damage. She even remembers going for surgery.

Just then a nurse comes in. "Oh my, little one. You decided to join us again, did you? It's so good to see those beautiful eyes of yours, finally." Evelina looks up at me with a bit of a frown on her forehead, not really knowing what's going on. The nurse checks Evelina over and then Dr. Davis comes hurtling through the door. I've never had much to do with him. He's the night doctor, so I'm usually asleep.

"Well, look at you, Miss Evelina. So lovely to meet you." She looks at me again.

"Hello."

"Do you mind if I sit with you and just ask you a few questions?" She looks at me for confirmation.

"It's okay. This is Doctor Davis." I nod at her.

She sits up and puts her hands on her legs. "Yep sure."

"Ok, then. Can you tell me your full name?"

"Evelina Rose Tourney." She looks at me as if to say, 'Is he silly, Daddy?' I smile at her. I feel like I'm dreaming.

"Very good. Now, a couple of things. Do you know where you are and do you know how old you are?"

"You're silly, Doctor. Of course, I know. I'm in the hospital, and I'm ten years old. I have a twin brother who is also ten, Evander, but he is older than me." Dr. Davis can't help it, and he laughs loudly. I laugh with him because god, I love her so much.

"How much older is he?"

"Four minutes. Can you believe that? Why didn't I come out first so I could be the eldest?" She crosses her arms as if in protest and pouts. I lean in and kiss her head. She is adorable.

"Now, a serious question. Do you have any pain anywhere? Like on your body, in your head, anywhere at all?" She thinks about it and by the way she's sitting up and folding her arms, I'd say no, which is fantastic.

"Just my hand, where this thing is sticking to me and this thing hanging down." She points to the cannula in her hand and the tube attached which has been keeping her hydrated and fed throughout her coma.

"That's good, Miss Evelina. Just those and nothing else?" She thinks again and shakes her head no.

"Except my throat feels scratchy, and I'm hungry too." She never ceases to amaze me. She is so resilient. The doctor notions with his head for me to follow him out of the door. I really don't want to leave her. I'm terrified I'll wake up, and it will all be a dream, or I'll come back in, and she'll have gone back into a coma. I kiss her head and tell her I won't be a minute, and the doctor says goodbye and what a pleasure to meet her. She lies back down and watches us walk out of the door.

We stop just outside. "Well, Mr. Tourney, she seems to be just fine. No memory loss and no pain. Given the amount of time in a coma, she has healed just fine. I will make sure Dr. Cassidy knows she's awake as soon as she comes in. She will be so pleased, and I think she may want to do a couple of tests. That's one amazing little girl you have there, Mr. Tourney."

"I know and thank you." I'm beaming. I'm so happy. I rush back into her room to make sure she's still awake.

I send a silent thank you up to Evelyn. I'm convinced she did this. Made our angel sleep all this time so she could heal fully and not feel any of the pain from surgery or the sickness from the chemo. I'd stake my life on it.

She's asleep when I walk in, but I stroke her cheek and she smiles. She's never done that in the coma, so I know she's out of it. I crawl on the bed next to her, needing to be close and holding her. "You have no idea, little one, how happy you have made your daddy. I was so worried about you, poppet. We've all been worried. I love you and Evander with everything I am, baby. You have just made this one of the best days of my life," I whisper. I don't want to wake her even though she's been asleep for weeks.

I must have fallen asleep next to her when I feel a hand shake my arm. It's our usual morning nurse. I wake and then it hits me like a ton of bricks. The dream I had about Evelina waking up. Oh fuck why? Why do that to me? I look at Evelina, expecting her to be in a coma still, as she has been every morning, but she's lying there with the biggest fucking smile on her face.

"You snore, Daddy. You woke me up a few times with loud grunts." She snorts like a pig showing me how I sound. I'm in shock. It's real. She did wake up. I wrap her in my arms and hug her.

"Poppet, I love you so much. I thought I'd dreamt that you woke up. But you did. You've made daddy the happiest man alive. Do you know that, baby?" She can't shake her head because I'm hugging her too hard. I let go.

"I did wake up, Daddy. Like I normally do after a sleep. I love you too." We just smile at each other. She has no idea how long she's been asleep.

"I need to phone your grandma and grandpa and Evander so they can come in and see you." I get up and let the nurse do all the checks. I go and stand just outside the door, and I phone Sonia.

"Good morning, Theon. Is there something you need me to bring for you?"

"She's awake." It's all I can manage to say. I have an enormous lump in my throat and tears start flowing down my cheeks.

"Sweetie, did you say she's awake?"

I can't answer. "Theon, are you there? Theon."

I nod, but she can't see me. I try to clear my throat. "Yes," I manage.

"Oh, thank the lord. Thank you. Thank you. ARNOLD, EVANDER!" she screams, and I can hear her running

"She's awake. Our princess is awake." I hear her say then Arnold comes on the phone.

"Theon, is that you, son? Sonia's in tears. Is it right? Is she awake?"

I'm nodding again. "Yes. Yes. Arnold. Can you all get down here? Bring Evander, please." It's all I can manage. The emotions swimming around me right now, the relief I feel like the weight of the world has been lifted from my shoulders, are just too much. I fall back against the wall then slide down to the floor.

A couple of nurses pass, and one stops. "Are you okay, sir?" I nod and smile.

I must look like an idiot, sitting here crying and smiling. "My baby woke up," is all I say. She smiles back at me before they carry on. I hear more footsteps and look up to see Dr. Cassidy almost running down the corridor. She stops in front of me.

"I was just told Evelina is awake. Mr. Tourney. That is the most wonderful news. And Dr. Davis said all seems perfectly fine with her." I just smile and nod again. I wipe my eyes then stand up.

"I can't believe it. I keep thinking I dreamt it. I have to keep checking it's not a dream."

"Come on. Let's go back in, and I can speak to her." We both go in, and Evelina is sitting up in bed. The TV is on, and she's cuddling her new teddies, Lotso bear and Sulley, along with Stitch and the turtle.

"Oh Dr. Cassidy, I'm sorry I thought Evelina was in here, but I don't see her. All I see are teddies. Maybe she left to go for a run," I joke then hear the most beautiful sound in the world that melts my heart.

"I'm here, Daddy, silly. Look at my new Lotso and Sulley. I love them, Daddy." She squeals trying to hug the three teddies all at once.

"Well, look at you, Evelina. It's so lovely to see you awake."

"Everyone sleeps. I must have been tired after my surgery. Did it happen, Daddy? I don't feel any pain. Or haven't they done it yet?"

"Well, poppet." I sit next to her on the bed and tuck her under my arm. "You did have the surgery, yes. But you were asleep more than a few hours, and you have healed all up, so you didn't feel any of the pain. It's a good thing in a way, but daddy didn't like it."

"Why?"

"Well, because I didn't get to speak to you for a long time, or hear you laughing and giggling, or see your beautiful smile and your beautiful eyes. However, I didn't miss your sass." I smile so hard at her, she grins at me and pulls her tongue out at my remark. That's my girl.

"So how long did I sleep for, Daddy, if I'm all healed?" I look to Dr. Cassidy, and she nods slightly.

"Well, it was four weeks." I see the shock slowly appear on her face as she registers what I just said.

"Silly, Daddy, no one can sleep for four weeks. They need to eat and use the bathroom and go to school and …" She looks up at me and realizes I'm serious as she's reeling off the things she has to do.

"So did I not go to school for four weeks?" I shake my head no

"Aww shucks, Daddy. I missed having four weeks of school, and I didn't know about it." She lifts her shoulders up and drops them in a huff being very dramatic and pouts as she sulks. I burst out laughing. That is the sweetest thing ever. I pull her into my chest laughing.

"Oh, poppet, I love you so much, and I've missed you, sweetheart." I explain how she's also had chemo and how her body kept her asleep to allow her to heal.

We are watching TV when we hear running before the door bursts open, and Evander practically leaps onto the bed, pushing me out of the way to get to Evelina. He grabs her and kisses her all over her face.

"Eww, Vander, that's gross. Stop it. Stop kissing me." She's trying to push him away.

"God, I missed you, Lina. I missed you so much. I was so scared. I didn't think you were going to wake up."

"Well, I did, Vander, and I'm all better now. I guess I missed you too, I suppose." She hugs him back, and my heart just melts. Sonia comes barreling in the room, followed by Arnold and that's it, I'm kicked off the bed so they can all get in there and lavish Evelina with affection. We all missed her. I grab Arnold's elbow.

"I'm just going to use the bathroom and wash up then I'm going to pop in to see Alana while you're all here making a fuss of Evelina. Dr. Cassidy is really pleased with everything and even talked about us going home in a day or two."

"No worries, son, we're not going anywhere. You go."

I wash up then head to see Alana. As I get to Caroline's room, the door is slightly ajar, and I can hear Alana crying, "No, Caroline, no, Caroline, please no, no, no." She sounds in pain, so I tap very quietly and edge the door open. The sight before me kills me. Alana is on the bed, holding a very limp Caroline in her arms. She's rocking her back and forth and hugging her to her chest. Caroline's arm is dangling down, lifeless. She's gone. The poor kid has gone. I'm heartbroken for Alana. There are no monitors beeping, so a nurse or doctor must have turned them off after she passed away. Alana looks up at me, still rocking with Caroline in her arms and tears streaming down her face.

"She's gone, Theon, my baby girl has gone. They didn't get a liver for her. What am I going to do? She's gone." I have no words as I watch her hugging and rocking backward and forwards. I walk over, and I hug her to my chest.

"I'm so sorry, Alana. So very sorry. God, I wish I could have helped. Baby, I'm so so sorry." She nods in my chest, acknowledging me. I don't know what to say. I know when I lost Evelyn, I got sick of all the 'I'm sorry's', but all I can do is comfort her. I feel so bad that she's in here on her own coping with this. What a shit thing to happen. Good news and bad news all in the space of a couple of hours. Life sucks. So I stay and comfort her by hugging her while she hugs Caroline, and I silently cry for the loss of this amazing little girl.

Chapter 38

10 Years Earlier

I CAN'T GET OUT OF DEBORAH'S OFFICE QUICK enough after finding the courage to say the words out loud – that I wanted to see my babies, that's all I can focus on. I thank her for all her help. I don't say it, but I don't think I will need to see her again.

I run to my car and sit for a minute. I just want to rush over to Sonia's and see them, but my heart is beating out of my chest, and I need to calm myself down before I attempt to drive. I sit and rest my head on the steering wheel, and I feel the tears slowly trickle down my cheeks. I'm nervous, but excited and scared. So very fucking scared. I can't believe how selfish I've been. It's all been about me. I know Sonia and Arnold have been suffering from Evelyn's death, but then they've had to look after my babies too because I was wallowing in self-pity at MY loss. Mine, me, myself and I. As if it was just my loss. Not anyone else's. Not Sonia's, Arnold's or the babies'. What a fucking selfish prick I've been, and I couldn't see it at all.

"I'm sorry, Evelyn, please forgive me," I say out loud. I calm down, wipe my eyes, turn the car on, pull out and head to Sonia and Arnold's house.

I pull into the drive and park by the garage doors. My nerves are shot, but I approach the door. As I go to knock, the door flies opens to reveal Sonia there, crying.

"What's wrong? What's happened? Is it Arnold? Is something wrong with the babies?" She shakes her head no then wipes her eyes on a handkerchief she has up her sleeve.

"Sonia, you're scaring the shit out of me. What's wrong?"

"Oh, sweetie, I'm just so happy to see you here. Every day, I've prayed you would come." She pulls me to her and pulls my head down to kiss my forehead — then she hugs me. I hug her back, taking the comfort. It puts me at ease. I'm ready to do this.

"Thank you, Sonia, for everything. For being patient with me and for believing in me. Thank you."

"I knew you would come in your own time, Theon. You had to be ready for this." I nod, hanging my head in shame. "Are you ready to meet your beautiful babies, Theon?"

I nod, all the mixed feelings are there: nerves and fear. I'm terrified and feel as though I'm going to panic. She must see it in my face as she grabs my hands. "You are their daddy. It's understandable to be scared and nervous, but they will love you unconditionally, no matter what. You will fall in love when you see them. Come on, Theon, they are both awake and very bright after their nap. Don't be afraid."

We walk, hand in hand toward the rear of the house to the study. I stop dead at the door and freeze. I can hear them. I can hear gurgling noises. I swear there's a giggle as well.

"Grandpa is tickling one of them by the sounds of it. I'd guess it's your daughter. She's getting to be a right little character. Your son is so good. He hardly ever cries."

I just stare at the door. Can I do this? Sonia pushes the door open enough for me to see into the room. Arnold is on the floor and in front of him are two tiny humans. They are on a blanket, one in pink, kicking her legs and arms about as Arnold is tickling her gently. The other in blue, also kicking, but silently. I stand in awe, my heart melting.

I'm walking towards them before I realize I'm moving. Then I'm staring down at the two most beautiful, precious little things I've ever seen. I fall to my knees just to the side of Arnold, and I break. All the guilt, remorse, and sadness mixed with elation, love, awe, and excitement is too much for me. I feel broken inside. How could I have stayed away from them? How could I have blamed these two precious things? How could I do that to them, to me, to Evelyn? I've missed the first month of their lives. I will never get that back, and I don't think I will ever forgive myself for it.

I look at them. The pure love I feel is immense. My daughter has stopped and has turned her head slightly towards me. I'm crying hard, looking at her perfect features. She looks just like Evelyn. She's got her eyes and her mouth. She is gorgeous.

"Hello, poppet," my voice breaks trying to speak.

"I'm your daddy. You are my little Evelina." I hear a gasp behind me and turn to see Sonia crying.

"Oh, what a beautiful name, Theon. Did you just decide on that or was it one you and Evelyn had already picked?"

"We had two names for each. We were going to see which name fit first, but I can see straight out she's an Evelina." I hold my finger out, and she grabs onto it, her tiny little fingers wrapping around my big finger. Just then my son makes a noise, and I look at him and again hold my finger out. He too grabs it with his tiny hand.

"Hello there, Evander. I'm your daddy too, my little man. So pleased to meet you." I smile down at the two of them. They are perfect. We created the two most amazing, gorgeous little people ever. Evander looks a bit like me but still has the look of Evelyn.

"Theon, what beautiful names. Finally, they have names. Thank you. Here, do you want me to show you how to pick them up?"

"Yes, please, Sonia. I'm terrified. Look how tiny and fragile they are! What if I hurt them? Look at the size of my hands. I could hurt them."

"You won't, sweetie. Here, let me show you."

I spend the day with Sonia who shows me everything she can, and I stay with Sonia and Arnold for a week until the day arrives to take them home. We keep one of the nannies on, and she is going to stay and help me through the day, thankfully. This is one of the scariest things I have ever done in my life. These two perfect tiny humans are going to solely depend on me. As I drive off with the twins in my car, I can see Sonia wiping her eyes. I know Sonia and Arnold will miss them, but I'm sure they will be relieved they can be normal grandparents now and spoil them. It's now my turn to step up and be the best daddy I can possibly be to these two precious beings. They deserve it.

Chapter 39

ALANA LEFT THE HOSPITAL RELUCTANTLY yesterday with Susan after the mortuary came to collect Caroline. My heart broke for her, and I didn't have it in me to tell her the good news about Evelina.

I hugged her, burying her face in my chest so she couldn't watch them take Caroline away. It took a while to calm her down afterward. I sat in the chair with her on my lap tucked into my chest. I didn't speak, just held her. There wasn't anything I could say. I offered to drive her home, but she said Susan was on her way to pick her up. I waited until Susan arrived, then gave her a hug and kissed her mouth. I held her face in my hands making her look at me. "You need anything, and I mean anything at all, you ring me. No matter what time of day. Even if it's just to talk. I'm here for you, Alana. You don't have to be alone. Do you hear me, baby?"

She nodded and held my hands, then she kissed my palm. "Thank you, Theon. Thank you for being there for me throughout this. You will never know what it meant to me." She was talking like this was it. Like I wouldn't see her again. Like hell I wouldn't.

"Hey, this isn't goodbye, you know? Do you hear me? I will come and see you." She nodded, stood on her tiptoes and kissed my cheek before gathering the bags of Caroline's things and heading out with Susan. It broke my heart seeing her like that.

All Evelina's scans come back clear, and we all sigh with relief, elated that Dr. Cassidy says we can go home. Evelina has to take it easy for the next seven days. No running, jumping, dancing, boyfriends, to which Evelina pulls her face in disgust with no fighting or arguing. She has to have complete rest, no matter how bored she is.

We pack everything up, get Evelina dressed and head out. She's able to walk, but Evander keeps hold of her from the hospital door to the car. Sonia and Arnold follow us home. It feels like years since we have all been home. Evelina has to go back to see Dr. Cassidy for a final check-up, and as long as everything is still okay, then she can go back to school. I'm not sure if she's upset or happy at the thought.

We soon get into a routine. Sonia or Arnold come and sit with Evelina, and I take Evander to school. I owe him my attention for a bit. He's been a star throughout this whole ordeal and never once moaned. The first day, after I drop him at school, I pull into a restaurant car park to phone Alana. She doesn't pick up. I try a few times after that, waiting a few minutes in between, but no answer. On the last try, I leave a message.

"Hey, baby, it's Theon. I just wanted to check in on you and see how you were doing and if you needed me to do anything for you. Can you ring me when you get the message, so I can hear you and make sure you're okay? Speak to you soon." I head home, praying the phone will ring, but it doesn't. All day, I wait for the call but nothing. When the Evs have gone to bed I text Alana, and I sit with the phone on my knee, waiting for a text back, but nothing.

The next day after dropping Evander, I do the same thing, and she still doesn't pick up. I'm torn. I need to be with Evelina, but I also feel I needed to be with Alana. I want to see Alana. I want her to know I'm here for her. I decide to get back to Evelina and spend the day with my angel. She's on complete rest still, but I ask Sonia if she wouldn't mind spending more time with her tomorrow, and I will go and see Alana.

The next day I do the same thing. Drop Evander off then pull into the car park at the restaurant to call Alana. She still doesn't pick up. She's definitely avoiding me. She doesn't know we are home from the hospital, and she doesn't even know Evelina woke up as far as I'm aware. I feel bad.

Last night, I asked Patrick if he could find an address for Alana for me, which somehow he did. As Sonia agreed to stay with Evelina for the day, I decide to visit Alana. If she doesn't want to see me, then that's fine, but I need her to know I'm here for her.

She lives about thirty minutes away from me. As I approach, I can see she lives in a nice neighborhood and has a lovely family home. Not huge, but enough for them. There is only one car on the driveway. I don't know if it's Alana's, as I have no idea what she drives. In all honesty, what do we really know about each other? I pull into the drive and park at the side of the other car in front of the double garage.

I pass a window as I approach the front door, but I can't see inside as the curtains are closed. I knock on the door, and I wait. Nothing. I knock again and wait. Still nothing. Shit, what now? Maybe she's staying with her sister. That must be it! Alana, Bailee, and Bryan must be staying with Susan. There's no noise in the house. I knock once more just to be sure. Nothing. I head back to my car. Just as I pass the window, I see the curtain suddenly close. Well, someone is home.

"Alana, baby, are you in there? It's me, Theon. I just want to see you and make sure you're okay." I peer into the window, but I can't see anything. I tap on the window.

"Alana, please open the door." I head back to the door and knock. Nothing. I come out of the porch and head around the side to see if I can get around the back. There is a gate at the side of the garage. I try it, and it opens. I cautiously walk down the path to the back of the house. It's quite a small garden, but it's enclosed and tidy. I see a flowerbed toward the back with lots of different colorful flowers.

There is a door I see leads to a utility room. There are also sliding doors that lead onto a small terrace. I walk up to the doors and look in. I see a living area with a couch and the kitchen to the side.

Alana is slumped on the couch with her head back, looking up to the ceiling. She looks like she's in PJ's. Maybe I woke her. I tap lightly on the door, trying not to startle her, but she jumps at the noise and looks straight at me. It breaks me. She looks haunted. She's pale, hollow, and her eyes are dead. She doesn't smile like she usually does when she sees me.

She looks like she's going to just ignore me when she puts her head back on the back of the couch, but after a short breath, she starts to move and gets up and walks towards me at the doors. "What do you want, Theon?" Her hostility is a shock. I wasn't expecting that. She doesn't even open the doors.

"Alana, baby. I just want to see you. To make sure you're okay. Can I?"

"I'm fine, Theon. Thanks for checking," she says cutting me off. Then she turns and starts to walk away.

"Alana, can I come in, please?"

She stops and drops her head. She has her back to me, but I can see her shoulders slump. She turns back and comes to the doors, flicks the lever, and slides a door open. "Look, Theon, it's nice of you to drop by, but I'm okay." She looks anything but okay. She's like a robot with no feeling. Her face stays stoic.

"Hey, I've been there. I know you're not fine, or okay. You can't kid a kidder, Alana. Now, can I come in, please? I want to see you?" She turns and heads back to the couch but leaves the door open. I take that as my invitation to come in. She sits back down with her legs under her. It's so quiet.

"Where is everyone?"

"Bailee and Bryan are staying with Susan for a couple of days. I thought it would be best if they weren't around me at the moment."

I stand in front of her with my hands in my jeans pockets. I'm rubbish at this stuff, but I remember Sonia, Arnold, and Patrick all helping me when I was grieving. I crouch down in front of her so we are eye level. "Baby, don't push them away. You need them, and they need you. You all need to grieve together. They will be hurting so badly right now, losing their sister, and then having their momma push them away. What must they be thinking? Alana, sweetheart, they lost their dad, now their sister, don't let them lose their momma too. The same for you. You lost your husband and now your daughter, don't lose the twins now when you all need each other."

I stroke her cheek with my thumb, wiping away the tears that are slowly running down.

I pull her onto my lap and lean her head into my chest, and I hug her.

"Let it go, baby. Let it all out on me. I'm here for you. You are not on your own. You have two adorable kids that need you and a sister to comfort you." She cries hard, and it soon turns into sobs that leave her heaving to catch her breath. I hug her and stroke her back. We stay like that for some time until she calms down.

She lifts her head to look at me. "What is it about you, Theon? I just let it all go whenever I'm in your arms. With the twins and Susan, I feel I have to be strong, but I can't, that's why I pushed them away. I don't want them to hate me because they think I don't care, but I don't want them to see me fall apart like this. You know Bailee shouted at me yesterday, asking me why I wasn't crying for Caroline like they were. I just told her to get to her room. I was emotionless. You come, and I just break."

"They won't hate you, baby. Everyone feels grief differently, but you are allowed to show emotion. You don't have to be strong all the time. It's okay to break. If you all break together, you will all help in the healing process. I know you've had to go through this before, and they were all very young, but they understand more now. I've been so worried about you. I've left you messages, but you never got back to me."

"I'm sorry. You have enough to worry about with Evelina. I don't want to add to your burden and worries."

"She's home, Alana. She woke up that day. It was early in the morning. I was on my way to tell you when I found you with Caroline."

"Oh, that's wonderful, Theon. Is she okay, though? No damage or any effects from the coma?"

I shake my head no. "All normal. She's just like she was before she got sick." I smile but try not to be too happy given the circumstances. "Hey, have you eaten or drunk anything?"

She looks down, and I know she hasn't. "Right, let's go into the kitchen and see what MasterChef Theon can cook up for you."

I look in the fridge and see some milk, eggs, cheese, and ham. Omelet it is. Perfect if she hasn't eaten for a while.

"Baby, why don't you go have a shower and get changed while I make you one of my famous omelets? Then, if you feel like it, we could drive over to Susan's to see them all. Let them see you're okay." I put my finger under her chin to tilt her head up so she looks at me, and I gently kiss her lips. She nods okay. "Are you sure? You should be at home with Evelina?"

"It's fine. Sonia is spending the day with her doing some girly pampering hair and nails thing. She's got a few more days of complete rest then she should be okay to start back at school. She's done amazing, Alana. You wouldn't even know she had cancer a few weeks ago."

Alana steps away from me. "I'll go for that shower." Shit, she looks hurt. I shouldn't have said that. Fuck, I need to be careful.

I don't start to cook the omelets until I hear the hairdryer turn off. I'm cooking them in two separate pans so we can eat together. Alana appears, looking so much better. I work out the coffee machine and pour us both a cup. She sits at the table in the corner near the back door and nurses the mug in her hands while staring out of the door window.

"Alana, can I ask, where are you up to with funeral arrangements?"

She doesn't look at me or even acknowledge I spoke. I dish up the omelets and go and sit down opposite her.

She looks up. "I'm supposed to go to the funeral home today to finalize everything and decide on the date. I couldn't do it the other day, and to be honest, I'm not sure I still can. With Bailee and Bryan not being in school, it would mean me going on my own with Susan looking after them. There's no way I would take them."

"I can go with you."

She looks straight into my eyes, looking for what, I don't know. "You would do that for me?" I look at her. "Of course I would, Alana. I told you, I'm here for you, no matter what. Let's eat our brunch," I say looking at the time, and noticing it's 11 a.m. "We can go to the funeral home, sort out everything for Caroline, and then we go to Susan's, and you can spend time with Bailee and Bryan. Deal?" She nods her head yes and tucks into her omelet.

"Mmmm, Theon this is lovely. Best omelet I've ever had. Thank you. Thank you for everything. I'm so sorry I was shutting you out. I didn't want to be another burden for you with Evelina being poorly. I'm also sorry for the way I reacted before my shower. I am truly happy she has pulled through. I'm happy for you and for her. She's an amazing little girl. Just like her daddy." I stare at her, but she puts her head down and doesn't look at me. I reach across for her hand, and I squeeze it.

We go to the funeral home to sort out the details for Caroline. I know how hard this is and why she was putting it off. Choosing caskets, songs, order of service etc. is not enjoyable. She sorts out the date for five days time. I will make sure I am there to support her.

After an emotive time at the funeral home, we head to Susan's, where there is more emotion as Alana hugs Bailee and Bryan and they all cry, hugging each other. I leave them in the living room and head to the kitchen with Susan.

"How did you manage this, Theon? Getting Alana out of the house and bringing her here? I'm so grateful to you."

"She just needed a reality check, I think. I've been ringing her and leaving messages, which she never returned so decided to go and see her. She was in a bit of a state, but we talked." We talk while Alana spends time with the twins, and I tell her about the funeral arrangements.

A little while later Alana comes into the kitchen. "Susan, I'm going to take them home with me. They want to come back home. I'm sorry for pushing you all away. Do you want to come and stay with us?"

"Yes, Alana, I think it would be a good idea. We both need support through this, sweetie. I want to be there for you and the twins."

I drop Alana off at home, with Susan following behind with the twins. We make small talk before Alana asks, "Theon, will you come to the funeral with me, please?"

"Of course I will, Alana. I have every intention of coming. I told you, I will be there for you no matter what. I need to go now to pick up Evander from school. I'll call you later, and I'll see if Sonia or Arnold can spend a bit of time with Evelina tomorrow morning and call in to see you — if that is all right with you?"

"Yes, that would be great, Theon. Thank you."

Chapter 40

Present

I CALL TO SEE ALANA EACH MORNING AFTER dropping Evander off at school. She doesn't think she's doing well, but to be honest, I think she's doing remarkably, considering the circumstances. Her, Susan, and the twins are all supporting each other, which is great to see. They are all grieving in their own way, but also together — they need that. They were all doing well but the healing process won't start until the funeral is over. Bryan isn't going to school because of his grief, but Bailee wants to be at school to keep her mind occupied, and that's her way of dealing.

I spend the mornings at Alana's house and then spend the afternoons with Evelina. She is doing great, and now she's up and about as though nothing has happened. She's even getting excited to be going back to school although she claims she isn't. I think she wants to show her scars off to her friends. I haven't told the Evs that Caroline didn't make it, but I'm going to sit with them tonight and tell them I am going to her funeral tomorrow.

Once the funeral is over, I want both our families to spend time together, so they need to know.

Evelina comes with me to pick Evander up from school, and I take them out for dinner. I let her choose because she hasn't been out anywhere for so long, and I shouldn't be surprised it's The Cheesecake Factory. She loves having the Ultimate Red Velvet cheesecake after her meal.

Later on at home, I decide now is the time to tell them.

"Hey, Evander, would you come into the living room for me, son? I need to speak to you and Evelina." I go and sit down with Evelina who is lying on the couch watching the TV. I sit down, lifting her legs then placing them on my knee. She looks a little exhausted, but it was her first trip out today.

"You feeling okay, poppet?" She nods

"Just a bit tired, Daddy." I stroke the hair from her forehead. Evander comes in, so I turn the TV off. "Hey, I was watching that."

"I know, poppet, but I need to tell you something."

She looks at me a bit worried. "What's wrong, Daddy?"

"I just needed to tell you that I'm going to a funeral tomorrow. Do you know what that is?" I look at each of them, and Evander nods.

"It's what happens after someone dies. They put you in a box and either burn you or put you in a hole in the ground."

"Eww, Vander, don't say that. That's horrible. They don't burn you, do they, Daddy?"

"Well, yes, sometimes, it's called a cremation when they do that. Evander is right. When someone dies their soul goes to heaven, and the body is left behind. There are a few ways to deal with the body, but the most common are burial in the ground like mommy when we go to her grave to put flowers on or cremation. The cremation is to burn the body then the ashes are given to the relatives, and they decide what to do with them, like scatter them over the loved ones favorite place like the ocean or they keep them on a shelf in a nice vase. There are lots of things. Anyway, this is a burial I'm going to tomorrow."

"Who died, Daddy?"

"You remember my friend Alana at the hospital?" They both nod yes.

"Did your friend die?"

"No, not Alana, but you remember her daughter, Caroline? You both met Alana's children, but Caroline was sick."

"Oh no, Daddy. Did Caroline die? She had cancer like I did but in a different place in her body."

"That's right, poppet, she had cancer in her liver. No, she didn't make it.

"Oh, that's so sad. I'm sorry she didn't make it. Was her liver too poorly to fix?"

"Yes it was too poorly, she needed a new one, and unfortunately the only way anyone can have a new organ is by somebody else dying and letting someone who is alive have an organ."

"That sounds terrible, Dad. So for Caroline to live someone else had to die. That doesn't seem fair?"

"I know son. On this occasion, Caroline was in real need of a new liver, but no one died in time for her to get one. That meant she passed away and got her angel wings. It is very sad, and Alana, Bailee, and Bryan are all very upset as you can imagine."

"Daddy, it doesn't seem fair." I move her to my knee and cuddle her as I see tears trickle down her face.

"I feel bad for Alana and the others. She's a really nice lady. I remember her from before my surgery, and I remember hearing her talking to me when I was asleep, I think." I wipe the tears from her cheeks and kiss her forehead.

"Yes she did, poppet. That's right. Your grandma is coming to look after you tomorrow, and I will go to the funeral. Alana will be extremely upset and because she's my friend, I want to be there to help her. Is that okay with you two?" I look from one to the other, and they both nod yes to me. God, I love my kids so much.

"I needed you to both know, so that when you next see Alana, Bailee, and Bryan if they are a little sad, you know why."

"Daddy, can I make a card for them, please. Will you get my craft box out for me and help me?"

"Of course I will. You want to do it now? You're not too tired?"

"No, I want to do it now, please."

We spend the evening making cards. She decides she wants to do a card for Alana and one for the twins. She draws pictures on the front of each card. For Bailee and Bryan, she does a colorful pony with a rainbow tail and wings sitting on a cloud in the sky with a rainbow behind it. Inside she writes:

To Bailee and Bryan
Please don't be too sad your sister has gone away,
She is in heaven now with her angel wings,
She will always watch over you both.
Lots of love from Evelina and Evander. X xxx

Then she draws a picture of a lady with a child either side of her. The lady and one child have a dress on, and the other child is wearing shorts and a t-shirt. They are holding hands. Above them is another child with wings, in a cloud, with a halo above her head. Inside she writes:

To Alana
I know you are very sad that Caroline has gone away
She is now an angel just like my momma
Angels watch over us always so are never very far from our hearts
My daddy will look after you too
Lots of love from Evelina and Evander. X xxx

I help her put some glitter on the rainbows for each color.

"Daddy, I want them to be sparkly and colorful to make them happy and smile when it's a sad time." This kid makes my heart swell so badly that sometimes I have to pinch myself. Both of them have me in awe sometimes. I guess I'm doing something right.

"Poppet, they will surely smile at these. They are beautiful and very thoughtful. You make me so proud." I kiss her head.

The following day I'm up with the Evs so I have time to get ready for the funeral. I want to get to Alana's as I know she will be in a state. Sonia arrives early to help. I'm going to drop Evander off at school then go straight to Alana's. The funeral isn't until noon, so I will be there in plenty of time to help her. Sonia's going to take Evelina out.

"Nothing too strenuous, Sonia. She's still supposed to be resting, but at the moment it's a bit like keeping a wild tiger inside. I took her out yesterday to pick Evander up, and we ended up out for dinner, she was exhausted when we got home."

"No problem, Theon, it's not like I can do anything too strenuous at my age anyway. I'm just going to go to the mall and then back to mine. I thought if they wanted to, as it's Saturday tomorrow, they could stay with us tonight if you don't mind? That way, you can have as long as you need with Alana today." She winks at me. I know what she's saying. "Arnold is picking Evander up from school and bringing him back to ours anyway, so they may as well stay, and if Evelina is up to it, we can have a movie night." She's a lifesaver

"That would be great, Sonia, thank you. It means I don't have to feel guilty being away from them for the day then. I think Alana is going to need a shoulder to cry on."

I get my black suit on and put my tie in my pocket then drive Evander to school. "You okay staying at your grandma and grandpa's tonight? They would like you both there, and if Evelina is up to it, they said about having a movie night."

"Yeah sure, Dad. That will be great. You know we love staying with them. I hope Alana is okay today. It's a very sad day for her. She will need her friends and family. I know it's going to be hard. I know we lost momma, but we never knew her. I feel sorry for Bailee and Bryan. They lost their dad and now their sister. I was going crazy thinking I might lose Lina, so it has to be really hard on them. Maybe we could hang out with them sometime? I know they like video games, so they would love our cinema room, Dad, with the X-box on the big screen." I'm in awe of both my kids and of how accepting they are of others.

"That would be great, son. Maybe give them a little time to get over the funeral, and I will invite them over for a BBQ one weekend. They can play in the pool and play games. How does that sound?"

"Cool, Dad. I can't wait. It will be great having someone that likes games the same as me."

I drop Evander at school and head straight over to Alana's. Susan opens the door, she's crying.

"Oh thank god, you're here, Theon. Alana has locked herself in her bathroom and won't speak to the twins or me. I'm terrified in case she's done something stupid?"

"Where's her bathroom?"

"Up the stairs, first door on the right is her room. Her bathroom is in there."

I run up the stairs taking them three at a time. I barge into her room and stop dead. She's sitting there on her bed in just her underwear. "Shit sorry, Alana, I didn't mean to barge in. Susan said you were locked in your bathroom and wouldn't answer. She was worried." I turn away from her to give her some privacy." I'm really sorry. I'll wait downstairs for you."

"No, Theon, don't go. Just one second." I can hear movement and rustling.

"Ok, you can turn round now." I do slowly. She's dressed in a plain sleeveless black dress.

"Hi," she says as I look at her. She looks stunning. I move over and stand in front of her. I take her face in my hands and tilt it, as I lean down and kiss her on the lips softly.

"Hi, yourself," I say pulling away.

"How are you feeling? I know it's a daft question, but seriously, how are you?"

She's looking me in the eyes. "I don't know. I don't seem to be feeling anything. I'm numb. Honestly, I just want the day to be over. I know it's not Caroline there. I know her soul has left and this is just the day to say our goodbyes." She moves away from me to a set of drawers, on top sits the turtle trinket box I bought her. She opens it and takes out a simple diamond stud earring for each ear. I love she is using the trinket box I bought. Her hair is tied up on top of her head in a simple bun. I know it's a really sad day, but she looks beautiful.

"Alana." She turns to look at me. "You look beautiful, baby." I look away quickly. I start for the door to head downstairs before making a complete idiot of myself.

"Don't go, Theon." She walks towards me. She stands in front of me and takes both of my hands. "Thank you. It's been a long time since anyone has said anything like that to me, and I'm flattered. It means so much you being here for the twins and me today. Outside of Susan, I don't have any other support. You are such a kind gentle and loving man, Theon. How have you not been snatched up already?"

I look her straight in the eyes. "No one has ever interested me since Evelyn."

She looks down when I say that. I lift her chin with my finger. "No one until you that is. Let's say our goodbyes to Caroline today. This day is for her, you, and the twins. I'm here for you all day and night if you need me." Did I just say that? What is wrong with me, and my mouth today? She raises an eyebrow at me.

"Shit, I didn't mean anything by that, Alana. Just that I'm here for you. Sonia has got Evelina and Evander until tomorrow. So what I meant was, I don't have to rush back anytime soon. If you want company afterward, I'm here for you." I squeeze her hands. She rises on her tiptoes and kisses me on the lips this time.

"Oh, before I forget." I reach into my inside pocket and pull out two plastic bags. I hand the one that says Alana to her. She takes it from me and opens it. The card Evelina did for her is inside, and she pulls it out. The glitter falls everywhere.

I laugh. "That's why it's in a bag, or I would be covered in the stuff." She laughs with me, and it warms my heart so much to hear it. She studies the picture on the front and runs her finger over it. Then she opens it and reads inside. I can see the tears falling down her cheeks. I take her head in my hands and wipe away the tears with my thumbs from both cheeks.

"I'm sorry, baby. I didn't want it to upset you. Evelina thought it might bring a smile to your face on this sad day. She's done one for the twins too. Should I not give it to them? I don't want to upset them." She looks at me and shakes her head.

"No, you should give it to them. It wasn't that the card upset me, more because of what it's for. I love it, Theon, honestly. Make sure you tell Evelina she did make me smile. The tears are happy tears when on a day like today there shouldn't be any happy tears. I think it's the most perfect gesture ever. She really is an amazing little girl. Did she think of these all by herself?"

I nod yes. "Her drawings and her words are amazing for a ten-year-old, Theon. She is so caring and thoughtful, just like her daddy. Make sure to thank her for me tomorrow."

"Well, I was hoping if it wasn't too soon, and if you and the twins were up for it, that maybe you could come to my place either tomorrow or Sunday. I just thought it might be nice for the kids to be kids, yours and mine, and they can spend the day in the pool. Evander asked me this morning if you would all like to come over. He wants someone to play games with and knowing Bryan plays has Evander excited. Maybe, if you want to get away, then you could come over tomorrow and stay over. I have a summerhouse that you and the twins could stay in? If you think it's too soon, then I won't be offended, and we can take a rain check." I still have her face in my hands looking at her.

She nods. "I think that is a wonderful idea. I will ask the twins first though. They might think it's too soon. I know, after losing Gary, there is no use wallowing. I know life goes on for the ones that are left behind, and for the sake of us all, I know we have to go on and try to be as normal as we can. What did I ever do to deserve meeting you and having you in my life at this particular point? It's like a miracle."

I hear a commotion outside Alana's door, and she opens it to find Bailee and Susan.

"I'm fine, you two. No need to worry. I just needed a few minutes to myself." Susan just looks at Alana with a skeptical look on her face.

"Ok, Momma, as long as you're okay. Do you want a coffee, Mr. Tourney? Aunt Susan has just made a fresh pot?"

"Please call me Theon, Bailee, and yes, I would love a coffee, please."

"Ok, Theon." With that, she bounds down the stairs.

"I'll head down and help with the coffee. Would either of you like one?" I ask, heading out of the door. I feel a bit embarrassed, not sure what Bailee or Susan heard at the door.

"Yes, please, Theon. I'm almost ready now, and will be down in a minute." I head down the stairs. Bryan is on the couch playing on his Nintendo Switch.

"Hey, buddy, how you doing?" I say ruffling his hair. It already looks like it hasn't been brushed.

"Ok, I guess," is all he says without looking up from his game. He may be struggling.

"What are you playing there, buddy?"

"The Legend of Zelda. I only got it last week, and I'm dope at it." Huh? Dope? What on earth does that mean? I'm getting old. I sit next to him and watch him play. I got Evander the Switch before it hit the shelves because we'd created a game for that and we got a few other consoles before they went on general release. Evander loves that he can play it almost anywhere and with anyone.

"Evander has the switch. Maybe you could hook up and play together?" He looks up at me a bit confused.

"We already do. We play a lot of the games with each other. I thought you knew that. I saw him playing the Switch in the hospital one time, and we got talking about it and have played ever since. I just need some more of the games like he has, then we can play a lot more. Only, I have to save my pocket money for them, or my Birthday and Christmas money. Momma can't keep buying me the games, they cost too much." Hmm, I will ask Alana if she minds me giving games to Bryan before I suggest it. I get all the new games before they are out, and I get quite a few copies of them, so it's no problem me giving him them. I don't want to step on Alana's toes by promising if she doesn't agree. They still don't know I own one of the biggest gaming companies in the US.

We talk a little as I watch him playing and because I know the game, I give him a few of the cheats that I know and helped create, but I don't tell him that.

"Great, thanks, Mr. Tourney. I didn't know you knew how to play games. Don't tell Bailee. Now I can beat her at it. She usually beats me at most of them."

"No worries, buddy, it's our secret. Anytime you're stuck, just let me know, and I will help you. I know a lot about these games." I wink at him then get up to go and make the coffees.

It's time to leave for the funeral home. There is no procession, just the five of us in my car. I wanted to drive us, as I have an eight-passenger Escalade there was no problem us all fitting in. We arrive at the funeral home, and I can feel the tension coming off Alana and the twins and can see that Susan's trying to keep it together for them all. I squeeze her shoulder as she gets out of the car to let her know I'm here for her. She takes Bailee and Bryan's hands, and I take Alana's. I can feel her body getting more rigid with every step we take towards the home. I pull her into my side with my arm around her shoulders. I squeeze and look down at her. "I've got you, baby," I whisper to her.

She puts her arm around my waist, and I feel her grip getting tighter. When we walk into the funeral home and enter the room and see the casket waiting at the end, Alana stumbles. Her legs give way, but I catch her and hold her up. Her hand goes to her mouth to try and stop the cry that is escaping.

"I've got you. You can do this for Caroline. This is your goodbye to her, Alana. You can do this, sweetheart." I kiss the top of her head and help her to the seats at the front. The home is full of people here to help the family through this and pay their respects. I have tissues in my pocket, which I pull out and hand to her. I have her tucked into my side with my chin on her head. I sit us down next to Bailee, Bryan, and Susan.

It's very emotional. I can't help the tears rolling down my face. It brings back so many memories of Evelyn's funeral, and how I couldn't accept she was gone.

After the service, we all leave and follow the hearse taking Caroline to the cemetery to be buried with her dad. Once we approach the graveside, Alana's legs go again. I keep her from collapsing and sit her on the chairs next to the graveside. Out here, she can't hold it in, and as the casket is lowered, she's wailing as though in pain. I feel her pain with her. There are no dry eyes anywhere. I manage to get her up so she can throw a rose onto the casket as it lowers. I do the same, and we stand there and say our goodbyes.

"Can we go now, please, Theon? I need to leave."

"Of course we can. Come on." I keep my arm around her to help her to the car, and I have my other arm around Bailee, who is crying into my side and hugging me. I want to take the pain I know they are feeling away from them. I know this is the twins' first funeral, they were too young for their dad's funeral, so this is really hard for them, especially being at their dad's graveside as well.

There is no wake. We just go back to Alana's. Susan asks Bailee and Bryan if they want to stay at her house tonight. I think she wants to give Alana and me some alone time — to help Alana grieve properly as she holds back so much in front of the kids. Bryan isn't that bothered, as long as he has his Switch but Bailee is more concerned about leaving her momma. Susan tells her she won't be alone and that I'm going to stay with her. Bailee looks at me a bit funny, as though weighing me up. I smile at her.

"Bailee, it's up to you, sweetie. If you want to stay home with me, I am more than happy for you to stay. No one is forcing you to go anywhere, darling. I can't promise I will be good company tonight, that is all. I promise I will be better tomorrow. I just need to grieve for Caroline tonight." Bailee looks from her mom to me and back again. I don't interfere. This is her choice and her home.

I didn't give them the card Evelina made for them before the funeral, and it's still in my inside pocket, so I pull it out and hand it to Bailee. "Evelina wanted me to give you this today. She made it for you and Bryan last night." Bailee takes the card out of the plastic bag and, of course, glitter falls everywhere. She examines the front, and she smiles at the picture Evelina drew, then she reads what she put inside.

"This is really nice of Evelina. Will you thank her for me?" I nod yes.

"Actually, Bailee, Theon has invited us to his house this weekend, but only if you and Bryan feel up to going. We could go tomorrow and stay over, then spend the day there on Sunday as well, with Evelina and Evander, or we could go for a few hours either tomorrow or Sunday or leave it for another weekend. What do you think?" She looks over at Bryan who stops playing his game to listen. He smiles and nods yes to Bailee.

"Yeah, I think that would be nice to get away for a day or two. I think it's a good idea and Evelina can show me her Monsters High dolls that she told me all about in the hospital. I'm sure Bryan will be happy playing games with Evander. Those two are so alike."

"I thought you guys would like to play in the pool as well. Evelina won't be able to go in just yet, it's too soon after her surgery, but she can sit on the side of it and play a bit."

"You have a pool? Well, then, yes, I would love to come tomorrow and stay over, Theon." She smiles so wide at me that I melt a little.

"I think I would like to stay with Aunt Susan tonight as well, mom. Let you grieve and then see you tomorrow." She runs off to get her things together to leave. Bryan follows to do the same.

"Susan, you are more than welcome to come this weekend as well. I have plenty of room."

"Thank you, Theon. Don't worry about me, I have things planned this weekend and would appreciate some time alone to reflect."

I understand.

Chapter 41

I'M SITTING IN THE SMALL BACK GARDEN at Alana's house with a bottle of beer. The twins left with Susan about thirty minutes ago and Alana has gone to get changed, but she's been a long time. I don't want to search for her, as she may just want some alone time. She hasn't actually said she wants me to stay tonight, and I'm not going to push it. She may want to be alone to grieve. I decide to ring Evelina and Evander. I need to speak to them — to hear their voices. It's been such an emotional day and talking to them makes it better for me. Evelina wants to know if the family liked their cards, so I tell her they loved them and they all smiled at them. I ask them to put me on loudspeaker so we can all chat together. I need to make sure they are okay with Alana and the twins stopping with us this weekend.

"So, you two, how would you like it if Alana, Bailee, and Bryan came over to our house tomorrow, and they stayed until Sunday? They can stay in the summerhouse. There is plenty of room."

Evelina squeals. "Yes, oh yes, Daddy that would be lovely. Bailee can see all my Monster High dolls and the house and the DVDs. She loves Monster High like me. Yippee, I get a girl to play with."

"Yeah, Dad, that's cool. Now Bryan can see my room, and we can play games together. Cool."

"Evelina, you know it's still a little too soon for you to go in the pool, but I promise, next time they all come, you can go in. You can still put your bather on and sit on the edge and maybe throw the balls, but Dr. Cassidy said not to go swimming for a little while. Okay, poppet?"

"Yeah, it's okay, Daddy. I won't be sad, I promise. I'm just happy they are coming over to stay."

"Me too, sweetheart. Me too. Now be good for Grandma and Grandpa, and I will see you both tomorrow. Love you both to the moon and back."

"We love you back from the moon to us, Daddy," they both say together.

"Oh, Daddy, can Bailee sleep in my room? Please, Daddy, that would be so cool."

"We will discuss sleeping arrangements tomorrow. Love you both." I hang up and put the phone on the table.

I don't hear the door open, so startle a bit when I see Alana standing there, looking at me.

"Hey."

"Hey. I'm sorry. I didn't mean to eavesdrop. Those are amazing kids you have there, Theon."

"Right back atcha, baby." I wink, and she smiles, but it doesn't reach her eyes. I know she's thinking of Caroline. I pat my knee for her to come and sit on it. She hesitates at first and then comes over to me, and I pull her onto my lap.

"It's been a tough day for you today, baby. Just relax here for a bit. We can sit in silence, or we can talk about anything you want." She leans in and kisses me on the lips.

"Thank you so much for being there for me. I don't think I could have done it if you weren't there. You will never know what having your support means." She leans her head on my shoulder, and I lean my head on hers.

"You would have coped, baby. It's in us all to get through the bad stuff in life, no matter how hard it hurts. You did amazingly." We sit in silence for a while.

"Theon, will you stay tonight, please? I don't think I want to be alone here."

"Of course I will. I'm going to cook you some dinner first. Do you have any wine?"

"There may be a bottle in the cupboard, but I'm not sure. I very rarely drink. It's usually just me and the kids, and I never go out." I head to the kitchen and search the fridge to see what I can make for us. There is some chicken, some mushrooms, tomatoes and then some green beans and some milk. I look in the cupboard and find some rice and some herbs. Perfect. I'm just going to throw it all together in a pan make a little sauce to go with it and put over rice. I find a bottle of white wine in another cupboard. It's a Morning Fog Chardonnay from San Francisco. It's not like the Home Vineyard wines I like to drink, but its wine.

I take the wine into the living room with two glasses, and when I get there, Alana is asleep on the couch. I don't want to wake her. She must be exhausted after the events of today, and I bet she hasn't slept much since Caroline passed away. I take the wine back into the kitchen and put it in the fridge to chill. It's still early. I'll cook the food but not the rice until she wakes up — if she wakes up. I go up the stairs to her room to see if I can find a blanket to throw over her so she doesn't get cold. I see a throw on the chair in her bedroom, so I grab that and gently place it over her, trying not to disturb her. I sit on the chair nearby and watch her sleep. She looks so peaceful. I'm glad she was relaxed enough to sleep. I just watch, admiring how stunningly beautiful she is. She is so understated. I have never seen her with a face full of makeup. She doesn't have to plaster herself with the stuff because she is a natural beauty.

I must have fallen asleep myself while watching Alana because I feel something on my cheek, and when I open my eyes, Alana is crouched in front of the chair.

"Hey, sleepy." She laughs

"Hey, sleepy yourself. I guess you looked so peaceful you made me fall asleep as well, huh?" I look at my watch, and it's only 8.15 p.m.

"Are you hungry now? I made us some food earlier, but you fell asleep. I just need to put the rice on and warm up the rest of it and the wine should be chilled now."

Just then her tummy rumbles. "I guess that's a yes," she says. I get up, and we both head into the kitchen. I set about putting the rice on and warming up the chicken I made. I get the wine out of the fridge and uncork it, letting it breathe a little before pouring two glasses.

"Mmmm, that smells so good, Theon. You seem to know your way around a kitchen pretty well."

I pass her the glass of wine, and she takes a small sip. "I've had to learn with it just being the Evs and me. I couldn't take them out to eat every night, now could I? Although, if you ask them, I'm sure they would prefer that." I raise my eyebrow. Alana laughs again, and I love hearing it.

"I doubt its bad, Theon. I think most kids these days like to eat out. It gets expensive though. It was a once in a while treat for my three with not having a wage coming in." She looks down at her wine and swills it around the glass in thought. She looks really sad again.

"Hey, we could go out for a nice meal tomorrow night if you want? My treat. Then we could have a BBQ on Sunday, how does that sound?"

"Great, but I can't expect you to pay for all of us as well. It's bad enough you have your two." I look at her like she has four heads. She really has no idea about me. I think that will change once she comes over this weekend. I'm sure she's going to ask what I do when she sees the house.

"Alana, my treat, okay? No arguments about it. You're my guests for the weekend, so it's on me. Do the twins have a favorite place they like to eat at?"

"Ok, no argument this time. They both like The Cheesecake Factory but only because they usually get to choose a cheesecake between them."

I laugh. "That's Evelina's favorite place for that exact reason. You would think it's the only place to get dessert from the way she goes on. Evander likes a place we found called Button Mash, but we have to go in the afternoon or very early evening for that one. It's full of arcade games, which is why he loves it, but after 8 p.m. it turns into a bar, so no children allowed. We don't go to that one often because he would rather play than eat."

"Maybe we should put it to the vote tomorrow? With five kids, I'm sure we will—" She stops dead. She looks at me, her face full of anguish, sorrow, hurt, and pain. I see the tears pooling in her eyes, trying to escape down her cheeks. I'm at her side and pulling her into me before they start to fall. She hugs me, holding on tight to my shirt.

"It's okay, baby. Let it out. Don't bottle it up. You will have many of these moments, but they will get easier to handle, I promise you. Shhh, I've got you." We stay like that for a few minutes until I hear the rice. "Shit!" I move away quickly and just manage to grab the pan off the stove before it catches on the bottom. I spoon the rice out onto two plates. "That was a lucky catch." I look at Alana. She isn't crying now. "Are you okay now, baby? Ready to taste my amazing concoction?" I say, wiggling my eyebrows at her and she rewards me with a big grin and nod of her head.

We sit at the small kitchen table and eat, mostly in silence, but it's not an awkward silence, it's a nice peaceful silence. After we finish, I take the dishes to the sink, fill our wine glasses up, finishing the bottle, and take Alana by the hand into the living room and sit her on the couch with her glass of wine.

"I will be right back," I say kissing her head. I head to the kitchen and start to wash the dishes. I try to be quick so we can cuddle on the couch for a while, and maybe put a film on the TV.

I head back into the living room and find Alana is fast asleep again. As its late this time, I decide to take her to bed. I will sleep here on the couch. I lift her gently and start up the stairs. She doesn't wake but makes herself comfortable in my arms. I sit on the end of the bed and pull the covers towards me so I can then place her in the bed and cover her up. I'm not going to undress her. She can sleep in her clothes. I'm just covering her, and I lean down and kiss her gently on the lips. "Goodnight, sweetheart. Sleep tight," I whisper to her.

I turn to leave the room. "Theon, please don't leave me. Please stay here with me," she says very sleepily. I turn to see she has pulled the covers back on the other side of the bed — an invitation for me to get in with her. I rub my hand over my face, shit this will be hard, sleeping in the same bed. I haven't slept in the same bed with another woman since Evelyn. It will also be hard because I'm so attracted to her. But, I can do this. She needs me. She needs the comfort. I take my shirt off but leave my trousers on. She's fallen back to sleep, so I gently ease onto the bed and pull the covers over me. I'm lying on my back when I feel Alana move. She turns over and cuddles into my side with her hand on my bare chest. Maybe I should have left my shirt on. I lift my arm so she can snuggle in farther, and I place it around her, pulling her in tighter. I didn't realize how much I've missed simple contact like this. Nothing sexual — just the cuddling. The comfort you get from it. I lay in the dark listening as Alana's breathing gets more labored and she falls into a very deep sleep. It doesn't take long before I follow suit, taking comfort from Alana.

Chapter 42

Present

I WAKE UP SUDDENLY, FEELING VERY HOT and confused as to where I am. It takes me a minute to realize I'm at Alana's, in her bed, with her wrapped around me. I'm lying on my back, and she's facing me with her leg hooked over my hip, her knee at my groin area and her other leg between my legs. Her head is on my chest and her hand on my stomach. Shit, I have the biggest morning wood ever with her wrapped around me. She is still asleep. I can tell from her breathing. I turn my head slightly towards her and raise it to look down. Bad choice, Theon. Her dress has ridden up her body, and I can see her little black lace knickers. Shit, I need to think of something horrible before she wakes up and sees my hard-on. All I can see in my head are her lace knickers, and all I can think about is how I would love to take them off, which is not helping. I reach down to adjust myself, very gently, trying not to disturb her. I'm very uncomfortable in the confines of my trousers.

She moves. Shit, is she awake? I listen to her breathing, but I can't tell.

I daren't move. I daren't look.

I feel her go slightly rigid the second she realizes where she is and who she's with and the position we are in. She moves her knee slightly, and it rubs me. I inhale sharply at the contact and suck air in through my gritted teeth. She raises her head to look at me. "Good morning," she says with a knowing smirk on her face.

"Morning," I manage to say.

She moves her knee again. Rubbing me again. Did she do that on purpose? "Sorry." She smiles at me. God, she is beautiful.

"Why do I get the feeling you didn't mean that apology?"

"I have no idea what you mean, Mr. Tourney?" she says, coyly batting her eyelids at me.

"Baby, I don't think this is going to end well for me. I think if I don't move now, I'm going to make a complete fool of myself and embarrass myself right here in your bed. I'm sorry. It's a natural reaction when you're in bed with the most beautiful woman you know."

She lifts herself slightly and gently kisses me on the lips. In the state I'm currently in, I automatically open my mouth and kiss her right back. But this kiss is like none we have shared before, and it doesn't take long before the tongues come into play and the kiss deepens and sends me to new heights. She feels it too. I can feel her nipples hard against my chest with the material of her dress between us. I have to summon every ounce of resilience I can and pull back to look at her.

"Baby, if we carry on like this there may be no turning back. If you're sure this is what you want, then you will get no arguments from me, but I want you to be 110% positive you want to take this step. I don't want you to do it because you are grieving, baby. I want you to want this, as badly as I want this. As badly as I want you, and have wanted you since the day I met you on our bench in the hospital garden."

"Yes, Theon. I do want this. I want you. I have never wanted anyone since Gary, but I want you so badly. Please, Theon, take me."

I look deeply into her eyes to make sure she wants this. I see the lust and desire. That's all I need.

I reach for my wallet on the bedside table and take out a condom. Alana slowly pulls her dress over her head, and she is absolutely gorgeous in just her lace black panties and bra. She unzips my trouser and edges them down. I lift up to help her, and she pulls them down, along with my briefs. Here I am, in all my glory, watching her look at me.

"Wow, you are stunning, Theon. I had no idea you looked like that under your clothes. I think I just hit the jackpot." She's sweeping her hand down my body over my abs. I breathe in sharply as she gets lower. I reach over and unclasp her bra, and I return the favor of removing her panties. We both stare at each other in all our naked glory.

"You sure?" I ask to be certain.

"A million percent sure," she says with the biggest grin.

That's all it takes.

Much later, we are at the little table in the kitchen having coffee and scrambled eggs on toast, which Alana made after our shower together. I'm in my trousers with nothing else on, and Alana has a short robe wrapped around her. We are like two Cheshire cats, sitting and smiling at each other.

"No regrets?" I ask

"Are you kidding? I should be asking you that. Look at you? You're perfect in every way. Do you have any flaws, Theon? I mean, you're caring, loving, and supportive. You cook, and you definitely took me to new heights, four times or was it five?"

"Hold on there. You are way out of my league. Look at you. You're beautiful, hot as hell, sexy and devoted, and you, lady, took me to the moon and back a few times." I feel as though I just betrayed Evelyn and the look on my face must give me away.

"Hey, look at me. We both lost the loves of our lives, Theon. There is no way either of them would want us to stay celibate, and not find love and happiness. Nothing will ever take them away from us, or what we had with them, and in truth, I wouldn't want it to. But it doesn't mean we can't move on. We will never forget them, Theon. Never feel bad for thinking about Evelyn or speaking about her to me. She was your wife and the mother of your children. Just like I will mention Gary and think of him from time to time. I know Gary would want me to find happiness, Theon, and I have with you. We have to accept this or we will never work."

"I know you're right. It just feels weird thinking about Evelyn when we just did what we did and feel what we feel for each other. It will just take time to get used to it, that's all, baby, and I know Evelyn would want me to be happy too." She looks at me for a moment.

"What do we feel for each other, Theon? I mean, I know my feelings, but we haven't talked about this," she says motioning between us. I look her straight in the eyes and do what I do best. Tell the truth. "I love you, Alana."

Chapter 43

Alana makes to move past me, heading for the stairs, I know from her startled look that she wants to bolt, but I grab her by the elbow and pull her into me. "I did it again, huh?" I say with my chin on her head, which is on my chest. She nods yes.

"I'm sorry. I don't seem to have a filter when it comes to you. I just say things out loud. I have had all these emotions going around, but, to be honest, Alana, I think I knew the first time I saw you on our bench. There was something about you then. I was just drawn to you. It's been hard accepting the feelings I have for you, especially with all we have been through over the last month or so. They say you can't choose when and how you fall in love, and they are right."

She looks up at me and smiles. "You're rambling, Theon. Are you nervous?"

"Very and terrified."

"Of what?"

"You," I say simply and shrug my shoulders. I kiss her nose and smile.

"Am I that scary?" she laughs at me, and I nod yes. She gently slaps my arm.

"You just shocked me, Theon. I didn't expect you to say that. I was just going to take a few minutes to process what you said. I feel guilty like you said. I've never even kissed anyone since Gary, never mind fallen in love with anyone." I see the penny drop with the look on her face and her mouth forming an O. She's fallen in love with me.

I bend down and kiss her on the mouth. She responds immediately and before we know what's going on we are both naked on the kitchen floor, making love. Again.

After our session in the kitchen Alana decides she now needs another shower. Susan texts to say she will be dropping the twins off in about an hour. I follow Alana into her en-suite and get in the tub with her, and even though we only just did it in the kitchen, I'm ready again.

We are drying each other, Alana is behind me, and I feel her tracing over my tattoo, very gently with her fingertips. "This turtle is amazing, Theon — so colorful. It's just an amazing work of art. If I had a tattoo, I would have this exact one. It's perfect."

I turn to face her. "I love turtles. When we were in the Maldives, we went out swimming, and there were so many turtles. I was amazed at them and how majestic they are."

"It's perfect and fits your personality perfectly."

I bend to kiss her but have to stop before it gets too heated again. Susan and the twins will be here very soon.

We are sitting out back, waiting for Susan to get back with the twins. I phone the Evs and tell them I'll pick them up from Sonia's, and I'll have Alana and her kids with me. They are excited about that. I remember that I want to ask Alana about games for Bryan.

"I was talking to Bryan yesterday, and I wanted to run something past you before putting my foot in it."

"Why would you put your foot in it?"

I shrug because it's nothing to me but could be a lot to her. "Well, he was on his Nintendo Switch, and he was saying how he plays games online with Evander, but doesn't have many, and has to save up for new games. Well, I get all the new release games before they go out on general sale. A work perk. Evander always has every new game, and I felt bad that Bryan has to wait so long. I can get him any game, just like I do for Evander, but I didn't want to presume you would be okay with me doing that."

She has the cup to her mouth about to take a sip but stops. "No, Theon. It's about the money. I can't go spending money on games for Bryan or Bailee when I have groceries to buy. I do try to get new games when I can, for us all to play. So yes, he does save for games and sometimes he buys the pre-owned games because they are cheaper. If one of the perks of your job is that you get all the new releases and you want to share those with the B's then I have no problem with that. Thank you for asking though, and not just presuming it was a done deal. I really appreciate that. He will love you for that, just like his momma." She blushes.

"I love you too, baby."

"I never did ask you what you did for work. What do you do, Theon, when one of the perks of your job is getting games?"

Just then, the front door slams and the French doors open as Susan and the twins come out back. Alana gets up and goes to hug them all — conversation forgotten. I get up and head inside with Susan while Alana stays on the patio talking to the twins and asking them how they are and what they have been doing.

"How has she been, Theon? I see you stayed the night, which I'm really grateful for. She seems to come alive when you're around. I know we only said goodbye to Caroline yesterday, but Alana looks relaxed this morning. I can only thank you for being there for her."

"She's been okay. A couple of meltdowns, which was to be expected, but she is doing okay. You don't have to thank me for being around. I love being around Alana, even at the worst time in her life. I'm glad I can be there for her."

She smiles at me. "I like you Theon. You're good for her."

I just smile back at her. Alana and the twins come inside, and they bound off up the stairs.

"They are going to pack another overnight bag, ready to take to yours. They're really excited to be going somewhere new. It will be good for them. Thank you, Theon."

"No need to thank me. They Evs are excited too."

"I'm just going to go pack my overnight bag. I will be back in a minute once I've sorted us all out. Then we can get going." I lean in and kiss her, not thinking about it, or the fact that Susan is watching us. Alana looks at Susan and blushes. I love it when she blushes. I just shrug at Susan, who stands grinning. Alana disappears up the stairs.

"I knew it. I just knew you both had this glow about you this morning. I couldn't be happier. I haven't seen my sister like this for years. I know for a fact, if you weren't around, she would be wallowing and pushing us all away." She looks towards the stairs.

"God knows she's gone through so much. First her husband, and now her daughter. I don't know how she does it really."

"She is stronger than you realize, Susan. She has you and the twins to keep her going."

Not long after, we are all in my car on the way to Sonia's house to pick up the Evs. The nearer we get to the Hollywood Hills, the more I feel the change in Alana. I don't say anything. Instead, I sing along to the radio station. I keep glancing at her out of the corner of my eye, and I can see her playing with her hands in her lap. She's nervous. I reach over and still her hands with mine.

"You okay, baby?" She looks towards me then back out the window. She's watching the houses getting bigger and grander with each road I turn down. When I indicate to turn into a driveway, she looks at me.

"Where are we? Why are we here?"

"Picking the Evs up from Sonia and Arnold's."

"What, they live here? They live in this massive mansion?" She's looking up at the house in awe. Shit, what's she going to be like when she sees my house? Just then, the front door opens, and the Evs come out with Sonia and Arnold in tow. I can see Evelina taking it easy. She would normally be running for the car, but she is just walking down the steps slowly and carefully. I jump out of the car to help her.

"Hey, poppet. Are you okay? Are you hurting or in pain anywhere?" I ask worriedly.

"Hi, Daddy. I missed you."

I reach down to pick her up, and she wraps her arms around my neck, kisses my cheek, and hugs my neck. "Are you in pain, poppet? You were walking very slowly." I turn to Sonia and Arnold and raise my eyebrow at them in question.

"No, I'm okay, Daddy."

"She's been fine, Theon. She is just taking it easy like she's supposed to. We did a little shopping yesterday, but nothing much, then watched a movie last night. They have been as good as gold like they always are," Sonia says as she moves past me to go to the car. Arnold does the same. I can see Alana, but I can't see the twins as the back of the Escalade has blacked out windows. Sonia is at Alana's door before I can move to the car to put Evelina in. She has the passenger door open, and she's leaning in and hugging Alana. I can see the shock on Alana's face, but then she relaxes. Arnold approaches, and he hugs her too. I go around the other side and put Evelina in the back next to Bailee. They all greet each other excitedly, and the noise in the car gets louder and louder as each of them have different conversations. Sonia and Arnold, asking how Alana and the twins are doing after yesterday. Bailee is asking how Evelina is doing after her surgery and thanking her for the beautiful card she made them. Evander has gotten into the very back with Bryan, and they are talking about games. I stand there, taking it all in. I love it. Sonia is now telling Alana that they must all come and visit one weekend, and Alana is just agreeing, saying it would be lovely but I'm not sure she is that comfortable with not really knowing them. I just stand, leaning against the front of the car with my arms folded listening to it all. We all say our goodbyes to Sonia and Arnold and hit the road again.

It's only a few minutes to my house, and again, I watch Alana out the corner of my eye as she sees we are not leaving the Hollywood Hills but heading into them more.

"Do you live here as well, Theon?" I just nod, not looking at her. The back of the car is noisy, as I turn onto my road. There are only four houses along this road and mine is at the end. I turn into the driveway that leads to my house, and I can see Alana's hands in her lap again, so I grab them to still them. I come to a stop at my garages. I turn to face Alana, who is looking out of the window, trying to take in the house. I think back to the first time I went to Evelyn's house with her and how I felt, and understand how she's feeling.

The kids start to pile out of the car. "Wow, look at this place. It's huge. Do you live here?" I hear Bailee asking Evelina.

"Do you live here, Theon? Is this your house? It's bigger than Sonia and Arnold's. It's a mansion, Theon. Oh, god, who are you? Are you famous or something, and I'm too stupid to know who you are? Is that it?" I smile at her as she turns back to look at the house. "You never answered me before when I asked what your work was?" She's looking at me again, waiting. I take her face in my hands and kiss her gently on the lips.

"Baby, calm down. No, I'm a no one. I'm not famous. I just own a company. Why are you nervous about being here? Don't you want to be here with me? Does this bother you that I live in a house like this? Does it change how you feel about me because I have money?" She hangs her head down, and I tilt it back up with my finger under her chin so she looks at me.

"I'm just me, Alana. I'm Theon, who you fell in love with. What I have doesn't change how we feel, or it doesn't for me. Does it for you, baby?"

She's looking over my face and into my eyes. "No, you're my Theon. I don't know what you do or how you come to live here, but … Oh gosh, Theon, I'm sorry for my reaction. I'm just shocked, that's all. I've never been in a place like this. It just scares me."

"Well, if it makes you feel any better, I know exactly how you feel. I was brought up in a trailer park with my grandma. No parents. The first time Evelyn took me to her house, which is where Sonia and Arnold still live, I was in awe. I too had never been in a house like that. Evelyn and I set up a company Toureve Development. We create computer games. It grew, and it's now the biggest gaming creator in the US."

I see the realization hit her. "Oh my god. I used to test the games for your company. I used to work for you. Oh god, this is unreal."

"No, it's not, baby, and it doesn't have to be an issue. Please, tell me it isn't?" She's looking out of the window at the kids, our kids, happily talking on the steps leading to the front door. They are waiting for us, but they aren't in any hurry.

"Baby, is this a problem? You don't work for me now and haven't done for many years, so I'm not your boss — unless you want me to be that is?" I wiggle my eyebrows at her when she turns to me. She laughs at my suggestion.

"No, it's not a problem. I'm just a little shocked. I also feel a little intimidated."

"Why?"

"Look at you and what you have. I have nothing, Theon. I come from nothing, and I feel I don't have anything to give. I know I'm not making sense, but what do I bring to the table?"

"You and your beautiful children," I say without hesitation. "You don't have to bring anything else, Alana. This isn't about who has got what. This is about us and love and family. Look at them out there. They are all amazing kids. But, baby, I know how you feel, I really do. Trailer park to this …" I point outside.

"I have no airs and graces, Alana. I'm just plain, geeky computer nerd, Theon. Who just kept himself to himself all his life until Evelyn came along and we created a company. I'm still only thirty-seven and hopefully still have a long life ahead of me, and I'm hoping to spend it with you. I know it's too soon to be saying that, but Alana I've only ever loved one woman until you. When I love, I love for good. If you think this is all too much then tell me now, and I will gladly give this up for you and live a simple life."

She dives on me, crossing over into my lap and straddling me, grabbing my head and kissing me hard. "You would actually give all this up if I said I didn't want it? You would move into a little house for me?"

I nod yes. "Anything for you. The kids would adapt."

"The kids would kill us if you gave this up. All of them." She laughs loud. I can see all the kids looking at us in the car. Well, the secret's out now.

"I love you, Theon Tourney. I love you so much, and it scares the shit out of me."

Epilogue 1

I AM SO NERVOUS. I HAVE EVERYTHING planned out just perfectly. I'm nothing but meticulous in everything I do.

Alana and the twins moved into my house with us about four months after the first time they came to stay. We had the best weekend — the kids loved it. We took them out for dinner that night after they played in the pool and, yes, we ended up at The Cheesecake Factory by unanimous vote. Evelina struggled with the exertion, and she didn't moan once about not being able to go in the pool. On Sunday they all played games in the cinema room on the big screen, and me and Alana sat out by the pool and got the BBQ ready for them.

After that, they came over most weekends, much to my delight. I saw Alana as much as I could, and during school breaks, they stayed with us the entire time. Bailee and Evelina insisted on sharing a room. They didn't stay in the pool house. Bryan took one of the spare rooms. Bailee stayed with Evelina, and Alana stayed in my room with me of course. The kids all saw Alana kissing me in the car that first day, which was a good thing as it meant we didn't have to hide how we felt. I remember the conversation with the girls though as I was saying goodnight.

"Daddy, are you and Alana girlfriend and boyfriend now. You were kissing in the car, and only girlfriends and boyfriends should kiss?"

"No, it's not just girlfriends and boyfriends, Lina. Moms and dads kiss as well," Bailee tells her.

"Well, they are both a mommy and a daddy, but I think they are girlfriend and boyfriend now."

"Well, poppet, I think we will just see what happens but fingers crossed, Alana is my girlfriend. What do you think about that? Are you both okay if we become girlfriend and boyfriend?" I look at each of them asking them. It's important to me they are happy with this. They both nod vigorously and giggle with each other.

"Oh yes, Daddy, I really like Alana, and it will mean I get a mommy and a new sister and brother, and the best thing is, they are twins just like me and Vander."

"Me too, Theon. I like you, and I want my mommy to be happy, and I would like a daddy, and I get a new sister and brother." She looks a bit sad

"Hey, Bailee, it doesn't mean you ever forget Caroline. She will always be your baby sister, no matter what. She will always be a part of our family." I lean over and kiss her on the forehead then leave them. I start to close the door, and I hear Evelina.

"Bailee, I'm so sorry you lost your sister. It must be so sad. I would love to be your new sister, but not to replace Caroline. We will always talk about her just like I do about my mommy with daddy. They now have their wings in heaven, and they watch over us. Daddy says mommy is my guardian angel now, which means Caroline is now your guardian angel." I click the door shut and stand there with my back to it looking up to the ceiling. I silently tell Evelyn I miss her and to not be upset I'm moving on. I feel so guilty sometimes — when I'm away from Alana — but when I'm with her, it's completely different and feels natural. I love my kids so much and hearing Evelina fills me with so much pride and the fact that both girls are happy for me and Alana to be together, fills me with warmth.

"Hey, are you okay? What's wrong?" I hear Alana's panic. She just came out of Bryan's room and must have seen me looking up to the ceiling. I move over to her and put my arm around her waist and pull her into me. I bury my face into her neck and breathe her in.

"I'm okay, baby. Just in awe of the kids. Come on, let's go grab a drink and sit out by the pool, and I'll tell you how we are now girlfriend and boyfriend because we kissed." I wink at her as she laughs.

From then we have all been pretty much inseparable, so the only way forward was them to move in with us. Alana hesitated at first, thinking it was too soon, but I made my points, which she took in. I told her we were going to be together forever and I meant it. I did give Alana the option of us finding a new house together, but she was more than happy to live in our house.

That was three years ago. In that time, I finally persuaded Alana to let me help her with her dream of buying a flower shop.

We found a lovely shop right in the heart of Hollywood and we set about buying it. Alana refused to let me buy it for her, she's very independent but I paid for it and we drew up an agreement that she paid me back. Like I would even think of taking her money and the agreement is a waste of paper, it's not even legal, but she thinks it is. I know I'm terrible. We got it fitted out to a high specification. It needed to be prestigious in the neighborhood it was in, and we were hoping that once word got around, she would have some top end clients.

Having four teenagers in one house, all nearly the same age, has its challenges, but I have to say they are the best set of kids ever and I wouldn't want it any other way. Evelina and Evander are almost fourteen, and Bailee and Bryan are almost fifteen, so it's fun at times. Evelina has recovered remarkably from her Wilms tumor, and the cancer has never returned. She still has to be monitored every six months and will be for two more years before we get the all clear. That will be a day we all celebrate.

It's the day of the flower shop opening. The girls have been helping me plan the day, and I'm heading to the shop with all the kids, ready for the opening. We have quite a few big-named guests coming in and lots of locals to the area. Alana has been there working non-stop getting all her floral displays just perfect. She's hired two assistants to help her and a shop manager. I want her to have staff so she doesn't have to spend all her time working. I want us to have time to ourselves, and family time, lots of it, along with her seeing her dream come true. She agreed with me, thankfully.

We all arrive at the shop to bedlam. Alana is in a panic because she doesn't think she has enough time, her assistants are frantically putting all the flower garlands and ribbons everywhere, and the shop manager, Julie is helping Alana finish the displays. It looks amazing.

"Wow, baby, this place looks fantastic."

It's like walking into a fairy wonderland full of trees, flowers, and feathers. The walls are white with a splash of color coming from the displays Alana and Julie are working on. There is lots of sparkle about the place but elegantly done. It screams opulence, and it needs to in this area. Susan, Sonia, and Arnold are also here to support Alana. Sonia and Arnold love Alana and the kids, and they treat them as their own. I couldn't be more grateful to them. They often have the four kids at their house for sleepovers, which gives Alana and me the much-needed alone time that I crave with her.

It's time for the opening. A lot of people have gathered, which I'm really pleased about for Alana. She deserves this. She's worked so hard the last few months. We have a big red ribbon across the front of the shop with lots of silver balloons, and Alana is going to cut it.

"I want to thank every one of you for coming to the opening today. This has been a dream of mine for some time, and if it weren't for my wonderful boyfriend, Theon, this wouldn't have been possible. Thank you, Theon. I now declare Caro Petals open," she says, cutting the ribbon with a huge pair of scissors. Everyone cheers and claps and the boys holler and whoop. I have the biggest grin on my face as I move to stand next to Alana. The boys have started to move around the guests, with trays filled with glasses of champagne.

I whisper to Alana, "I just want to make a quick toast."

She looks up at me and smiles. She looks gorgeous at my side, with her arm around my back, clinging to my shirt. I kiss her forehead, then Bryan comes over and stands next to me. Evander has a tray and hands me a glass of champagne. I feel myself shaking. I don't like being the center of attention, yet here I am, about to do something that I hope I get the right reaction too.

"Ladies and Gentlemen. As Alana said, thank you all for coming today and making this special for her, and for us as a family. The name of the shop is a dedication to Alana's daughter, Caroline, who we sadly lost three years ago, to cancer." I lean down and kiss her forehead.

"Please raise your glasses and join me in wishing Alana every success with Caro Petals. To Alana." Everyone joins in with the toast, raising their glasses, then taking a sip. While they are doing this, I nod to Evelina and Bailee who are stood at the back of the crowd out of sight, then to Evander and Bryan.

"Just one more thing, before we go inside and see the beautiful displays." Everyone is looking at me. I put the glass I have in my hand back on the tray Evander has, as I step in front of Alana. She's looking at me curiously. I get down on one knee in front of her, and I grab both of her hands. The look on her face is priceless. If I didn't have hold of her hands, I know for a fact they would be covering her face.

"Alana, since you entered my life, just over three years ago, you have brought new light into my heart. Light, I never thought I would have again. I love you, Alana, and I couldn't imagine my life without you or Bailee and Bryan. Please would you do me the honor of becoming my wife?"

Just then, the girls come through the parting crowd, carrying a big beautiful floral display. The display is made up of roses and in the shape of a heart. In the middle, in white roses, it says, 'Will You Marry Me?' Bryan then presents a blue Tiffany ring box and opens it for me so that I can take out the beautiful platinum, round, brilliant cut 4ct diamond. Alana gasps at the ring. Her hands are at her mouth, and she has tears streaming down her face.

I take her left hand from her mouth and put the ring to the tip of her finger. "Will you do as the flowers say, baby? Will you marry me and make me the happiest man alive?"

She nods. "Oh, Theon. Yes, of course, I will. I would be honored to be your wife. You make me so happy. I will marry you, my love. I love you so much."

I'm still on one knee as I pull her down to kiss her long and hard, bending her backward. Everyone is hollering and cheering and shouting congratulations to us. Evelina is at my side.

"Dad, you need to stop kissing now. It's getting embarrassing."

I pull away from Alana, and we laugh. I stand up with her and hug her to me. People are passing us now to enter the shop, but congratulating us as they do. I get so many pats on the back. Sonia comes up and hugs us both. She's crying as well.

"Congratulations, you two. I'm so happy for you both. You both deserve happiness, and I'm so thrilled that I officially get a new daughter and grandchildren." She kisses us both then heads into the shop. It's just me and Alana left, grinning at each other.

"Are you happy, baby?" I ask her

"Theon, you have no idea how happy you make me. This is one of the best days of my life. Definitely up there in my top three."

"Three, huh. Well, I think I can safely say it's up there in my top spot, with the two other best days of my life."

Epilogue 2

THE DAY I LEFT WAS THE WORSE day of my life. Watching Theon fall apart on the floor, screaming, shouting, and slipping in my blood destroyed me. I've watched over him, when he was in despair, drinking and attempting to end it all. I couldn't let that happen. I had to intervene. The babies needed him.

I watched over my daughter as she lay sick in hospital. I couldn't let her feel the sickness any longer. Again, I had to intervene. I helped her sleep through it all. It was the least I could do because my babies had to live without a momma. I couldn't let Theon lose her. I don't think he would have survived that. They were my two allowed strikes at intervention, and to me, they were worthy.

I've watched them all grow. I couldn't be any prouder of them. I was happy Theon met Alana. She's a lovely person, and they deserve each other. They deserve happiness. I have met with Gary and Caroline, who both watch over them, and now we all join together to be their guardians. The family has grown. I'm now a grandmother. Evelina has had twins herself:

a boy and a girl. Thankfully, the birth was normal. I was on pins when her time approached. She is happily married to a lovely man, Joe, who adores her. He is a partner at the law firm she owns. They are a perfect match.

Evander now runs our company, Toureve Development, and it's gone global. He is due to be married soon, to one of the directors of a big gaming store.

Bailee has a boyfriend, and she now runs her mum's florist, only she has a chain of them across the USA. Her clientele includes movie stars, pop stars, hotel chains, and even royalty from different countries when they visit. Caro Petals is famous now.

Bryan helps Evander run Toureve. He is a lovely man, but can't seem to settle down with anyone. He travels all over the world with business, so I suppose that doesn't help. I hope one day he will settle down with his own family.

Theon and Alana travel a lot, and they still live in the same house we bought. They thought about moving, but with the family growing, they changed their mind. They are both so happy together. I'm so proud of Theon and the way his life turned out. I would never have wanted him to stay alone. I only wish happiness for him. I will see him again one day, and when I do that will be the best day of my afterlife.

Reviews

I really hope that you enjoyed this story. Reviews are lovely! Honestly, they are! And they also help other people to make an informed decision before buying this book.

I would really appreciate it if you took a few seconds to do just that.

Thank you!

Amazon

Goodreads

Bookbub

Lynda Throsby Xx

Also by Lynda Throsby

Catfish

Read on for a free sample of my
debut novel Catfish.
Catfish is a dark, gripping, romantic thriller.

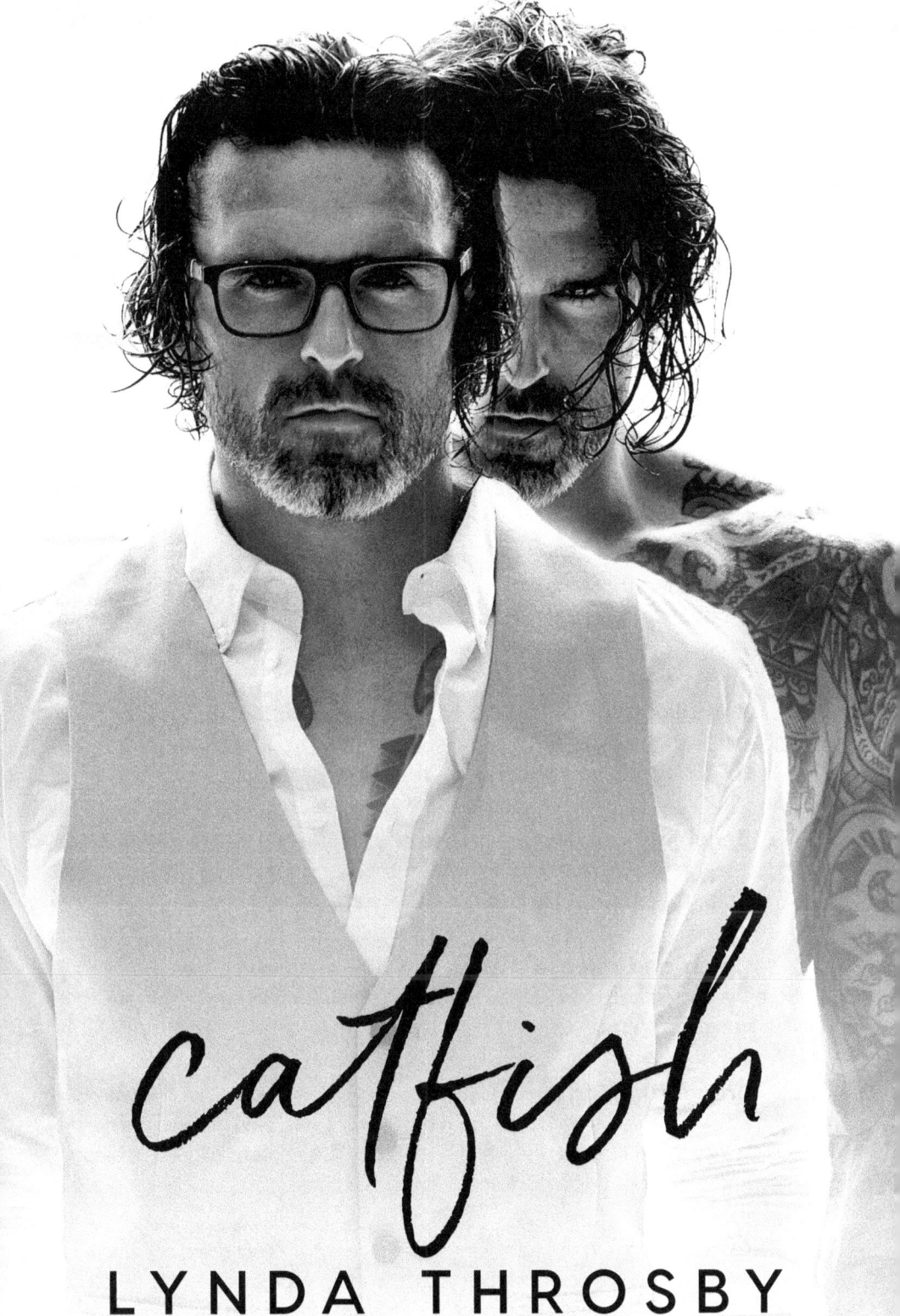

catfish

LYNDA THROSBY

Catfish

ONLINE DATING MEANINGS

Stashing – When you start seeing someone, but they keep you a secret and stash you away–usually because they are married or seeing other people. You are their secret.

Ghosting – When you start seeing someone, and they just disappear and vanish without a trace. They don't return your messages and even block you from social media and dating sites. This is so they don't have to tell you they are breaking up with you verbally.

Zombieing – If you have been ghosted the culprit may resurface back on the sites. This is usually a fair bit of time after they ghosted you. They try to make contact, only to probably ghost you again.

Benching – This is before you discuss exclusivity, and they bench you like in a football game while they look for someone better. You are their backup option. They may come back to you if no one better comes along.

Catch and release – Where someone persistently pursues you as they love the chase, but as soon as you agree to a date they release you, as you're not a conquest any more.

Breadcrumbing – This is where someone seems to be pursuing you, but really, they have no intention of being in a relationship with you. It could just be the chase they like, or it's a game as they are already in a relationship. They message and chase, leaving you breadcrumbs with no outcome.

Cushioning – When you're dating, but they know it's not going anywhere or will not end well so instead of cutting you loose they prepare you for the break up by chatting and flirting with others online to cushion the blow to you.

Kittenfishing – Someone who has out-dated images of themselves and lies about their age, height, job, hair etc. If you were to meet you would know they were lying.

Catfishing – The pinnacle of online dating deception. Where someone pretends to be someone else. They use fake images to lure you in and use false information to make them seem more interesting. This can be dangerous if you decide to meet up, although you would never know until you decided to go that far and by that time it could be too late for you.

George

IT HAS TAKEN ME A LONG TIME TO REEL this one in and get her to finally agree to meet me for a date. It's been too long now since my last catch, just over a year ago now. This one is going to suffer because i've waited for wait so long, I've missed out on others while I've been chasing her, and my need is growing more and more. It's getting harder each day—both figuratively and literally. The things I'm going to do to this bitch now... I can't wait, and boy will she regret making me. I am a very impatient man.

The minute I laid eyes on her profile picture while scanning the hordes of whores for my next catch, I knew I had to have her. It was the long mousey brown hair and the hazel eyes, although the others had looked similar, this whore was the spitting image of my fucking bitch of a mother.

My brow is wet from sweat, and I'm shaking, knowing I will finally have her tomorrow. I'm so fucking hard right now just looking at her picture. God help me when I get my hands on her. She will regret ever responding to my messages and playing with me, stringing me along. Why the fuck I get hard for these whores that look like my mother is a mystery to me. They should repulse me, but I can't help myself, and it makes me hate myself even more. I feel sick to the stomach. Now I need to take care of my fucking cock. That bitch, Katherine has done this to me yet again.

Katherine

W<small>HAT HAVE</small> I <small>DONE?</small> I <small>SAID</small> I <small>WOULDN'T</small> date for a long time, so why have I just agreed to meet this Lewis guy. Why am I doing this? Why do I put myself through this? It's not like I need someone. I have my own business, right here in the city, which takes up most of my time. But still… it's lonely, and his pictures are hot. I mean, those abs and biceps and the tattoos… Oh, god, they make me drool. But it's the bright, mesmerising, light brown eyes with long eyelashes and black curly short hair that made me succumb. He is just so pretty in a masculine way. I still think this is too good to be true. Why would someone that looks like him be on a dating site? Surely, he can get any woman he wants.

I've had such bad experiences with men in my life, going back to my family. I had no father to speak of. He left mum, my brother Brad, and me when I was two, so I never knew him. Brad is three years older than me, and although he did look out for me in school and was very protective as most big brothers are, he's an arsehole.

He has a wife now, Cindy, and he is mean to her like he used to be mean to me. Not the hitting, but he does have some serious anger issues, and I'm sure it stems from him being so young when our dad left.

Brad used to get angry a lot and hit me, and if I ventured into his room, all hell broke loose. He even broke my arm one time when I was eleven. He had a girl in his room; mum was at work as usual. He was on top of her, grunting away, and all I saw was his arse, but he jumped off that bed so quickly, grabbed me and threw me hard on the floor of the landing that my arm snapped. He was sorry, of course, and persuaded me to tell mum I'd fallen. That was just one of the times in my childhood that I ended up at the hospital, being told how clumsy I was.

Mum worked two jobs. She was the only one bringing money in for the three of us. She was a room cleaner in a hotel in London during the day, starting at 6.30 a.m., she finished that job at 3 p.m. just in time for me to get home from school and see her for half an hour before she had to work the evening shift from 5 p.m. to midnight down at the local petrol station.

She trusted Brad to look after me, being my big older brother, but it was best I stayed away from him as much as possible, or I ended up with bruises. I never told mum he did that to me. She had enough to worry about.

So yeah, men! Dad left—arsehole, and Brad hit me—another arsehole.

THERE WAS MY FIRST boyfriend at fourteen. Luke Jones. At first, he was really nice and made me feel special, but it became clear that was only because of what he wanted from me.

We were going steady for about three months and we'd only ever kissed, that was a trauma in itself the first time. I had no experience, and when he stuck his tongue in my mouth and tried to push it down my throat, I almost puked in his mouth, much to his dismay. Having never had a boyfriend before; I didn't want to go any further than kissing, although he did try to put his hand under my skirt or up my top a few times.

He even tried to put my hand on his erection over his trousers, but I was scared and naive, so in the end, he got fed up and called me a cock-tease because I wouldn't have sex with him or let him feel my boobs.

He told all the boys in school not to waste their time with me because they would get nowhere, and he told everyone who would listen that I was a frigid bitch. The girls in school picked on me anyway. I thought it was because I was quiet and kept to myself, but both Brad and Luke told me they were all jealous of me because I was pretty, and I had a good figure for my age, that the other girls felt threatened by me. When Luke dumped me, it just got worse with the mean girls. They had more ammunition to throw at me just because I wasn't a slut like them.

I REALLY THINK I should cancel on Lewis. It's just he is so sweet in our messages, saying how beautiful I am and asking if I've ever considered modelling. He wants to meet to talk and get to know me. Nothing more, he said he has no expectations as he respects me. I mean who does that these days? It's usually 'wham bam thank you, ma'am'.

I just can't see someone like him wanting to get to know someone like me. I don't think I'm ugly. I'm curvy in all the right places and in some not-so-right places, but I'm not a size zero by any means. I'm more a comfortable fourteen to sixteen in clothes.

I'm successful in my business, and it takes up most of my time, I've worked hard to get it where it is today. Porter Properties is one of the top property investor/developers in the city, and I'm proud of that. It's so hard being a woman at the top in a man's world, but I have this knack of knowing a good deal when I see one. I own several commercial buildings and apartment blocks.

I have a penthouse apartment in Knightsbridge, not far from my office, which I use during the week, and at the weekends I head to my five-bedroomed house in a lovely area of Chelmsford. I bought a big house because I was hoping mum would move in with me and quit her jobs, but it wasn't meant to be. It's very quiet where I live. I love the peace and tranquillity, and I know mum would have loved it too.

George

JUST ONE MORE NIGHT and I will have that bitch. My thirteenth catch. I may prolong it. Make her suffer like that bitch has made me suffer for weeks. I've checked her out on social media, and from what I can tell, she doesn't socialise much. There are some work references and a few pictures with work colleagues, that's it. After digging, I found she owns the company, but other than that, there is not much about family or friends. I just hope, as I suspect, she lives alone. They nearly always do or why would they be looking for love on these shitty dating sites?

In our messages on the dating site: LookingforLove.com, she never gave much away about herself. She was always quite vague and guarded, and I suspect she's had bad experiences with tossers who go on these dating sites purely to get free sex with no intentions of dating. I can't blame the wankers really. Why get tied down with some whore permanently when you can have pussy on tap? Looking for love, what a load of bollocks. I know why I go on the dating sites. It's to rid the world of anyone who looks like my useless mother. They don't belong here—don't deserve to live, just like she didn't. She used to say she loved me, yeah right, like fuck she did. What mother would let her waste of a husband do the things he did to me, do nothing about it, even joining in herself? Sick fuckers—both of them were.

Who needs love and all that crap when you can just take what you want and then do away with them? Love: what is it anyway? Is it what my father showed me when he used to punch and burn me while stubbing out his cigarettes on me when he couldn't be bothered getting off his lazy fat arse to find an ashtray?

He would make me sit in the room with him while he jerked off to his porn. I would have to sit on the floor next to his chair and get him anything he needed. I was his personal slave. 'Boy get me a beer.' 'Boy get me something to eat.' 'Boy get me my playboy magazine.' 'Boy, light me a cigarette.' The only thing I didn't do was shit and piss for him. I had to have tissues ready for him jerking off, or it would be my hands used to clean him up. He even made me suck him clean sometimes, telling me to lick every drop or he would beat me. He used to make me lift my t-shirt up, if I was wearing one that is, so he could pinch and twist my body when he was about to shoot his load. If I cried from the pain, he would kick me so hard that I would fall over and end up bruised, knocked out, or with broken bones. Once, he kicked me so hard, I sailed across the room, knocking the T.V. over. He flew out of his chair to make sure I hadn't broken it. I had never seen him move so fast, and for that, I got punched in the stomach and kidneys, a black eye and bloody lip. He never once looked or asked me if I was okay. Never. He didn't care what he did to me.

I never went to school. No one knew I existed. No one ever came to our house, and I was never allowed to leave except on the rare occasion I was allowed out to help mum with shopping when he'd severely beaten her and she couldn't move properly. When the man at the shop asked who I was, she just said I was a visiting nephew. I didn't know if we had any other family or not.

My mother used to work all day at a café in town to keep the money coming in for my dad's booze. God forbid if there was no beer or whiskey in the house for him, then he would lay into her with his fists—always on her body, never visible because she needed to go back to work. He couldn't have her staying off work and not bringing in the money. I would go days without food, and when they finally gave me something, it was only something basic like rice or porridge oats. Even though she sometimes brought leftovers from the café, I never got any. He got everything, and she was just as bad. She let him treat me like shit.

He wanted to watch me with my mother. I didn't know that what he had us doing was wrong. I had no idea. I thought all kids did it with their parents. He used to jerk off, watching me go down on my mother or with my cock in her mouth. He liked to join in sometimes and make her suck me while he ploughed into her backside. The bastard was sick. I know that now. I hated them both so much and the older I got, the worse it got. Being a teenager was a nightmare, but I was plotting in my head. Plotting to rid the world of the vile pair. I was plotting to fight back.

Available on kindle

BUY LINKS FOR CATFISH
Amazon UK https://amzn.to/2OmLYWc
Amazon US https://amzn.to/2zpwI5L
Also on Kindle Unlimited - KU

More about Lynda

Lynda lives in Cheshire in the UK with her husband Peter and cat Bailey also with two grown up daughters and an 11-year-old granddaughter.

She runs a successful financial business with her husband. As a young teenager Lynda used to read horror books with a love for everything Stephen King and James Herbert. She has always wanted to write and even wrote horror stories at age 13.

A little later she started reading Jackie Collins and Jilly Cooper and has always had a love of books. This then exploded with Twilight and Fifty Shades as it did with most people, oh, and the introduction of E-Readers.

In her spare time, she has a season ticket for Manchester City Football Club and goes to all the home games. Loves going to concerts and the theatre. She goes to the cinema at least once a week. Then when the weather is nice you can see her gliding down the road on her Harley Davidson 1200T motorbike. Travelling is also high on the agenda and her dream is to visit every state in the USA.

Acknowledgements

I wouldn't have done this without the help and support I got from a few people.

First my Husband who made time for me to write by running our business and the continued support he gives me, encouraging me to carry on.

My sister Jackie and friends who read the book and gave me feedback.

My Editor Claire Allmendinger for guiding me through and being patient with me, yet again.

Sybil Wilson from Pop Kitty for the amazing cover as always.

Stuart Reardon, Emma Hayes & Cathy Reardon for the cover pictures.

The adorable Marlie Brown & Sienna Brown for braving the cold, being in the pictures for my book.

Cassy Roop from Pink Ink Designs for the fantastic formatting and making my words look pretty.

Thank you everyone.